RISE OF THE SHAMRA

BOOK 1 OF THE SHAMRA

BY
LARRY HIGGINS

true_beginnings_publishing@yahoo.com

Edited, Formatted, and all artwork by True Beginnings Publishing. This
Work is Copyright Protected under US Copyright Law.

ISBN-13: 978-0692685624
ISBN-10: 0692685626

Ordering Information:
To order additional copies of this book, please visit Amazon or
CreateSpace, at: ttps://www.createspace.com/6186920

Rise of the Shamra, Book 1 of The Shamra.
© Larry Higgins.
First Printing 2016.
Printed in the United States of America.

This book is dedicated to my wonderful wife, Yvonne, who always believes in and supports me.

Table of Contents

Prologue

Epilogue

Prologue

Oh, poor Rasomite, Child of God. Look upon your brave men now. The innocents of the world pours out a great and silent weeping. Here is Persilius, who would daily rally the cry against the heartless men of the earth. And look also upon gentle Quibbus, who was so tender-hearted with the children. He knew they would one day be raised up to stand in his place. Oh, you brave men. And look, here is Garasom, your wise and seasoned leader who only sought peace, but now lies with his body torn apart and pierced through a dozen times with swords he was assured would never be raised against him again. Oh, you brave and wise and foolish man.

Across the Plains of Shazar lay his troops. The band of God's bravery that would have and could have brought peace, but it was not to be so. Look at you! Look with tears in your eyes. You were finally destroyed in a day. Nearly a thousand men who had been fighting the Lord's battle; vanquished. Not one man stood, no, not one man moved among the gore and sacrifice that had been a mighty army. The army of the Lord had been destroyed.

See how the smoke still billows from the bodies of Plantar and his men where they had been dragged and bound and burned alive. Can you still hear the cries and screams of anguish reverberate across the now silent plains? See his man, Rebus, who had his eyes blinded and his body kicked to death under the feet of horses. And Plantar lying beside him, his hands chopped off from his smoldering body and cast aside. His fingers are still curled and flexed as though they still clutched his grandfather's sword.

How could they have escaped or possibly fought back against an overpowering force of men on horseback and chariots? It was a battle of men with great swords against men with blades designed to butcher goats and sheep.

Look, over here is Meradin. His father had many brave sons. Meradin was the youngest and he was the last, for all his brothers were slain long before. Now, one could scarcely recognize his battered body. He had fought viciously until he had been tied to a horse and driven around the battle site a dozen times; much more than was needed to kill him.

And scores of others. Each had been brutally martyred by their enemy far more than death had needed. Now, was there any power on earth strong enough to turn aside the mighty force of the Atrocenes? The little spearhead of God that was called Rasomite had been the only bulwark against the evil Atrocenes. Now that "Sunlight of God" was gone.

The Rasomites had stood over this little corner of the earth for decades, defending the people and upholding the only true righteousness left. They had, however, tired of their chore for the Atrocenes grew stronger daily and the strength of the Rasomites waxed weaker and weaker. Therefore, Garasom had struck a deal with King Atrocene, leader of the Atrocene people, to lay down most of their arms and surrender their horses and chariots. In turn, they were told that they would be free to practice their religion and live in peace. Garasom had been blinded by the weariness of war.

Their fathers and grandfathers had fought against these people daily. There was little love between these angry men. It was true that Isoaten had left her brother's people and gone to live with the gentler Rasomites. It was also true that her beauty had so enraptured Garasom that he had married her and brought forth a daughter. Beautiful Aurora, whose skin was even fairer than her mother's. But Aurora, for fear of her life, had fled. None of the Rasomites knew for certain her destination. She had always been bitter for having to live among a strange-skinned people, for the Rasomites were grey-fleshed. There were no others like them. Their sons and daughters, when born of other women, were also grey. But Aurora was different as she had been born with a fair-colored skin. At last, however, came a good man and they had married. So, she felt at peace for a time. However, only briefly.

Now Isoaten, who had noticed the ranks of the Rasomites dwindling, had begun to fear. Therefore, she had pleaded with her younger brother, Atrocene, for peace. He had relented, it seemed, for respect of her. However, later, Aurora had told her the truth. Atrocene would betray them and kill every grey-colored man. That was the night Aurora had disappeared. That night, in desperation, Isoaten had killed herself and told her husband with her dying breath what Atrocene had planned.

When Garasom, now a leader of warriors without weapons, knew the truth, he had gone after Atrocene and had, unfortunately, found him. The Sunlight of God had been extinguished and now lay here in this battlefield never to rise again. But even as the sun reached the horizon and began to set, there was movement and one man stood.

Chapter 1
Mountains of Pitakae

The destruction had been total or so it would seem. Nearly a thousand men who had been, they felt, fighting the Lord's battle were vanquished. Not one man stood nor moved among the gore and disgrace that had been, only a few hours before, a mighty army.

The army of the Lord had been destroyed. No power in the world could possibly be strong enough, now, to turn aside the mighty force of the Atrocenes. The little spearhead of God that was called Rasomite had been the only strength on earth left which could have turned aside the evil of the Atrocenes and the apathy of the people. Now, that "Sunlight of God" was gone.

The Rasomites had stood over their little corner of the earth for decades, defending the people and upholding the only bastion of holiness left. The years and constant fighting weighed heavily upon them, and Garasom, leader of their people, had struck a deal with Atrocene, leader of the Atrocenes. They laid down most of their arms and surrendered their horses and chariots. In turn, they were told they would be free to practice their religion and live in peace. Garasom had been blinded by the weariness of war. With this foolish deed done, the Atrocenes slaughtered them like a flock of sheep led to the butcher.

The Sunlight of God had been extinguished and now lay here in this battlefield, never to rise again. Even as the dust began to settle from this fateful battle, however, there was movement and one man stood.

Anam's charcoal-gray flesh bore no marks of the battle that the Lord had delivered to the Atrocenes. He stood alone, gazing upon the horror of hundreds of dead, but he knew only peace. It had to be so, such that God himself could have the victory. Anam had been struck in the head at the first moment of battle and knocked cold. He ran his strong hands up and down his body and over his head and was assured there were no wounds.

His straight, black hair hung past his broad shoulders; shoulders that carried no other burden than to perform his Master's will. His eyes betrayed no hint of sadness, nor of joy. But to one who did not know his heart, they would appear cold and firm. Indeed, deep in his heart, there was sadness for his people; people who were no more. The scene before his eyes, now, had been shown to him by the Lord in a dream. For this reason, he never shed a tear for he knew he had a mission.

The only clothing this man wore was a brown, leather loin-cloth, unlike either his comrades or his enemies who always wore heavy and brightly colored uniforms and carried a sheath full of weapons. The only weapons Anam normally carried were a small bow and a quiver full of arrows and, occasionally, a knife. These he carried when he was not carrying the weapons of Garasom.

Closing his eyes to the ruin that surrounded him, he raised his arms up to heaven and sang in a voice that pleased God:

"Oh, my Lord,
thou art the victor this day, and I praise your name
because of it.
The army of the Rasomites has been destroyed on
earth but only to reach a higher calling.
The army of the Atrocenes has been victorious on
earth such that they may be better destroyed.
They shall be brought to destruction and also to
mockery.
Lead me, my Lord, show me now the way I should
go.
Teach me how I might be victorious for your
name, Father."

And then, Anam could hear a voice meant only for his ears:

"This day I have brought this destruction to your
eyes for you to understand the result of bending my
will.
This will be a new beginning for the Sunlight of
God and this time will be remembered throughout

history.
This day I bring unto you a new way to lead and
a new following.
They will hearken to your word and you will obey
me."

Even as Anam began to wonder in what way he would be shown to obey God, a gathering of people began to appear on the horizon. Not yet distinguishable to the eye, Anam knew this army. It was the parents, wives, and children of the dead men before him. The Lord would kindle a terrible fire in the hearts of these people, and the foolish Atrocenes would finally suffer for their wickedness.

The dead had not been buried for it would be foolish to leave a sign of the might of the new army. Rituals were not needed as the souls of the dead men were already protected.

Anam had been shown in his dreams that they should winter in the mountains and, in the spring, God would utterly destroy the Atrocenes.

The mountains provided a safe refuge for them, though the bite of winter came too soon. The Atrocenes were totally involved in exploiting the peasantry now that there was no protector. He felt totally confident of their speedy victory if only he could keep the peoples' anger from exposing them. Many, at first, were prepared to throw their ill-equipped bodies at the Atrocenes. But Anam explained to them the fatal error of his father-in-law and that they must be prepared and wait on God.

Their daily life now was one of preparation for the final conflict. Children were being taught the proper use of spears and arrows. Women were being taught by their children how to crawl on their bellies and scale cliffs as they did. Anam taught a select group of women advanced archery. Nothing could be done with an arrow that they were not learning to master. To this group he gave the name "Shamra" which meant "The Devil's Assassin." They had adopted another meaning for the word, as well: "Guardian Women."

They were as fleet-footed as the wind. If their eye could see it, their arrow could bring it down. Their brownish-grey skin blended perfectly with the rocks and sand, and it was said, if they were in hiding, a pack of wolves could pass them by and never see them. God was empowering them. Their arms and hands had become strong and able to climb sheer rock walls and bend the branches of the barboa tree where a normal man would be torn in half by those strong limbs.

Their sustenance was provided by the mountains; the soft buds of next year's pine branches, the roots of grasses and weeds, and an occasional berry. They were becoming a lean, quick-footed people and turned to the deer and the elk to teach them how to run, to eat and to survive.

But the women were without men. Their hearts would pound once for their anger at the Atrocenes and once for their passion that was never sated. Anam attracted many eyes among the people. To the old, he stood for the only way the past could survive into the future. To the young, he was a hero. His body rippled with the well -toned muscles that the Lord had provided him. His face, however, always appeared carved from granite as there was only one thing on his mind; his covenant with God. To the women, he symbolized these things as well as a direction for their ardor. However, he was not much interested in the fondness that they would be pleased to show him.

Anam's wife, the daughter of their fallen leader Garasom, was still a prisoner of the Atrocenes. The Lord had not shown him that she lived, but Anam knew in his heart that she must be in the Atrocene city, Rodan. His desire was to steal into the city, as he often did, and retrieve her without anyone's knowledge. He only awaited the opportunity.

On a day when the sun was burning much warmer than it had been all winter, his counselors came before him with Zeda, leader of the Shamra, at their head.

It was late afternoon and Anam had spent the day brooding over the deliverance of his wife, Aurora, as he prayed for a plan to free her. He sat between two large boulders and immediately behind him was the foxhole-home he had dug out in the side of the hill. From this position, he could see most of the Rasomite activity; however, it was seldom necessary that he become involved in the training or the daily activities around him. His presence was all that was needed.

Anam had put one of the women in charge of training the others and Zeda had managed, by God's grace, to take these women and forge them into a powerful force.

Today, Zeda stood before Anam clad in a white rabbit-fur loin cloth and a brassiere of black musk-ox hide held together by strands of gold. She was lovely, but physical appearance was of little importance to Anam. Her jet black hair rolled in waves down her neck and shoulders. She was strong and her almost ashen-gray skin was flawless and beautiful, at the same time, seeming as thick as the bark of a beech tree. She wore nothing on her feet, which had become the custom.

Anam sat silently, watching Zeda and the other two females flanking her as they approached him.

It was several seconds before she spoke. "You know that she lives?"

"I feel it is true. Can you tell me more?

"She lives," Zeda stated flatly.

He knew that this was not a truth that Zeda bore easily. He knew that she loved him. Throughout the winter, her attention had been devoted more and more to Anam. She was not overt or direct in her fondness, but she seemed always to be available. He could not, he told her, love anyone else now. The reasons for this were twofold and both were great. It was his feeling that Aurora must be alive and to be faithful to God, he must be faithful to her. He had also explained that there was enough on his mind now to satisfy the Lord's and the Rasomites' anger against the Atrocenes. He had told her it would be foolish of him to turn his feelings of faithfulness and duty to lust. After he knew the fate of his wife and when the final conflict was done, he would consider her affection.

Zeda in return had tried to explain that Aurora had not been faithful, for she had seen this in a dream. Anam denied it, but Zeda could not be turned from her heart-felt belief.

"The truth that she lives is good," Anam said.

"No it is not, because she has betrayed you. Aurora is in Rodan, but it pleases her to be there. She is the lover of Atrocene and stays with him of her own free will. Not only has she betrayed you, but she has betrayed God."

"How do you know all this?"

"This morning, my spies have returned from Rodan and given me this message."

"It is late in the day and the path from your tent to my den is a short one. Why have you taken so long?"

"I knew you would not believe me. I knew unless God showed you or you saw for yourself, it would be a mind not ready to know the truth."

"I do not like your words!" he spoke angrily. "You are afraid of my love for Aurora."

"I do not know fear, for I put my faith in God, not man. You know I lost my husband and have no children, so I have nothing to lose. You know I have trained hard and taken these women and turned them into the Shamra at your direction. They are now far more powerful than the men of the Atrocenes, but they cannot be victorious by their strength alone, for we are outnumbered by more than a little. It can be won only by the strength of God. You rely on his strength as do I. You deserve better. I am worthy of you."

"I have a wife."

"Your wife is dead. She is worse than dead. She is condemned beyond reproach."

"What has she done?"

"I cannot say. You won't believe me when I say she is unfaithful. You will not believe me when I tell you more."

"You do not know what she has done?" He asked this even as he knew her mind was clear. "Then, I have heard enough."

Zeda turned to go but hesitated. "What will you do?" she asked.

"I will pray and decide what I should do."

The entourage proceeded back down the hill to their tents.

Anam prayed throughout the night, asking for God's counsel. That steadfast God, who had promised to lead Anam in all things, withheld any real answer and simply warned him to let his spirit, not his heart, lead him.

The following morning Anam told Methibecham, his personal counselor, that he would need to be away to hunt as relief from the daily routine. He had said he would be gone most of the day. He felt the Lord calling him away and directing him, but did not clearly understand the mission. The only weapon he carried was his bow and one arrow. This he had brought as a sign to Methibecham that he would kill the quarry that the Lord had prepared for him with one shot. It would be foolish, he felt, to go with no protection. Zeda would know, but it would be too late when she discovered his disappearance.

As he descended towards the prairie, he pondered the words that Zeda had shared with him. Aurora was a prisoner of Atrocene. Of that he had been sure. It was easy to grasp the concept of her as Atrocene's lover, but it was inconceivable that she was living this way from her own desire. However, Zeda's words must be true, but he could not understand why the Lord had not shown or prepared him for this.

The day was very hot. Sweat had broken upon his brow as he reached the mire that separated the Atrocene city, Rodan, from the rest of the world.

His feet moved quickly through the swamp and never slowed despite the muck and twisted brambles. The Lord placed his feet where they should go to avoid any entanglements. Time was the critical element and could betray him. If he were gone too long, there would be no other recourse than for the Shamra to go after him. Zeda would make sure of that.

He stayed far from the well-traveled roadway. It was important that no one could see him, as his rescue attempt could be endangered by an eager shout from a stranger.

Eventually, he reached the foot of the city wall. The hour was still early enough that there would be little stirring within the city. The wall should be easily scaled in a few minutes, for it was less than fifty feet in height. It had been built rapidly with a variety of stones and was weak in several places. The lower wall, where he stood, was actually recessed several feet in from where the top jutted out. The Atrocenes were fierce warriors, but they were not wise architects. Actually, Anam was quite sure that they could not design a city to keep him out.

Anam grabbed the wall with both hands and placed his feet on outcropping cobblestones. Inch by inch he scaled the wall. He moved quickly and was sure-footed, careful not to alert guards to his invasion. In a few minutes, he had scaled the enclosure to this godless city. He knew where to go next.

Atrocene's palace was in the heart of the city. The city had been designed with the palace in the center and it was the tallest building. Each structure he came to was slightly higher than the one before it. He moved quickly along the top of the city leaping from one building to the next.

Finally, he stopped. His way was blocked by a chasm that surrounded the palace, over a hundred feet across and twice that height with a canal running through the depths. From his vantage point, he could clearly see that Aurora's bedchamber window was perhaps twenty feet higher than where he was standing. He had sat in this same spot many times in the past.

Then, he saw a face in the window. Aurora had just risen from sleep and was looking directly at him. She could not, at first, distinguish who it could be with the morning sun directly behind him, but his appearance must have been quite impressive with the rising sun illuminating him. Then, he sensed that she knew him. Who else could have been waiting in this fashion? One of her arms stretched out and pointed down, showing him where to go. Immediately to his right was a staircase descending to a deep courtyard. He looked across the distance once more at her and descended the steps.

His heart leaped, for he knew that she would soon be free. He crossed the bridge of the little canal and entered the courtyard. Within the courtyard it was warm despite being in the shade. Kiwatuan's furnaces were always in use. Anam stood at the foot of a marble staircase. At the top was a statue of Kiwatuan, the devil god of the Atrocenes. It stood, perhaps, eighteen feet tall, made of some black, very smooth, stone. Anam stared at its ugliness as he waited. To this devil, the bodies of children and peasants were burned as offerings to the stone god. It was a statue of a fat man, with a ring in its nose, bearing four arms. Two of the hands were extended in a sign of peace. The other pair were extended over its head and crushing the body of an unknown enemy warrior.

To Anam's left was the white plaster wall of the palace of Atrocene. It bore the flag of their army, six black and six white stripes with the face of the ugly Kiwatuan imposed over the top.

To his right were the poles bearing the heads of those great leaders defeated in combat. One of these rods carried the head of Garasom, his former leader, now rotten and deformed. An empty pole stood next to this. Confusion suddenly occupied his mind. Could they be aware of him?

Aurora entered and stood next to the statue. Its black lifelessness was in contrast to her cream-colored skin. She was not of the same complexion as the Rasomites, which is what had attracted Anam to her. Her skin radiated life, but seemed very different from what she had been before, and her blue eyes appeared to breathe love, showing that her heart was still Anam's. She wore over her blonde hair a set of bull horns that were the normal wear to deliver the blessings of these people. Her floor-length gown was bright red silk and fell from her neck to below her feet. It was emblazoned with various Atrocene war and religious symbols. As she stared at Anam, her guards formed behind her.

"I have come for you." Anam said, watching the guards carefully.

"We have waited for you. I knew that you would come. You have lived alone?"

"Does the Devil not show you how I have lived?" he said, looking at the lifeless head of her father.

"Kiwatuan knows all and directs life as he sees fit. He has brought you to us."

"I have come to you of my own will."

"I know," she said.

"How has your winter been? It was a cold year."

"Atrocene has kept my nights warm. The furnaces of Kiwatuan have warmed my days."

"Then you wish to stay?"

"I will stay and you will be near me always."

She looked in the direction of the remains of those who had been righteous and at the vacant pole. Her father's head stared blankly back at her.

"I and Atrocene are one, and we both lead these people."

"Then why did your eyes betray you when they first saw me?"

"The flesh is weak."

"But my spirit is strong."

In a second, Anam had let fly his arrow into her heart. She let out a gasp and fell to the ground. In another second, Anam had disappeared from the courtyard and was soon descending out of Rodan along the tops of the buildings. He was already near the wall before the guards were able to gather their wits and sound an alarm. But Anam was already gone, leaving his lone arrow buried in the breast of his wife and enemy.

Zeda was so very beautiful. Her hair had been brushed out as straight as it could be, though the ebony waves were still evident. Her bright, brown eyes sparkled and perhaps they were moistened from joy or from the agony she feared her mate must be going through. Her lips were full and still slightly parted from the surprise of grief and joy Anam had bestowed upon her. Her dress was made of the only silk left, taken from their home a few months ago. It was cream-colored, as she had had a husband before but had never bore any children. It fell to just above her ankles and was full and loose at the bottom. She wore no shoes but stood upon a bed of leaves that had been carefully strewn before her as she walked to the altar.

Anam stood on a mound of dirt also covered with leaves so that his bare feet should not have to touch the cold earth. He wore nothing elaborate except the black snakeskin headband which had been given to him by Garasom.

His eyes, which were still moist, were riveted on Zeda's as they prepared to exchange vows in front of the entire population. Not a single child was missing from this gathering today.

There were no others before them to act as counselor or to unite them in marriage. They had prayed all through the night before and chosen to simply exchange vows and allow God to be their chief witness. Anam had told Zeda everything and that he would be pleased to take her as his wife before the great conflict.

Anam spoke first. "Who am I? I am the child of God and the brother of man. This was why I was brought unto man, to deliver him out of the hands of the world and into the hands of God. We are now on the day of the great conflict between the people who are called the Sunlight of God and those who are called the Sword of the Devil and the scourge of the earth. And in this brief moment before that conflict comes, this lovely woman comes before me, who would be my wife, for I have none. Zeda, I will pledge to love you above all else, save God, and I will be your husband until the ends of the earth or until it is God's choice to take us out of each other's lives."

Zeda replied in kind, "I was brought into this world to be the wife and lover of the man who would save man from himself. I will, with God's blessing, always support you and always be by your side. I will do that which you ask of me and more than is asked."

"I will die for you," he said as he took her left hand in his and they turned to the gathered Rasomites.

"To die is good," she said to him, "but to live is better. If God calls me, I am willing to die for you to be a sign for you or to protect your life."

"I declare this woman to be my wife and I her husband!" he said to the people. "God is our witness in heaven, and you are our witnesses on earth."

He turned back to her and spoke quietly so that only she could hear.

"The world is being turned upside-down, Zeda. In a day, it shall be over and all good people will have a chance for a new beginning."

"Can it work so quickly?"

"We are but a distraction to the Atrocenes. It will be God's victory."

"But men will doubt."

"Men will always doubt. That is a worldly gift, but it shall be God's victory, nonetheless."

"I feel that very soon the Lord will use me to make you stronger."

"I will be blessed. In a few hours, we must start our trek to Rodan. There is no time in this age for proper ritual, but I want you."

Zeda blushed, and a touch of pink could even be seen through the gray flesh on her cheeks as her eyes seemed to sparkle even more brightly in the afternoon sun.

"I want you," he said again, "then, we shall fight God's war."

Anam looked up at his people who were anticipating his final words. He spoke in a loud voice so that all could hear. "Go ye, my people, and prepare for God's war. Soon, we go to Rodan and to our victory. Prepare for this with my blessing and render unto us this one hour of peace."

Then, he and Zeda turned and ascended the stony path to Anam's habitat in the rock wall above.

It was still dark, though one could see the light beginning to form at the horizon. The stars were shining brightly, but it was a new moon. There was not enough light to allow the enemy to detect those who would put them under siege. Anam looked upon the main battery of the Atrocene army. Their tents and night fires spread out across the valley as far as the eye could see.

Anam had sent Zeda to Rodan. The Atrocene army was sleeping in the valley between them.

He had brought himself and four others to the camp that lay before them. They were all men, his comrades, though none were yet sixteen years of age. God had prepared a gift for them that would be written and spoken of throughout the generations. They stood a few feet behind Anam, not afraid to gaze at the enemy, but in awe of the anticipated outcome.

Anam raised his right hand to the sky and said in a loud voice, "Evil men who would kill children for play. You who have worshipped Kiwatuan. Prepare to meet your true Master."

There was a rumble and the ground began to shake. The noise continued to build up to such a volume that his four companions fell to the ground in fear and covered their ears. Anam spoke to the smallest warrior, a boy of only six, and asked him his name.

"My name is Togorasom. It means the light shall shine again."

Anam picked him up and placed him on his shoulders. As he did so the stars shimmered, becoming indistinct, as if even the sky was shaking. Suddenly a beam of light flashed across the heavens.

In the encampment of the mighty Atrocenes below, men had begun dashing from their tents, shouting and screaming out for their god of stone.

The sky was becoming a mass of light that began piercing the atmosphere. Suddenly, it became like a round of giant fiery boulders smashing down upon the earth. There was no escape. The fire from the sky pelted the powerful army below and, in only a few seconds, the entire camp was in flames.

The smell of burning flesh finally drove Anam and his band back from the edge, and they began the eager run to the city of Rodan.

By this time, the entire city was alert and pointing up at the dazzling light display. None realized the reasons behind this or what lay in their immediate future.

Deep within the bowels of this city, Zeda had crept in with her accomplices to show the Atrocenes the power of a true God.

In the midst of the courtyard where Anam's former wife had

been slain and laid to rest, King Atrocene stood. His arms were raised above his head and he spoke in a religious language unfamiliar to the Rasomites. Even in these shadows, the early morning sunlight glittered upon the fresh blood that covered his pale white skin. Their ritual was to pour the blood of fallen warriors over their heads in the belief that they would gain their strength.

It would have been so easy for Zeda to pierce Atrocene with an arrow and flee, but that was not what Anam had told her to do. She must destroy the statue.

Kiwatuan sat at the top of the steps, very near the edge. He wore a gold nose-ring in his fat face and this was Zeda's target. If she could hook that ring with the line she had on her back, they should be able to pull it forward enough to topple it. If not, Atrocene and two others in the yard would have to die before the task could be completed.

She handed the line, with its ball and hook and arrow, to Anna, her best short-range archer. Anna picked up the thin line and rolled the ball tied to it in her hands. She would have one try to get it right. She tested the ball by throwing it up and down in her right hand.

One of Atrocene's men, alerted by the movement, turned and gazed into the bushes. His mouth fell open, and he turned to grab his spear but fell to the ground. He twitched once in the dirt and moved no more. Zeda's arrow had entered the back of his neck and reappeared in his forehead.

Anna, unfazed by this, let fly the ball with her arrow. It hit Kiwatuan near the top of the head and rolled over the bridge of his nose. The hook did not catch the ring, but the ball did. Zeda and the others pulled the line with all their might. The statue was amazingly light, as though it was as hollow as the promises of power. It inched forward a foot and then began leaning over the steps.

By this time the other Atrocene guard had become a witness to this flurry of silent activity. He grabbed his spear and flung it into the bushes in a wild, unaimed movement. It met Anna's arrow halfway and glanced off to fall harmlessly at her feet.

The intensity of Atrocene's prayer increased. He sensed a disruption, but his involvement in his activity was so total that he paid it no heed. Suddenly, the statue tottered over the edge of the stairway. The guard, understanding Zeda's plan now flailed at the line. All he succeeded in doing was adding extra weight to the line. Kiwatuan fell over into the courtyard.

The guard and Atrocene barely got out of the way to avoid being crushed. The statue's torso was solid, but most of its arms had broken off, and it had been decapitated. Its head now lay on the earth near the body of the dead guard. Zeda and her contingent had, by now, fled up the stairway and were escaping from the city.

As they reached the wall of the city, they were surprised not to hear the noise of Anam's attacking army. It was not until Zeda reached the edge that she could see exactly what Anam had done. Instead, he had with him the leaders of the Shamra and many of the archers but had left nearly everyone else behind. His attacking force consisted of less than two hundred female archers and perhaps thirty positioned leaders. Anam stood in their midst with a circle of open space around him. As she peered over the edge of the city wall, a smile flashed across his face. In a moment, she had descended the ropes, left earlier, and she stood at his side again.

"The city of Rodan houses perhaps fifty thousand with an army of at least ten thousand. This is your attack?" She motioned towards the gathering.

"Today, we shall win the Lord's battle. There shall be no doubt who the victor is."

Togorasom, clad in a goatskin tunic, moved closer to Anam's side. His face, in spite of the moderate heat, appeared to be sunburned.

"This boy," said Anam, placing his hand on the lad's shoulder, "I have taken as my son. He is the only witness of the defeat of the Atrocene army. Atrocene is a fool. All he has remaining are his horsemen, and there are fewer than two thousand of them. If he wants to fight a war, he has only a few minutes to raise a new army."

"The city is large. The people are many, even without an army. We are few. Show me."

Anam raised his arms into the air, and the earth began to shake as it had earlier. The rest of the Rasomites began to flee into the surrounding swamp, leaving the three alone. They began backing away from the wall. The wall stood like a giant monolith before them and, though it appeared to be solid, a fissure began to form in it near where they had been standing.

The entire earth seemed to be shaking. The weaker branches of dead brush stuck in the mud behind them began breaking off, but the main force was concentrated at the wall. Blocks and pieces of stone began to fall from it along its entire length. Suddenly, a large crack appeared at its base and shot up to the top, as giant slabs of rock caved both inward and outward from the structure.

Anam was sitting peaceably enough on a log nearby witnessing this destruction. Zeda and Togorasom, their new son, sat at his feet. He heard a voice, inaudible to anyone else.

"Flee!"

He shook his head, denying the word. He thought this was too great an opportunity. Atrocene had no army, his city walls were crumbling, and what remained of his horsemen would be in total confusion. It was time to enter the city, take captives, and end the battle without firing a single arrow. He would be a fool to turn his back and run, allowing the horsemen time to organize and overtake them. It would be a worse defeat than his father-in-law had seen the summer before. No, he could not run.

Even as his troops began to advance on the giant gap that left the city open to them, the archers of the enemy were forming to protect what remained of Rodan.

Indeed, they were not soldiers, only craftsmen and family men who had organized to protect themselves. Since they were few in number, he called out for them to lay down their arms even as their arrows began whistling past him. He pulled an arrow from his quiver and retaliated as his female archers had reformed their ranks and had, also, begun firing.

It seemed, however, for every one of those he felled, five more took his place. This would not be an easy battle after all. Already, several of his archers had fallen and there appeared to be no end to those appearing on the inside of the wall.

He raised his arm to signal a full-forward running attack as he glanced at Zeda. Her eyes were fixed in determined concentration on the enemy, when suddenly, she stopped. Her mouth fell open and then shut as she began to fall. He could see the arrow in her abdomen and even as he leaned toward her to catch her, three more entered her body.

Anam quickly raised her over his shoulder and called a retreat to the tattered remains of his army. They now consisted of a few dozen, mostly unarmed women and one boy, and they ran with all the speed they had left in their feet.

The dirt road across the swamp was the path they chose, and beyond the swamp lay a wide belt of grass. They ran with the prairie lying between them and the safety of the mountains. Even if they could maintain their strength, it would take at least two hours to reach its safety, and Anam could imagine he heard the horses of the Atrocenes already leaving the city.

They had no weapons, but for their bows, for which they had almost no arrows. The mountains seemed to loom further and further away as the strength fell first from Anam's mind and then his body.

He stopped near a pile of boulders and, laying down the woman he loved, fell to his knees to prepare for prayer, but there was not even time for that.

The earth shook around him for the third time this day, but it was full of dust turned up by the heels of approaching horses. They were not two hundred feet away when they stopped and one horseman came forward a few paces.

He wore the skin of a bear, partially white. His hair was long and hung over his shoulders that were still red with the blood of Aurora's corpse. He called out in a strange language but one Anam understood.

"You have turned our world upside-down, arms-bearer. It will take much time to repair our lives. It would be wise to take you as a slave for you are strong and could repair the statue of Kiwatuan in a short time. However, my anger is too great and so you must die!"

He raised his spear, and Anam, still on his knees, could almost feel it enter him as he sat there facing the angry enemy.

The earth shook and Anam gazed into the sky as tears began to form in his eyes.

"You have not forsaken me, my God!"

As he watched, the sandy earth under Atrocene's horses gave way. He watched the terrified faces of those men and horses as they slowly and helplessly sank into the quicksand and disappeared. Anam raised his hands to the sky.

"Oh, my Lord,
thou art the victor this day.
I praise you, my God, for I am weak and you are
strong.

Nothing in heaven or on earth has the strength
of a mite when compared to you, my Lord.
Forgive us for not always following your will,
but we are only men.
I cry for you, and for your word."

Then a voice that could be heard by all filled the air.

"You are my children, and it is you I raise up.
Heed my cry when I speak to you.
You are my glory upon the earth.
There will be other wars to be fought, and I will
not always be at your side. It will not be
because I have left you, but because you have left me
though, I will not be far away.
Prepare yourselves for a long trip, for there are
things you must see and things you must do.
Now, go ye, and find the scattered flocks."

Chapter 2
Crato

The uncomely-looking man rocked back and forth on his legs as he changed position. He was weary. It had taken him and his family nearly four days to travel across the desert and the mountains to arrive in Crato. His flesh was dirty and his clothing, if it could be called such, reeked with a variety of foul aromas. He wore a robe that might have once been white and it hung to his knees; on his feet were leather sandals. His robe had worn through in many places and bore several snags and tears from the handling of his goats.

He was not old, perhaps thirty, but one would think that this poor, elderly-looking beggar must be nearly sixty years of age. His face was dry and pocked with crevices. It looked, in many ways, like the desert he called home. His legs were hairless and calloused from the desert storms. The hair on his head was nearly white and thin and short. His wife, Shabulari, had barbered him only moments ago to lend a little to his appearance; however, it had not helped.

The court in which he stood was, to most observers, only adequate. However, to his eyes, it suggested luxury. As he studied the plain granite walls and the wooden chairs with cushions of different colors, it was the slate floors that kept him in awe as he had not been in a place like this since childhood. His father had been a king over a populous city far away.

This place reminded him of his little sister who had played games and ran with him through a palace that he could scarcely recall now. He had been only five or six years old when the Atrocenes had raged through, destroying everything.

All his childhood family and friends were dead now, butchered by these men of war. His people had been destroyed but for a tiny number who had been slaves of these devil worshippers. He had been saved once from the glowing flames of Kiwatuan's furnace, though his back still bore the scars of the fire. Because he had entertained the Atrocenes with his snakes, they had spared him his life. They were fond of one who could control these little animals called Slatu, little blood-sucking snakes with fangs of death and skin like iron. He and his wife had eked out a meager living on his snakes and goats and her pottery.

Shaktar, the snake charmer. Shaktar, the King of the Corasites. Shaktar, the beggar. His poor, tired people, now numbering only a few hundred, were the cause of his mission to this place. He had a simple request to ask of Queen Beamu, and he prayed he would soon be on his way. If his request was granted, he would have his only child, Ramona, returned to him and his trip home would not be so far as the one here had been.

A door opened and several well-dressed courtiers and one elderly but well-kept woman entered. She sat in one of the chairs and cast a forced smile at Shaktar.

"All right, desert dweller, you have traveled far afoot to see me. I shall show you the courtesy of a few moments of attention. I see no gifts or decrees in your hand, so I trust you have not made a long journey to give me anything. I can only assume that you expect something from me. Speak up, quickly, tell me what you wish so I may dismiss you."

Shaktar needed a moment to gather his wits. He had not seen Queen Beamu since before the fall of Rodan and, though she was not a generous woman with her gifts, she had always been generous with her time. Now, perhaps not having to live in fear of King Atrocene had gone to her head in such a way that she needed no friends.

"Oh, good and generous Queen of the North. Though you were not a belligerent in the great battle against Rodan, you have risen in the ashes of their defeat as the victor. Except for Anam's meager band of mountain dwellers, there is no other power on this piece of earth than your Excellency.

I come now before your grace as a man freed from the great tyranny of the Atrocenes. A man who bore the full weight of their insolent attitude and cruelty. You know my family and people are few in number. You also know we are not afraid of hard work or of its benefits. There is a small piece of property near here commonly called the Plains of Shazar. This is not a plains, at all, but little more than a desert. However, it is better than the desert that I now call home, because we can find water in this place, good woman, and this shall benefit us all."

The Queen sneered. "Cast aside your flowery speech, beggar. I am not impressed by that or your foolish request. What should I gain from letting you raise your sick goats at my doorstep? For that is what you wish, is it not? I am quite satisfied that you stay in the desert and die. Why should I want you to prosper in my own back yard such that later you may burden me with more requests? There are still the mountains. Go there with your friend, Anam. You can entertain each other with your goats and deer. You are dismissed!" She rose from her seat to leave, but stood awaiting his response.

"Anam is my friend, your Excellency. However, he will soon be leaving your kingdom and this domain. I am not a mountain man and I could not survive there for the harsh winters. We have suffered long under the yoke of the Atrocene people. We have been treated like insects and turned from royalty to poor desert dwellers. Thankfully, we have no need to fear the Atrocenes anymore. As a power, their time has passed."

He stopped for a moment to control his tears. "We are weary, your Excellency. My request is a simple one that can cause you no harm. Should we be successful in the plains, there will be prosperity for all. I beg you," he fell to his knees, "grant us a tiny piece of land in the plains."

She stood a moment, considering his request. Her face was stern and without mercy. Crato was one of the few cities left unravaged by King Atrocene, and this was only because she had raised his statues and prayed to his ugly god. Since she did not believe in any god, it had been simple for her to go through the motions to please this man, but her kingdom had stagnated during his reign. Her people were not allowed to prosper. Their young men and women were hauled off to fight Atrocene's wars and pleasure his soldiers, and their children were fed to the furnaces. She had done little to openly oppose him for fear of losing everything. Now, however, she was in control.

They had toppled the sanctuaries and statues of Atrocene's god only hours after hearing of his death and Anam's victory. Anam had retreated back to the mountains, she supposed, to lick his wounds. Nothing had been heard of him since his retreat a few weeks before, except that he would soon be leaving the area.

She was a bitter woman who would not live long, so she would wreak her anger on anyone she did not need.

"Bring me the head of Anam in a basket and I shall grant your request, and more."

"But your Excellency!" He could not believe his ears. "Good lady, no! Anam is my friend."

"The easier it will be for you to betray him."

"This cannot be. From youth, I have revered this man. I could not. Besides he is, my good woman, protected above all men by the hand of God. The Lord would not allow such an outrage. I beg of you, Queen Beamu, ask me not to do this thing and we shall be your slaves. I shall be your personal servant. Or let us return to the desert to die a decent death under the sun, but not to die for anger of God."

"Shaktar, you have a young and beautiful daughter who is nearly of age. Ramona has lived in hiding for all these years, under my wing, and is still undefiled. I have kept her and lived in fear of my own life because of that foolish King, so you might see her when you will. I tell you this, Shaktar, if you do not betray and destroy Anam and bring me his head in one day, at the setting of tomorrow's sun, the girl shall die."

Shaktar screamed and fell on his face, beating the floor with his hands and his feet. He lay there for several minutes and finally raised his head. The court was empty and such was his heart. Slowly rising to his feet, he stumbled from the room. His mind was numb and his body shaking for he knew not what to do.

At the doorway was Shabulari, who had heard all. She shared his grief, and she wept for her husband who had made this trip, so sure that it would come out well. She also wept for her daughter who would soon be dead.

They would go to the edge of the city where they had encamped and rest for the night. Tomorrow, they would return to the desert and mourn the death of Ramona. There was nothing else to do.

It was not real sleep, at all, but more of a torture. Shaktar slept fitfully that night. Waking many times, he cried out to God to destroy him so this would all be over. Other times, he thought of destroying himself. His dreams, when he slept, were filled with dreadful images. He saw his people, lean and hungry, dying in the desert without even the Atrocene garbage to live on now. Many times he saw Ramona, in all her beauty, dressed gracefully and without knowledge of her imminent death. Each time, he awoke as Queen Beamu or one of her men brought Ramona down with an axe or sword.

He saw Anam. He composed in his dream how the man could be brought to an end, but always too soon either God would pull him away or Anam would sense the danger and save himself. Afterward, he would feel the burden of guilt that he could not control his dream or his wretched heart.

Then, it was morning. Shaktar sat up in his tent, feeling numb and empty in his body and mind. There was nothing he could do. They could not storm the city, for they were too few and their bodies were too weak. Besides, Shaktar's people had no weapons or the knowledge of their use.

All his life, Shaktar had lived in fear for his life and in anger for his people's lives and suffering. He had prayed that, after the conflict, things would be so much better. He could cry no more, for his eyes were so red and sore from crying, they could weep no longer.

Something blocked the rays of the sun in the entrance of his tent. He slowly raised his head, expecting to see his wife. His heart leapt and a smile crossed his face as tears again welled up in his eyes for before him knelt Anam, arms outstretched.

"Come, my friend, your wife has prepared a feast for us this morning, and I am tired from running through the night."

"I feel I have already partaken of a greater feast for seeing you, my good and faithful friend."

They grasped each other by the shoulders, and the tears of Shaktar rolled down Anam's bare, gray flesh. Shaktar felt strength come back to his limbs, and they both left the tent to dine with Shabulari and the others.

The good wife of Shaktar had prepared for Anam, at least in his eyes, a feast. There was cereal of hot bran and oats mixed with fresh goats' milk. There was wine that some of the Corasites had brought from Rodan when they made their escape. There was pudding of cheese curd, cranberries and honey. Anam had not had a breakfast such as this since the morning Garasom's army had been ambushed by the Atrocenes. There was also coffee, in the end, that had been given to one of Shaktar's men by one of Queen Beamu's consorts. As they dined, old times were remembered, but the present was left unsaid.

"My good friend, Shaktar, you do remember the first day we laid eyes upon each other?" Anam said.

"That I do, we were both only boys made old before our times. I wanted to kill you, for it had been a bad day. You know I was not truly angry at you?"

"No, you were just walking aimlessly and stumbled into me. You would not have killed me. You were not made to be a killer. But you would have been satisfied to knock a bit of sense into my head. We were both stubborn youths."

"I tried to bludgeon you with a log." Shaktar laughed. "It broke against your arm. I must have been mad to attack a man thrice my size. I didn't know you or even have a grudge."

"I raised you up and said I would pull off your head unless you prayed to my God. I would never convert someone that way again."

"Aye, but you made your point well, and I was a good student."

"And you told your people and they praised you for it in the end. Let us talk of your good and prosperous future."

"For me, my friend, there is no future. I feel as a dead man who has been brought back to the flesh. Last evening, I wished I were dead. Nothing could have made me more joyful than to see your face this morning except, perhaps, that of my daughter, Ramona."

"The face that you shall see this day."

"Perhaps her face, but without her body."

"Shaktar, you speak of foolishness. Have you besought God's advice or prepared a plan? Or do you only wallow in your self-pity and allow life and death to happen and choose not to participate?"

"There is no hope, if only you knew of..."

Aman cut him off. "Thanks to the kindness of my Lord, I know your plight far better than yourself, for such cause I am here."

"Then you are here to rescue Ramona? I wished it but dared not ask."

"Nay, you are her rescuer!"

"I am a goatherd; you are chosen by God," Shaktar said, sitting back.

"The Lord and I have a covenant with each other. If you choose to honor the Lord and not the Queen, such can also be yours."

"I do not honor this ungodly Queen," Shaktar mumbled.

"You fear her and she controls you this day. How long will you allow other people to control you and your destiny? If you fear God and allow him to control you, then you shall be victorious."

"This very day, my daughter shall die. If you would aid me to be her rescuer, then I would take a covenant out of desire and not from fear."

"I am now returning to the Mountains of Pitakae, which I call home. For you, I have a plan. It is a plan of danger, but you are a man with much to gain and little to lose. The Queen knows you as a beggar and a man afraid, whom she can do with as she will. On this day, you shall no longer be Shaktar the beggar, but King Shaktar, Lord of the Plains of Shazar and of this territory. My plan is a simple one, but it will not work without much prayer."

"My Queen," Shaktar cried as he knelt before Queen Beamu, "this day, my heart is broken. My friend, who I loved so, is dead." He motioned toward the wicker basket that sat with a bloodstained base on the floor between them. He moved forward slightly and removed the cover to reveal its contents. "I shall never forgive you, my Queen, for driving me to this crime. I shall never forgive myself. I only pray that this evil will be matched by your honesty and allow us the gifts you promised and also to return to me my daughter." He turned the basket so that the Queen could clearly see Anam's bloodied face. Her mouth fell open and she failed in her attempt to swallow.

"I cannot believe that you have done this," she spoke falteringly. "Tell me how it came to pass."

"I sent a messenger into the mountains to tell Anam of my plight and the grief you caused me, and so he came. We sat in my tent and drank Atrocene wine all night and then he slept. In the morning, I chopped off his head with his own knife." He gestured to the knife on his belt. "Now, give me my child so I may go and mourn and repent of my crime. I do not know to what lengths my mind shall drive me, for I feel I am insane."

"Give me the basket."

He wiped his tears away and slowly rose to hand the basket to the Queen. "No, to him!" she said, pointing to a guard beside her. He halted and then, reluctantly, handed the basket to the man.

The man touched the head and a piece of soft clay fell away from the side of the face which Shabulari had quickly formed that morning. The guard's face contorted into a grimace of anger as he pushed in the side of the clay replica.

"You have insulted my Queen. She is no fool. Did you not think we would investigate this object? Why have you done this?" He pulled the head from the basket, goat blood dripping down his arm, and threw the basket at Shaktar.

"So!" said the Queen, "Since we could not have the head of Anam, we shall have the head of Ramona. I will not kill you, goatherd. You are so weak, little man. This is so sloppy, you have not even the wisdom to be a little bit creative. Bring her in!"

She raised her hand and a beautiful young girl was brought in. She walked gracefully, at first, for she did not know what the Queen had in mind, but this changed as she took in the dark look on her Queen's face. She was just before her fourteenth birthday. Her hair was bright blonde, her skin light as she was not much exposed to the out-of-doors. This was a healthy girl as Queen Beamu had pampered her and treated her as her own daughter. Her height measured well over five feet, so that, even at her young age, she was taller than many of those around her. Large diamonds set in gold studded her fingers, wrists and ankles. Her dress was of fine -spun silk, the like of which was no longer made in these parts.

"Father!" she called out when she saw him standing there. "Why do you cry so? Have you come for me, at last?"

"Off with her head!" screamed Queen Beamu. "Teach this treacherous beggar to treat me like a fool."

The guard who held the replica of Anam's head picked up a large sword that lay next to the Queen's seat, an ugly smile crossing his face. Unthinkingly, he handed the clay head to the Queen and she, equally unthinking, took it from him. In quest of a hand-hold on the slippery object, she placed her forefinger into the object's mouth. Instantly, a tiny sliver of black shot up across her finger and wrapped itself four times around the woman's wrist. In fear, she cast the clay head away and screamed.

Ramona ran to her father as Queen Beamu slowly raised her hand near her face and gazed horrorstruck at the tiny black snake. Its head was smaller than the fingernail of her tiniest finger. Its fangs were so tiny she could barely see them, but she knew the instant death that their venom held.

"Get it off me! Get it from my hand!" She gazed first at the guard, who stood transfixed, and then at Shaktar. Fear gripped her entire body. Her face had turned white, her mouth hung open, and her breath had nearly stopped. She looked back at the snake. "Please, get it off me," she whimpered, barely able to speak.

Shaktar put his arm around the shoulders of his daughter and smiled at her before addressing the Queen.

"The tiny Slatu is a victim of its surroundings. Few learn to handle these snakes and keep their lives. This one is fond of women and so will bond quickly with you. It does not need much to stay alive. Only a few drops of goat blood or milk will satisfy its hunger for a day or so. Of course, if it becomes too hungry, then it will seek another close source of nourishment. Its skin is as tough as brass tubing, and it prefers not to travel but to seek the warmth of another animal body. They seem to live forever. I pray you do not make it nervous, for it could attack. I believe it is nervous now, so perhaps you might cautiously stroke its body to insure it of your good intentions. If you treat it well, it shall be like a pet. It may also attack if its host feels fear or hatred as, I said, it is a victim of its surroundings and those whom it comes in contact with."

"Please, Shaktar. I beg of you. If you will get this animal from my wrist, I will show you honor and generosity. You were a king, so be the king of this domain. It is yours if you only spare me this retribution. Please."

"I shall never remove it, my lady. It will live with you always. Should you try to remove it, it shall kill you. Even should you become so desperate as to remove your arm to be free of it, it will immediately release its hold and find you; that is its nature.

You can live. Your life shall be a good one. The Slatu will ensure that you are always cheerful and well-tempered. Otherwise, as I said, it may become nervous. In time, you may become quite good friends with this little one, but it will never release its hold."

Queen Beamu sat back in her chair and let her hand fall limply on its arm but she did not move her gaze from the snake.

"It shall be this way, Madame. My God and, also, my good

friend, Anam, have chosen this to be a sacred region. It is a good thing. They believe that all should live free to love one another and to praise God. That is all that is required. Anam desires that all your people and all those here roundabout should be thankful for this day.

Now, it is my time to lead once more. My city shall be near here in the Plains of Shazar and my court will be a simple one. The people here desire a new kind of home and a new beginning. This is the gift that they shall receive. I go now with my family to build my kingdom here on earth and, I trust, you shall soon visit me to speak of honor and the Lord's generosity. Then, I shall tell you of another kingdom yet to come. Good day."

Shaktar and Ramona bowed low, turned about abruptly, and left the poor woman, still in a state of shock as she stared at the snake nestled on her wrist.

Chapter 3
Cursed

Anam sat quietly, watching Togorasom draw shapes in the dirt and build designs with pieces of gravel. The designs seemed to be of no special significance, but the boy sat with two older boys who were intently watching his artistry upon the earth. They would whisper to each other occasionally upon some aspect of this work but, other than this sound, there was great silence. It was quiet time, as it was each day shortly after noon, unless Anam or one of the counselors directed otherwise. The people were directed to pray and consider what had happened at Rodan and what God now desired of each one of them. Anam had kept Togorasom by his side almost constantly since the fall of the Atrocene army and the death of Zeda.

Below him sat the survivors of the Shamra. Many of the people had moved to Crato after Queen Beamu had been subdued. The tribe now numbered thirty-nine women, including Anna, who had been long before selected by Zeda as their leader in the event of her death.

All of these women were beautiful, but Anna's beauty by far surpassed any of the others. She was not interested in ornamentation such as bracelets and gold chains, as were many of the others. In fact, except when required, she never wore jewelry. She also dressed simply. Today she wore a goatskin tunic, her long jet-black hair, usually tied up in a bun, was brushed out and fell nearly to her waist. In spite of her well-toned body, her face was still childlike.

She sat now slightly apart from the others, with her head bowed in prayer. Her grief had been as great, or greater, than Anam's upon the death of Zeda and the other women. At first she had been bitter toward Anam when she heard of God's warning and how he ignored it, but the bitterness appeared to have passed. She had been away from the village several times in the days after the battle but, recently, had seldom strayed far from where she now sat. No one knew where she had wandered, though. They assumed she had been in the wilderness to pray and find peace as her countenance had improved more with each return home.

Anam scanned the small valley that he had called home for nearly a year. This had once been a mighty nation, spread out across the Plains of Shazar and into Kektar woods. They had ships that had set sail from Crato and returned with many fine goods, though Anam had not been a witness to this power for he had grown up far from here.

As a baby, Anam had been anointed by God and so had lived in the Temple of Teka many days from here. The priests taught him to know God, blessed him daily and laid hands on him to drive into his being the power of God. They had taught him well until the Atrocenes had come burning the temple and slaughtering the priests. Anam had fled with an elderly priest, Mebiktu, who was still with him today, but being the age of ninety-two, his words and visions were a gift seldom received, as he slept more than he was awake.

Anam's people were few in number because of the repeated Atrocene victories, which had brought great loss and suffering to both sides. There were the elderly and children but no young men and few young women. Instead of joy after Rodan fell, there was only mourning from those who had survived. Perhaps it was these cold, bare mountains that lent to the depression or not knowing what would happen next that had made the people spend less time in training and more time in prayer; if they really were in prayer at all. Perhaps they only cried and actually slept in a show of prayer. Even depression had gripped Anam and would not seem to release its hold.

Togorasom stood up and smiled upon his playmates. He leaned over and whispered something to them, and they slowly got up and walked back down to the main camp. Then he stood, feet apart, hands on hips, staring at Anam.

"Father, are we still called the Sunlight of God?"

"Yes, my son."

"Are you still anointed by His hand?"

"Yes."

"Then we should be happy. Perhaps, we should not have a

quiet time so we can feel sorry for ourselves. Maybe, we need a noisy time." He smiled at Anam. "You have been thinking of when you were a little boy?"

Anam blinked, surprised that his son knew of his thoughts. "I have been thinking of much."

"I wish I had a priest to teach me, but all the priests, except grandfather," for such he called Mebiktu, "are gone. Can we have new priests?"

"That is for the old priest and for God to decide."

"But what will happen if grandfather doesn't make a new priest? Can God do it without grandfather's help?"

"I do not know. You ask many questions."

"I know, but I want to be like you, because you need my help. Can I ask grandfather about the priests?"

"Perhaps on a day when he feels well."

"Can I be a priest?"

"That, I cannot answer. You ask too many questions."

"I'm sorry. I will go and make sure grandfather is asleep."

"But don't awaken him!"

"Yes, Father." Togorasom lowered his head and walked down the path.

"My son." He turned back. "I am going on a hunt. You stay at camp and watch for me."

"Yes, my Father. Goodbye." He turned and headed down toward the circle of women, and as Anam watched him go, he laughed inside about a noisy time. Perhaps the boy was right in his own way.

Anam arose and prepared to go, but a hunt was not in his plan. He wanted to go see Rodan.

As he descended the mountain path, he stopped to gaze across the desert-like prairie. The sun was still high in the sky. There was so little life in this place. Once, one could see a city from this promontory where Anam sat. It was not so much a city, but rather a busy village but, now, there was no sign of this place. It had been levelled to the ground by the Atrocenes, the pieces used to build Rodan and the people destroyed. It had been one of several villages of the Rasomites and their allies. They had lived in peace with even Queen Beamu, whose circumstances now made her as bitter as Anam.

For a moment, he wept and wanted to level the city of Rodan, killing every man, woman and child there. He wanted to be ruthless.

It seemed now as though everything was over. The handful of survivors still remaining would take many generations to grow and rebuild, even if the Lord were generous. There was nothing in this place to keep Anam here. He would go to Rodan, condemn the city, and return. Then the Rasomites would leave.

If only the Lord would lift him up and tell him what to do. He, of all men on earth, knew he had been chosen by God for a glorious mission. But, now he felt like the weakest man on earth and the most alone. He lay on his face and wept bitterly into the barren earth before exhaustion overcame him and he slept.

When he arose, the sun was beginning to set beyond Kektar Woods. It seemed every color on earth had filled the sky with the sunset and Kektar Woods was aglow, seeming almost to be ablaze from the drenching of this sun. Never had Anam seen an evening of such beauty. He praised God for letting him see this and arose to begin his journey. He would walk to Kektar Woods and, in the morning, find a horse to carry him to Rodan.

The forest was peaceful, and the Lord had prepared for him a dry bed of pine needles and soft grass. He thought of nothing in particular, but felt satisfied from the sunset and long walk. Eventually, he closed his eyes and slept soundly with a faint smile on his lips. He had not smiled like this for many days.

There were others in the forest that night eagerly anticipating his sleep. Two men from Rodan had also planned for this to be a day away from their troubles and, instead, God had brought the enemy to them. They only waited for darkness and Anam's sleep. It was their belief that this man of God could not have walked passed and not seen them except that Kiwatuan had delivered him to his death at their hands. The man's mind was clearly far away, and he was totally unarmed.

One drew an arrow from his quiver and notched it, training his unsteady sights on the sleeping man. Both men were intoxicated, having drunk to victory over this man before it had been granted, and so they did not realize that another set of eyes was trained on them.

A small shadow dropped from above them and a knife entered

the archer's neck in the curve of his right shoulder. The injured man's scream woke Anam instantly but the danger had passed. The man lay on the earth, near death. The other man, in great fear and confusion, had fled into the forest. The shadow had fled, as well. Anam did not know his rescuer for, though the weapon had been left, he did not recognize its make or origin but cleaned and kept it for the future.

Togorasom was still terrified when his legs gave out from running. He felt vulnerable and alone and wished he had taken the knife with him when he ran. Although going home was tempting, he didn't want to risk running across the unprotected grassland with an unseen enemy still out there. Instead, Togorasom curled up behind a dead stump and despite shivering from cold and fear, slept.

Early in the morning, he was awakened by a sound nearby. He opened his eyes to see only a pair of legs in trousers blocking his view. Terrified, he looked up at the angry man standing over him, a large sword strapped to his side.

"Now, little charcoal-colored boy, you shall die. Did you think I would not track you? You have killed my friend horribly and so you shall die in the same way. And after I have finished with you, I will find Anam. It would have been a good thing for Anam to be slain, for he has slain our good leader and his wife."

Togorasom spat at his feet. "Your leader was the son of the devil and wicked and she was a whore." He spoke bravely in spite of shaking with fear.

The man drew his sword, and Togorasom scrambled up and looked quickly around for rescue but there were no saviors in sight. The boy snatched up a branch lying near him, and the Atrocene began laughing.

"This will be a fine duel, little goat."

The giant sword swung down and would have lopped off the boy's head had he not pulled back. His weapon however, raised to block the stroke, had been sliced off only an inch from his thumb.

The man saw the terror and shock on the boy's face and threw back his head to laugh, rocking on his heels in his mirth.

Togorasom leapt forward with the shaft sharpened by the Atrocene's own sword. Throwing all his slight weight into his thrust he pierced the evil man's throat, shoving the wooden blade in as far as it would go. Blood spewed from the man's mouth as he fell to his knees, gagging, but the boy was gone before he had drowned in his own blood.

Never had Togorasom ran so hard. He was still being pursued, and fear would not allow him to look over his shoulder at the attacker. Suddenly, he felt a hand on his shoulder. It was only when the hand pulled him from his feet and into an embrace that he knew who it was.

"Father," he cried as he threw his arms around Anam's waist. "Oh, Father." Tears rolled down his tiny cheeks, and Anam raised him to his neck and embraced him.

"My glorious little son. How I underestimated your power. You have saved my life and again your own. God bless you. How I esteem you now."

Clutched safely in the big man's arms, Togorasom's fear slowly melted and his tears ebbed.

"I am still afraid of your anger, Father. I am sorry that I disobeyed you."

"I will forgive you but, first, tell me how you came to follow me."

"I went back to Anna and the others, but they were no fun. All of my friends were busy, so I thought I would see if you had gone far. I climbed over the ridge and, if I could not see you, I would go back, but I found you asleep. So I watched, and then I slept. When I awoke, you were gone and it was starting to be dark, so I thought that you were further on the path. I followed as I got too scared to go back, but then, I found you. I was afraid of your anger, and so I climbed up a tree until I could think of something to tell you. Then, those men came…"

"I think I know the rest, little boy, and I forgive you of it all. Does anyone know where we are?"

"God."

"I mean of our people." Anam laughed.

"No."

"Then we must fulfill my mission quickly and return so they will not worry long. They will think I have taken you somewhere for teaching."

"Where are we going?"

"Rodan."

Togorasom's eyes grew large. "Father, they hate us. They will kill us. No, let's go home."

"God will be by us. Should we go home and be sad and depressed with the others?"

"I think I like sadness more than death."

"We shall not be sad or dead. I must go to Rodan. If you don't want to go, then you can go back home." He put the boy back on his feet and aimed him toward the mountains.

Togorasom quickly thought of the two men he had fought and all of the terrible people there must be in Rodan. He also thought of the long walk home all by himself.

"No. I will go with you in case trouble finds you again."

Anam laughed. "I didn't believe that you would prefer to be alone, and if you continue to offer me the kind of help you did last evening as I slept, then I will be grateful."

"I was never so afraid. Everything I did was in terror."

"Whether you acted from terror or not, I know you saved me from death or a grave injury and, for that, I am thankful. I also know that you are no longer a child. You have grown many years in one night but do not let this action turn you into a fool taking brave chances. I want you to live long."

"Then why must we go to Rodan?"

"You ask too many questions. Did you sleep well in the night?"

"No."

Anam looked across the prairie at a herd of wild horses. These horses knew Anam, and one white mare had been watching them since they appeared on the edge of the woods. Upon Anam's shrill whistle, the horse eagerly ran to her master and bowed her head. After they had mounted, he showed Togorasom how to hold on such that he could get an hour's rest before they reached the city. It was not a comfortable sleep, but it was better than nothing.

Even from a distance, Anam could see that this empire was almost done crumbling. No one had bothered to repair any of the damage that his God had brought down, and smoke arose from various parts of the city, indicating that the Atrocene's had turned their destructive urges upon each other.

When they were near the city, Anam awoke Togorasom and dismounted. The horse walked along beside the man, and the little one remained mounted as they entered a break in the city wall.

No one met them, but Anam knew many eyes were trained upon them as they strolled through the carcass of the city. It had been only a few months since the collapse, but the destruction appeared like it had always been such. Wild dogs and rats battled each other for the garbage left to accumulate along these once-proud streets. Buildings had collapsed and pinned the half-exposed bodies of the dead. No one had gone through the wreckage or bothered to bury the dead. More dead were strewn along the streets, some with festering sores, and others with protruding ribs and swollen bellies; all were the meals of marauding animals. The living people, it appeared, ate nothing. Their eyes were tired and their bodies depleted. Disease was clearly rampant.

Not everyone was a part of this living death however. The inns and whore houses were still doing a lively trade, and raucous laughter flowed from these places, though it was early in the day. The laughter would last as long as the liquor.

There was no need to bring a greater condemnation down on this people. Nothing more could be done to further ruin this civilization and as they reached the heart of the city, Anam considered simply turning back and returning home.

He found himself near the palace and the sepulchers used by the priests. They entered the courtyard where once mighty Kiwatuan had stood. The pieces of his statue that had been laid waste by Zeda and the others were already partially covered in weeds and moss. The palace of Atrocene had collapsed but where once the statue had towered now stood an elderly priest clad in white linen. He spoke to them, his voice heavy with righteous fury.

"Why have you come here to this place, man of God? Have you not done enough, or do you gain pleasure from seeing an empire die? These people are not dead yet, grey one, for their king lives." He paused to laugh, an eerie sound.

"You heard me correctly. Their king lives. The son of Atrocene and Aurora has been spirited away by his protectors and, someday, this great man will return and bring a terrible vengeance down on you. I urge you to multiply and become a great people, for the more pleasure it will cause the King when he returns. You shall never find him until he is ready to be found.

And upon this future curse, I pile another one. The woman that you would want to love has betrayed you and your god. She cannot be forgiven; Kiwatuan has seen to that. Now, I urge you to depart before my anger can bring down more despair upon you. Perhaps, the boy on the horse..."

Confusion and anger were building inside Anam's mind, but the threat on his son cleared his mind. Before a further curse could come down on them, the knife he had taken from the dead man earlier flew from his hand and entered the old man's chest. No further curse would ever leave his lips and, as he sprawled on the ground, Anam saw the dagger the priest wore at his side. He now knew the source of the dagger Togorasom had used; it was that of an Atrocene priest.

"Togorasom, where did you find that weapon?"

"It is Anna's, Father. I saw it last night and knew that it was not her own, so I borrowed it for protection. Was I wrong to do this?"

Anam shook his head, unable to speak, for tears were welling up in his eyes as he wondered what further trouble these people would cause him. He quietly mounted the horse and they departed the city.

In one day, her beauty had noticeably faded. There were red spots that covered her body. Her lovely black hair was matted and stringy from sweat. Anam had sat by Anna's bed throughout the day. Occasionally she would call out for help, but never opened her eyes. Anam had tried to feed her, but either she would not accept it or, if she did, it would always come back up. Anam attempted to sleep at her bedside but he could not. Finally, as the day was coming to an end, she quietly opened her eyes and stared at the ceiling of the tent.

"Anna." Anam took her hand.

She blinked twice.

"Anna, can you hear me?"

"I can hear, Anam, and my head, I believe, is clear. I have sinned." She spoke quietly as a child who might be afraid of a parent. "What will you do with me?"

"I have thought all day of what we can do now. I am not sure."

"You are our leader."

"You are a leader, also."

"The Shamra do not need a leader. They are fighting no wars. They certainly do not need one such as me to lead them."

"Do you think that is all that matters? To fight wars? You need to lead them more than ever now."

"You and I know I shall never lead again."

"Tell me why you did it?"

"Is that so very hard to understand? I have never been loved by a man. I could not have you, so I sought one elsewhere. I did not know that the very food they fed me would infect me so. I allowed them to feed me. I allowed them to give me the antidote, and I didn't even realize it."

"So, you've been going to Rodan? I could have loved you but, sometimes, as you have proven, emotion leads us to foolish desires."

"No one could be so foolish as I. Anam, I do not believe that you shall ever find a woman good enough for you. There was only one – Zeda."

"Perhaps you are correct."

"What will you do with me? I cannot stay here or you shall all die."

"I do not know. I must think."

He got up and headed away from her tent and toward that of Mebiktu.

Mebiktu sat cross-legged in front of a small fire. His eyes were closed. Anam sat across from him and waited. Eventually, the old man's eyes opened and he stared into Anam's sad face.

"Do not speak, my son, for I know why you are here. You have a problem and you want for me to supply an answer. Sadly, you have waited too long to come to me for counsel. Before, my answers may have cheered you, but now I must give you stronger medicine. You must do what I say.

The woman must either die or be driven away. She will inflict more on us if she remains, even if she should be cured. There will be no more joy for you or our people on this side of the desert. We must leave. The old may decide to stay here or live in Crato or with Shaktar. You must take the women and children across the desert and far out of this place. I will go as far as my strength will allow. You must choose a new leader for the Shamra, for the Devil is still alive and must always be chased away. You need a woman. The women need men. I do not have all the answers, but I know someone who does. He is waiting for you to speak to Him. Why do you neglect your Lord? Do you wish to lead us in mourning or in the challenge that God himself laid down for you?

But, I am old and I am tired. Perhaps I am wrong. But go and send me the boy, Togorasom." He lay down on his side, on the grass, closed his eyes and went to sleep.

Anam arose and, having no alternative plan, decided to do everything as Mebiktu had instructed. He found Togorasom with his friends and sent the boy to his grandfather. Anam returned to Anna.

She lay with her eyes closed as if sleeping, but something disturbed Anam.

"Anna, are you awake?'

"I am, my Lord," she whispered, but she did not open her eyes. Even speaking seemed a laborious task to her.

"Have you gotten worse so quickly?"

"My Lord," she said, slowly opening her eyes. "I have brought down upon you and my people an insult." She was obviously in great pain but spoke on. "My sin is one with which I cannot live and so, while you were gone, I drank poison."

Anam's mouth fell open in shock.

She spoke on. "I knew that you would either be forced to drive me away or kill me in some manner. If you did not, the disease the Atrocene's infected me with would eventually spread. I have no right to bring any further pain upon you. Of this death, you are innocent." Tears were flowing down her cheeks, and she spoke slowly. "My God, I can hardly bear the pain."

Anam knelt beside her and held her close, so close that their tears became one. She began uncontrollably shaking and choking.

"Oh God, save my soul!" she cried and stopped shaking suddenly. Anam sat up and believed that she must have died. His grief began to fill his chest. She did not move, not even appearing to breath, but her eyes opened, locking on Anam's. "Please, I beg of you only one thing. Lead my sisters out of this place. Lead my sisters..." and she spoke no more.

Anam closed her eyes, rose slowly and stumbled out into the dusk. He fell into the sand on his face.

"Oh Anna. I would that you were alive. I would have loved

you." He screamed as he buried his face deeper into the sand. "What is to become of me?" Many watched him, but his grief was so great he did not care. He did sense, after a bit, that someone approached, and he raised his head. Before him stood Mebiktu and Togorasom.

"What is this that you are doing? You are shaming us," Mebiktu said, looking down at him. "Everyone is standing about watching you. They know what Anna has done. She was our enemy for she went to our mortal enemies and now you mourn her death?

Why do you not proclaim her sin or have you gone so far from God? We are your friends, why do you choose not to lead us? I do not understand you anymore." The old man turned and hobbled towards his tent. Togorasom stood over Anam, staring into his uplifted face. Anam reached out his hand toward the boy and he fled.

Anam rose shaking the sand from his hair, and slowly walked up the path to his burrow.

"Anam. Anam, it is I. Look upon me and do not be afraid."

Anam had slept soundly, but lifted his head when he heard a sweet voice call his name. His eyes grew wide and his mouth fell open in disbelief when he saw Zeda before him. Her wounds had healed and she was as beautiful as she had ever been. However, when he reached for her, she stepped back.

"Do not lay hands upon me for I am no longer of your world. He who loves us has sent me unto you. You must listen and you must obey."

"I will do whatsoever you ask. How came you now to this place?" He looked around and, though he remembered falling asleep on the ground in front of his foxhole, they were now in a place he could not recognize. They stood in a pool of light which was surrounded by darkness. There were a few scrub bushes, though everything seemed indistinct and unreal. "What place is this?"

"It matters not. Now listen to me. In the morning, you must gather the women and the older among the children and tell them that on this day they shall cross the desert. Then you must go to the old and very young and send them to live in Crato. They must leave this day. Some will want to travel with you but they must not, for they will only slow you down and keep you from your mission. Mebiktu will accompany you as far as he may."

"But what must we do in the desert? Why should we leave in this rush?"

"Because your heart is heavy for all your losses. If you tarry then you may never depart. It is now that you must lift up your heart and carry your remnant out of this place."

"Across the desert, will we find a home and peace?"

"God has many things that he must reveal to you. You have far to go before you will find peace and a home."

"Anna is dead." A tear trickled down from Anam's cheek.

"Weep for her sin but do not weep for her death. She is in a better place now and forgiven. One more thing, bury Anna with the other warriors. She is my sister and had been forgiven."

"These are like the words Mebiktu had said."

"Yet, you did not hearken to him. Do not be a fool any longer, except that if you do not depart from this place, the Rasomites will surely sit on this mountaintop and weep until they die."

"I love you." Anam reached out to her again.

"I love you, my husband. Now go and be about those things that you must do."

She stepped back a few paces into the darkness and was gone. Anam stood up and stepped forward as if to follow her and realized he was again in front of his burrow with the sun beginning to light the edge of the horizon. There was so much to do this day and he must begin immediately.

"Maftu, Elamuna, Zabikta, Crazon. All of you must quickly bring together as much as you can carry on your backs. Fill many flasks with water and prepare to depart. On this day we leave this place forever and go through the desert."

There was much murmuring as to what could be going on but, as Anam had already moved on, the women rolled out of their bags and their tents into the early dawn to begin preparation.

"Listen to me! Today, God has given me a mission and these are the things that must be done." He proclaimed these words from atop a large boulder in the middle of the camp, a stage used often for announcements. "Gather your bundles and go to Shaktar or go to old friends in Crato and there you shall live.

You shall be a lamp to these people who need to know the real God. On this day, I take the strength of the Rasomites and head across the desert. This is the day for which we have waited. I know not what the Lord has laid down for me but this is His will and it is our duty to do His will. Now go quickly and prepare your things."

At that moment, an old man and a young boy appeared on the scene. They walked arm in arm, the younger one supporting the elder, but their faces seemed to shine from the excited smiles that emanated from them. As they approached Anam, he leapt down from the boulder and dropped to one knee. When they were in front of him, he looked into the old man's eyes and lowered his head.

"Forgive me, Father, I have sinned. I ask for your blessing."

He was surprised to feel the hand of the boy lay upon his head.

"You have not sinned," the boy said softly, "you have merely erred in your understanding of those things around you and acted from your weakness, not from your strength. We all honor you and are gladdened that you have chosen to lead us. Now arise, for there is much to do."

Anam stood up and looked down at the little boy. His eyes showed no longer a quiet little boy, but those of a prodigy. He looked to Mebiktu in wonder.

"It has been a busy night, my son," the old man said to Anam with a smile. "It seems that leaders and priests and prophets were born last night."

"Can the child be a priest? He is so young and unknowing."

"I suppose he can learn to prophesy and lead in worship and such. All good things take time, it seems." He looked around at the gathering of the elderly. "I have chosen him, and he I, and the Lord has blessed it. When he speaks, you should listen."

"By God's grace, I shall."

There had been only a few tears upon their departure. Most of the people were going to Crato and would help Shaktar found a new city someday soon. A small band headed south from the mountains across the plains. Anam, Mebiktu and Togorasom led this group of travelers. Its numbers were this: thirty-eight beautiful warrior-clad women, sixty-five boys and forty-six girls whose age ranged from six to sixteen. Several of the children and all of the little ones had departed with various adopted grandparents.

Mebiktu was the only one of the elderly left to accompany them and Togorasom, the youngest. Anam represented, of course, the only man. They traveled light, carrying their weapons, a flask of water and a days' supply of food. They left their extra clothing, bedrolls, tents and nearly everything else they had ever known. They prayed for God's generosity to keep them supplied. They had no idea of what adventures awaited them beyond the edge of the desert.

Chapter 4
Oasis

Lear crept quietly through the grass, picking the large, juicy strawberries from the plants spread across the ground. Occasionally, he would freeze in position as he heard the "Caw! Caw!" of the not-so-distant blackbirds. Once one swooped through the air near him, but he remained unnoticed. Eventually, his hunger temporarily satisfied and his kerchief full of fresh berries for his family, he crept out of the grass toward his adobe brick house.

As his head emerged, he gathered all of his strength for the twenty yard dash across the open space. Sweat formed on his brow and he shook all over. His back was so sore, now, he could bear no more physical abuse.

He ran. His sudden appearance startled those birds who were watching, and they immediately took flight, six of the huge blackbirds in pursuit.

The first one to see Lear was in front, his talons poised to sink into the man's back. Lear reached the door that his wife had just opened when he felt the bird sink his razor like talons into his back. The animal was too late to stop him, though, and the door almost slammed shut on the bird's legs. The man had escaped, this time.

Fresh blood trickled down Lear's back across the scars from previous attacks. He braced himself for a moment, and then he showed his wife and three young children his treasure, two dozen large, firm strawberries. Their eyes lit up and they reached out hungrily.

"Now, eat slowly. I have had my fill, but I cannot go out again today. I am too sore."

The family was thin and withered. Lear was the only one who still appeared well fed, but his arms, legs and back were covered with sores and scabs. He was a tall, black man, over six feet in height. He wore only an apron of a canvas-like material. His face was weathered and lined from his ordeals, his lips quivered with the pain, fear and hatred he had for the birds. He leaned against the wall, gazing out across the gardens and beyond toward the trees where the birds maintained their vigil. From this position, he could see all six of the adobe houses and knew he would not be the only one looking from his window.

The corn was nearly ready. He could see the plump, juicy ears on the stalks, sometimes three or four ears to a plant. Around the corn crowded the cucumbers and squash. There were also several orange and fig trees, but those were not ready yet. How he craved an ear of that corn.

His wife came to him and began to apply cream to his new wounds. It was cool and felt good. He reached behind him and wrapped an arm around her waist.

"Sona, what are we to do?"

"I do not know, Lear. My head hurts from hunger, and I cannot think."

He kissed her on the forehead. "Go and rest. I see Mapho is in his yard and I need to talk with him."

"Don't go near the garden."

"If I get a chance, I must."

"But you are so sore."

"You and the children need to eat. Go and rest, Sona. I love you."

The frail, little woman kissed Lear and walked to the corner where the furs were lain. Lear walked to the sink, pumped a bit of water into a bowl, and poured it over his head, the water running to the floor. He went out the door. As he appeared, the birds, who had been watching Mapho, directed their attention to Lear, but as he walked away from the garden toward his friend they settled.

"Has your family eaten today, Mapho?"

"I am too afraid to go near the garden and we are all so hungry, my son is sick in bed. I do not know what to do."

"My wife is also sick in bed." He looked towards the garden. "Perhaps we can go together, after dark, and gather some of that sweet corn, eh?"

"It looks so good," said Mapho. "Oh, to sink my teeth into a fresh cob of corn; that would be real nice. Perhaps we can do that."

Lear gazed around at their tiny paradise. They had fled into the desert from the Atrocene tyranny three years ago and found this beautiful little oasis awaiting them. They had the seed to start gardens, and the fruit trees were already here. The first two years, the ground had sprung forth with abundance and they lived in peace and ate well.

Then, last year, the birds had come. They had taken over the bounty, but they wanted to toy with their victims as well. As long as the people stayed away from the gardens and orchard, they could walk unmolested but, if they ventured too near, the birds would drive them back and feast upon their harvest. The people had survived so far by night raids and craftiness, but the birds were always watchful.

Soon, the people would starve to death in the middle of this bounty. They were too weak to head across the desert and there were too many birds and they were so large that Lear and his friends could not protect themselves or destroy them. They had managed to beat a few of the birds to death, but there were simply too many of them and these battles were fought with much human loss as well. Lear thought of Relana, who had traveled into the garden to get food for her husband and children. Her body was found torn and gouged. There was Songa, who had helped them kill a bird one day. That same day she emerged from her doorway with no thought of the garden and the birds had descended upon her. Her body now lay buried only inches from Lear's doorway.

Lear let out a frustrated scream, startling Mapho. "There has to be a way! We cannot surrender to those creatures. It's not fair."

"Go home, Lear, and meet me here after dark. Then, maybe, we can get a bit of corn."

Mapho went back into his house out of the heat. Lear stared across the garden to the tree, black with birds. If only there were a way to defeat them. He turned and went to the backyard of his house. The grass was knee high, and he broke off a few spears and began chewing, knowing the birds would allow him this. He looked out across the desert and began thinking that they might depart anyway. Better to starve in the desert. But far off, his eyes were, he thought, deceived. The desert was moving.

He rubbed his eyes and looked again. A black mass was moving across the desert towards him. Fear and anxiety began to build up in him. Was this another plague? Locusts or more birds, here to finish the destruction of his people? He watched for a long time and finally realized that a large group of people had seen the oasis and was coming his way.

When they were about a half mile off, he ran across the desert to greet them. As he approached them, he began to realize who these people were. Though he had never met Anam, he had heard his name spoken of many times in awe by his people. They believed that he was a prophet. When his eye met those of the stalwart leader of the band, he fell to his knees.

"Anam, prophet of the most high, I salute you."

"Arise, brother, I and my family greet you."

By this time, the rest of the people from the oasis were standing behind Lear's house to greet the newcomers. The Rasomites could not understand the physical depletion of these people, considering the bounty of crop they were surrounded with. There was enough here to supply food for many men for many days, yet they were greeted by a party of about twenty haggard looking men, women and children. They appeared to have suffered a great conflict for many of them were sorely wounded. As the Rasomites began to wander the grounds of the oasis, guided by the natives, Anam looked to Lear for an explanation.

"We are an unfortunate people. This is, we supposed, our land. Fleeing from the hatred and slavery we suffered under the Atrocenes, we chanced upon this generous piece of property and promptly settled. Then, last year, the birds came." He gazed across the fields to where the blackbirds had been eyeing this new activity. "They will not suffer us to eat of our own work."

"We are a hungry people. Three days have we walked across the desert. My people hunger, and God promised us a meal and so, we shall eat." Anam turned and began to walk towards the new corn. The birds began stirring and finally as he grasped an ear of corn, four of them dove in his direction. The talons of the first made to slash at his shoulders. In a flash, Anam had the bird by the legs and, using it as his weapon, fought off the other three. As each attempted to strike his body, he would grab its legs and, once caught, would release the other one by flinging it to the ground. In the end all four of the birds had their heads crushed against the ground and their bodies thrown into a pile. Finally, Anam selected a good ear of corn and walked back to Lear.

"Tonight, my friend, you eat sweet corn and fowl. Tomorrow, I will show you a proper way to train your pets."

Anam had spent the next morning teaching the desert dwellers how to create a variety of shafts from the cornstalks. The dried cornstalks, heavily lacquered, did not make a very fine weapon though they were abundant. Lear had at his disposal several types of darts, either to be thrown or blown from a tube. He had fashioned a magnificent spear; however, it was only for show as it would shatter easily against a tree or rock. They also had several arrows, guided by the feathers of blackbirds. A good lacquer could be made from the corn oil and they were shown how to carve fine bows from the orange trees. By the end of the third day, Anam and Lear had assembled an incredible arsenal to wage war against these deadly birds.

Several of the birds had been killed during the preparatory time and they were summarily cooked and eaten. Now, the birds merely watched this activity and waited for conditions to return to normal.

The corn was now fully ripe and Mapho crept from his doorway and headed toward the crop. The birds watched this activity and also had a sharp eye on the rest of the surroundings, no one else was in sight; it was time for revenge. The travelers who had encamped behind the houses had apparently not yet arisen and no one else stirred. A flock of about twenty bloodthirsty birds bore down on the lone figure.

When Mapho saw the birds, he turned and ran back to his house although he knew it was too far to reach in time. He could feel the air from the giant wings of the pursuers when, as if from nowhere, the air was full of arrows and blow darts. Before the birds realized they were under attack, many of them had been brought down. The survivors made a hasty retreat.

Lear leapt from the top of his house. He waved his spear over his head and shouted, "Today, birds of death, we are the victor. Today, what is ours is ours again. From now on, you shall live upon our spoil and we shall live upon your flesh."

Anam emerged from behind the house. "Today, you are the victor, but beware. Look over your shoulder for the birds will wait and seek the opportunity for revenge. Now, I have something else to give you."

"Already, you have given us so much: weapons to defend ourselves, hope, our very lives. Can there be more?"

"You do not have God. If you had, perhaps this would not have happened."

Lear shook his head, "I know that there are gods, but I have only been taught of the hateful god, Kiwatuan. I know no other."

"Kiwatuan is a broken stone, and his religion is evil and death, but I can give you the God of goodness and life, if you want Him."

Lear fell to his knees and those around him did as well. "Give us this greatest gift."

So Anam began to tell Lear of all the things God had shown him from birth. Lear was a good and faithful scholar and learned abundantly that day. In the morning, the Rasomites were gone.

Chapter 5
Faith

Ulyana sat staring out across the arid nothingness of desert that totally surrounded her and the other Rasomites. As far as the eye could see in every direction was only sand. No tree, no rock, nor crevice met her perception only flat, tawny, sand. It had been four days since they had departed the oasis. They had left quietly during the night, making their departure known only to Lear and his family. Their water flasks were filled, and he had given them as much to eat as their pouches could carry. But now their flasks were empty and their food pouches bare.

Ulyana was young, only eleven, but already in her life she had seen two kingdoms fall and one begin to rise. Perhaps, she would also see the Rasomites prosper again. In Anam, she trusted totally. In her personal counselor, Elamuna, she trusted totally. In her God, she trusted totally. However, now she was very tired and very thirsty.

She stood up and scanned the horizon once more. There was no flaw in what she saw, it was totally desolate with no irregularity. It was good that Anam led them, because she was totally lost. She sat down, for it was better to conserve her energy until it was time to move on. Despite the appearance of the desert, it was not starkly hot. In fact, at times, it was rather cool.

Anam, Togorasom and several of the women sat in a circle conferring on the next direction. The boy did not speak, but sat quietly listening. Occasionally he would bow his head, either in prayer or in thought, she knew not.

She wondered if it were really possible for a person so young to be a priest. Of course, it had to be possible; he was a priest, but the boy was the youngest in their tribe. Though he was only six, and there were others both older and younger than he who had remained behind, it had been Anam's decision that no one younger than Togorasom would accompany them. There were still several older than he who had been left behind. Some would not have been physically strong enough to stand the ordeal of crossing the desert. Some were not spiritually strong enough. She felt great honor for having been chosen to go, even though she also knew those left behind had a mighty and worthy chore to bear up the survivors of the war.

The discussion among the elders was very animated, but hushed, so she could not discern what they were saying. She looked from the group to Elamuna, who sat with the group near her. When the woman looked up from her contemplation and saw Ulyana looking at her, the girl's thoughts were understood. Elamuna nodded and smiled at her, giving her permission to come closer to the huddled elders. Slowly, Ulyana arose and walked nearer until she could hear what was being said.

"We have been seven days across this desert," said one of the women, "and there appears to be no end."

"I tell you there is an end, nearby. Did our Lord send us out to this place to die? I think not," said Anam.

"Perhaps we could again return to the oasis and, after refreshing ourselves, begin again in a new direction," said another. "Perhaps we began wrong."

"Nay," said a third. "We have no food. We have no water. In a day or two, we would begin to perish. We must go on."

"I await a sign from the Lord or, in a few moments, we will arise and try again," said Anam.

"Perhaps Mebiktu could offer some counsel," said the second again.

"Mebiktu is not to be with us for much longer. I only pray for a decent site to tarry for him to die," said Anam.

Suddenly, the boy raised his head from prayer. His face seemed to glow. He opened his eyes and, although his gaze fell upon her, Ulyana felt he looked right through her. He stood up, turned partially about, and pointed off in the distance.

"It is time to depart," he said quietly. "One day in the desert and we shall find water and grandfather shall find rest." He began walking away from the circle into the desert, alone.

Ulyana looked about. No one moved; they sat watching the boy. Ulyana, knowing this to be the sign Anam awaited, stood up, snatched her belongings from the ground and followed the boy into the desert. Upon her decision to follow, the rest of the Rasomites began to rise also and follow her.

The sun beat down hard upon her that day. She did not sweat; it seemed as there was no moisture left in her body. Her lips were dry and cracking, and her lungs and throat hurt each time she breathed the dry air. For the first time in her life, her feet bled from the sores inflicted by the sand that felt like nails under her with each step, but she did not stop. Her pace was about twenty feet behind Togorasom, and she maintained the distance from respect. She did not look to see if anyone else followed, but she knew for, occasionally, she heard a cough or a voice, but still she did not look away from the boy in front of her. She had decided to follow him until she died or until she found his vision to be correct.

It was not a day, though it seemed like many days. From the position of the sun, she knew it to be only five or six hours when Togorasom stopped. He turned, waiting for the rest to reach him. When Ulyana saw his face, amazement took her. His face still glowed and, though a few beads of sweat had formed on his brow, he showed no other sign of his desert march. She knew, though, how red and weathered her face and body must appear from the scorching sun.

Then she looked about. Before them, for hundreds of feet, lay the skeletons of dozens of poor, dead souls who had gone this way and finally given up and died. No shred of flesh remained on any of them. Many lay only partially exposed, with sand filling vacant eye sockets and rib cages.

She looked Togorasom in the eye and said, "God bless you." Then, she fell on her face before him.

By this time, the rest of the Rasomites had begun to appear and, when the sight of death that lay before them was known, the murmuring began. Finally, Anam arrived. He had fallen behind because Mebiktu was being borne on his shoulders. Now, he stood before Togorasom. His expression was neither contempt nor pleasure, but he had also been much maligned by the desert heat.

He lay the elderly priest on the ground before Togorasom and said, "He thirsts."

Ulyana watched as Togorasom walked towards her and felt wonder as he placed his hand on her head and, pointing to the ground beside her, told her, "Grandfather thirsts."

Ulyana sat down. Tears had formed in her eyes. They were

tears of joy because she so totally trusted this boy. She sat up and, quickly using her hands to dig into the sand, she began to form a hole. At six inches, she pulled her hand out of the hole and held it up, for the sand was sticking to her skin, which it had not done at first. It felt cool and damp, and she dug more hurriedly. At a foot, she found moist sand and, finally, a pool of water. The water began to well up from the hole and sprang forth onto the dry lifeless sand. Ulyana was immediately soaked in cold water, relishing the feeling on her burnt skin. The others around her moved back because the force of the water became so great as to surprise them. She quickly filled her water flask and moved to Mebiktu.

The old man's neck was cradled with one young hand, and she tipped the spout of the flask into his mouth, but he did not swallow. Water overflowed from his mouth, trickling down his neck. And, still, he did not move. His life had gone out of him. His eyes were open and the lids motionless, but the pupils were aimed at the boy-priest. Slowly, his pupils lowered towards the ground, seeming to set as the sun until only the white of his eyes remained. It was, Ulyana thought, truly the "Sunlight of God" setting for this priest.

She looked about at Togorasom and Anam. She could see the measured sadness in Anam's eyes, but also, a sense of peace that Mebiktu had gone on to his reward, but not before he had chosen his replacement. Anam now stood ankle deep in water as it continued to rise and spill out onto the sand. Looking beyond Anam into the distance, she saw the sun finally begin to settle into the horizon. Night would soon follow. The coolness of night would be a pleasure. She stood up and realized now how much water was flowing and how deep it was becoming. Stooping over to rescue Mebiktu from this flood, she felt Anam's hand upon her shoulder.

"You have done enough." She looked into his eyes and saw compassion for her. "Your trust was greatest. Go, refresh yourself and be with our priest. For he and you have saved us. God bless you."

Still numb for all the happenings, she climbed to a place out of the water and sat next to Togorasom, taking turns with him at her water flask.

Mebiktu was buried at a place above the waterline on a dry promontory away from the corpses of those who had died before.

Above him was erected a simple cross, for there was nothing great in their possession. Finally, Anam took a drink from Ulyana's water flask. They named this place Metaseeno, which means "where the water sprang up".

It was dark now. Ulyana lay on the sand. She had dug a small crevice for her body and made a mound of sand for her pillow. All of her possessions lay beside her. They were few and included a bow and leather quiver of arrows, a water flask, and a knapsack. There were only three objects contained in the knapsack. She had never seen her father. Her mother had been told of his death on the day Ulyana was born. The messenger who came returned his personal possessions including a shell necklace. Ulyana had the necklace. Most of the shells were cracked and broken now, but it was all that remained of her father.

When she was a toddler, she was with the women at the river when they came under attack by the Atrocenes. It was a speedy battle. All six of the older girls and women were taken away, never to be seen again. She had hidden behind a log and held a small piece of gravel in her hand, intending to throw it at any Atrocene warrior that saw her. It seemed very foolish now, but she had saved that piece of gravel. Ulyana's mother and two elder sisters were in that group. She had no brothers and so Elamuna had cared for and taught her, ever since. The third object in the knapsack was a small wooden cross held together with a wrapping of vines. She had constructed the cross during the previous winter when they were hiding in the mountains. She often held it while she prayed.

Without the use of the cross she lay praying now, staring into the night sky. She contemplated the events of the day, speaking softly to herself and God.

"Heavenly Father. What a glorious day this has been. So many changes have happened that I am hard put to understand it all. Thank you for using me to be part of it. I wonder where we will go next and what we shall do. But that, I suppose, is not for me to know yet.

Lord, right now, I only ask for healing. My face is burnt and cracked. My body sore. My feet are worn and bloody from the march. If it be possible, I ask that I be healed. If it be not possible I ask only for the strength to bear the pain. But I know also that others hurt more than I, so I would ask that I be the last to be healed."

She rolled over on her side until she found a more comfortable position to lay. Now, she could see many others also lying on the sand. Many of them slept, but all had a restless sleep from the pain of their bodies.

She could see the cross which had been erected over Mebiktu's grave. He rested well tonight. She thought of Togorasom. He was probably sleeping well as his body alone did not bear the wounds caused by the excesses of the desert.

She wondered of Anam. He was the wisest man she had ever met. She wondered if he had ever felt weakness.

Ulyana felt very weak. From outside she felt weak because of her burns and sores, but she had a greater weakness. She felt weak from within. She wondered, when would life slow down so she could begin to understand it?

All of her existence, from the day she was born, she had known only war and sadness. Was there a day that she could remember when someone had not died, or they were not warring or preparing to war, or running or hiding? It seemed too hard to continue to be thankful. She wanted to ride wild horses and play with her friends on the streets of Crato. She also thought of boys. Wasn't a girl her age supposed to begin to notice and be noticed by boys? Maybe even begin to court? There was never time. But she could never let herself become interested in a boy, because he could be snatched away and sacrificed to the Atrocene wolves.

It was never right, for some reason. If the Rasomites never stopped fighting and running, soon there would be no Rasomites. Perhaps on the other side of the desert. Surely, there, they could find peace. She wondered what lay across the desert as she closed her weary eyes and began to dream.

Ulyana leaned her head back. The sun was bright, however, the breeze was cool. It was so refreshing to feel the fresh salty air blow by her. She opened her eyes and looked around. Standing where she was on the sandy beach near Crato, it was calming to know that there was no one around for once. She was totally alone. The water lapped the sand near her feet and, looking down, she noticed a large, very beautiful, conch. The young girl stooped down to pick it up, letting her fingers run across the pleasingly smooth inner surface of the shell. It was nearly white in color but had a faint trace of blue as well. Larger shells were always found along this coast but never had she seen one as pretty as this. She again ran the tips of her fingers along the inner lip, and it felt so very smooth. Some conches could be used as horns, but Ulyana was not sure how to blow it, nor did she want to destroy this magical quiet that surrounded her. She did, however, place her lips to the lip of the conch. The inside of the shell was so soft that it held the girl in amazement.

Suddenly, she realized that she was no longer alone on this beach and, turning around, was excited to see a beautiful white horse. The shell was gone. The animal stood taller than she. It was, in fact, a giant of a horse, but Ulyana felt no fear as she stared into the animal's eyes and a smile crossed her lips. She reached out and touched the horse's forehead and pet its nose for a moment. Then, she was startled when her new friend shook his mane and lowered his head to the ground. He looked her in the face again. The white stallion was eager to be going.

She could not recall climbing upon his back, but was thrilled to suddenly be astride him and holding onto his mane as she rested her head on his neck. Sitting up, Ulyana looked into the distance where huge rocks stretched out to the water's edge. It would be wonderful to go for a ride, but there seemed no way around the barrier. Suddenly, the horse bolted and ran, whipping up water and sand. She closed her eyes and let the animal have control.

The salty air tore through her hair, and she could feel herself getting delightfully wet as they ran through the mist. Wondering of the rocks, she opened her eyes to discover that there was nothing before her but sandy beach. She lay her head down on the back of the horse's neck and continued to let him keep control. The lurching seemed to rock her to sleep and when she finally opened her eyes, the daylight and the beach and her wild horse were gone. Instead, she was back in the camp of the Rasomites, and a sense of despair gripped her as she sat up.

No one else stirred about her. In the half-light of early morning she could see a few others were also sitting up, but no one moved; no one spoke.

She reached for her water flask and brought it to her lips. It was at this moment she realized her lips were no longer cracked and sore, nor was her throat dry. After taking two long swallows, she placed the flask back on the ground next to her. By force of habit, she swept the palm of her hand across her forehead, expecting to feel the sting and sweat as she touched sunburned skin. She could tell her skin was no longer red and peeling. Bewildered, she brought both her hands to her abdomen and ran them across her body. There was no burn, no blister, no bloody feet. A feeling between fear and excitement took hold of her.

She wondered if she were still sleeping and this was part of the dream. As she leapt to her feet, to proclaim her healing to all, she saw the young boy sitting beside her. His eyes seemed to sparkle in the moonlight as he put his index finger to his lips, indicating she should be silent, and then motioned for her to sit.

"Today," he began, "we will arrive in a strange city filled with a race of people with strange customs. Those who were called by God to lead the people will seem to be filled with the spirit, but they are filled with disgust. We must destroy their foolish faith and make the people aware of the truth. Will you help me?"

"I will follow you anywhere. I will do whatever you ask. But I do not know the words to say."

"God will tell you what to say."

"I am excited, for you have healed me."

"Not I, but God has healed you. I am only a child through which God can perform. He is no respecter of persons so it does not matter if he uses an old man or a young boy or a young girl. When the need arises, let God use you." He got up and walked away, his white tunic seeming to glow in the moonlight.

Chapter 6
Foramen

They had seen the rock wall from far across the desert and had headed for what appeared to be a gateway. Now standing before the entrance, they realized there were no guards posted and with good reason. The wall and entrance were only about thirty feet high, but were so sheer, Anam knew that only few of their number could scale it and that with difficulty.

Togorasom, standing before Anam, called out if there were anyone present, but his young voice did not carry far enough. Anam repeated the call and also received no response.

"Perhaps," he said, "this is a dead city. If a few of us scale the entrance, we can open the gate."

"This is a very live city," said the boy. "The main entrance is on the other side of the city, facing the countryside, that being where all normally come and go. However, the residents of this city seldom leave the confines of these walls. This is a back entrance into the desert and is seldom used. They feel no need to post a guard as it is so hard to scale, and I am sure very few visitors arrive from this direction."

Anam called out again. This time he heard a voice call back that they should stand back and wait a moment.

The procession moved back about thirty paces, which gave plenty of room for the gateway to lower. As it neared the ground, Anam realized it was made of highly-polished marble. The near-white surface against the noonday sun was very hard on the eyes. Anam closed his eyes against the brightness for a moment and then reopened them. The glare was almost unbearable, but he could detect the presence of two men before him.

"We are a people seeking peace," he said. His eyes, by now, were getting quite adjusted to the conditions. The gateway, once lowered, became a ramp that rose slowly to the point where it met the wall and then, apparently, descended likewise on the inside of the city. The portion that had been lowered was not wide, perhaps wide enough to pull an oxcart through. But it appeared the gate was fashioned in such a way that a considerably larger portion could be lowered.

The two men standing before Anam were both fairly young. The one appeared to be about sixteen years old and looked bright and well cared for. He was a tall, thin boy, but quite muscular, especially in his lower legs. Anam could sense that he was a boy prone to running. His legs were exposed by the blue shorts that he wore. He wore nothing else, and this showed his well-tanned body. The boy's face showed much of the innocence of youth, it being filled with curiosity.

The older man was perhaps in his early thirties. He wore a pair of white pantaloons, slightly dirty, that bloused out at the bottom, and a black pullover shirt. On his feet was a pair of black leather sandals.

Neither of these people impressed Anam as a decent gatekeeper or guardian of the city. He had expected to face a guard or a detachment of soldiers. These men bore no weapons and probably were not even familiar with their use. The three men stared awkwardly at each other as Anam awaited one of them to take control of the situation.

The boy extended his hand to Anam. "Hi," he said. "My name is Nathan. As I was passing by the portal on my daily jaunt, I heard you calling out, so I lowered the gateway." Anam reluctantly took his hand. "This is..." he motioned with his free hand to the man standing behind the boy.

"Ovey," the man spoke up. "I was preparing to go out for a bit of tobacco when I noticed the boy climbing the stairway to the parapet. I trusted he might need some help with the latches."

"We come in peace. My people are tired and hungry. Their flesh is sore. Even their spirit is weak. Is it possible to get in out of the heat?"

"We are sorry for apparent foolishness. We are not the greeters you are deserving of," said Ovey. "Nathan, run to Andre and tell him we have visitors of a bit more than a hundred in number. Tell him their condition. He will know what to do." The boy was gone. "I should have delivered your name. I am again sorry."

"I am Anam. These people are the remnant of the Rasomites."

Ovey's hands fell to his side, his body trembled and his face seemed to pale. He fell to his knees and clutched Anam's leg. "Savior," he whispered.

One of the women helped Ovey back to his feet. The man's breathing was irregular; the tear-filled eyes did not stray from Anam as his body trembled. No discernible speech came from his lips, only an occasional babbling in an attempt to speak.

"What has come over you, man? Tell me," encouraged Anam.

All Ovey could do was stutter in his vain attempt to say something reasonable. They all sensed a disturbance at the entry to the city, and Anam directed his attention to the gathering of people who began to appear there. The people were witnessing the unusual action that was taking hold of Ovey's body and the oddly dressed, strangely colored Rasomites who had arrived at this city. The Rasomites also thought the city inhabitants a strange group. They were all dressed in light attire, but in a spectrum of colors and types of clothing. They were a fair-skinned but well-tanned race, though many seemed thin and sickly to the Rasomites.

Nathan pushed his way through the crowd, dragging an older man by the hand who wore a heavy black robe with black shoulder boards. His chest was embossed with a symbol of a yellow cross lying on its side. Also around his neck hung a heavy gold amulet with a large, round pendant upon which was the same symbol. The sleeves of the robe went to his wrists, the hem fell to his feet, upon which he wore an old pair of leather sandals. The man's grey beard and grey, though balding, head attested to his age. His face portrayed no hint of emotion, but only calm seriousness, in contrast to his following who seemed dimwitted. He faced Anam, but neither of the men spoke for a few moments as they studied each other's faces. Finally he spoke.

"Welcome to Foramen. The word I received is that you come in peace. If so, you are welcome to remain as long as you wish. While you are here, I will do my best to play the part of servant. It is obvious that you are now much in need of bodily refreshment. You shall be attended to and, I hope, our generosity will encourage you to remain with us or continue your march in peace. From whence do you travel?"

"We presently travel from the Mountains of Pitakae and the city of Crato near the sea. It has been ten days across the desert. We have no destination except to move as the Lord would command. He has led us to you and promised us your generosity and, I hope, we can share in each other's fellowship."

"I am called Andre and am the priest over these people you see gathered here." He glanced at Ovey, who was being supported by one of the women, and again at Anam and raised his eyebrows as a question to this circumstance.

"Upon our exchanging of names, he began acting in this manner and I do not know why. Our race is of the Rasomites, who were once a brave and powerful people and covered the whole area we call home. The women you see here are called 'The Shamra'. Their purpose is to pursue and destroy the devil in his many guises."

"And you are called?"

"Anam."

Andre's mouth fell open. He looked Anam up and down and slowly closed his mouth. His words were slow.

"Tell your people to follow me." He turned back toward the city and his charge. Raising his arm with anger and determination in his voice, he shouted, "What are you fools staring at? This is not a museum piece. Go to your homes and ignore these proceedings."

The people slowly began to disperse as Andre walked back up the ramp with the Rasomites following him, Ovey being aided by several there. It was then that Anam noticed Nathan, who had been standing alongside listening and getting the attention of Ulyana, and now had fallen to his knees at the sound of Anam's name. Ulyana helped him to his feet as Anam turned and followed Andre and the others inside. Eventually, all had retreated out of the heat and into the city, save one. Togorasom remained in place until Ulyana and Nathan disappeared into the city wall.

"We have a mighty work to perform," he said and hurried to catch up with the rest.

Anam slid further down into the cool water. They had caught only a glimpse of the city before they were led into an underground passageway which brought them into the bath house wherein they were now. The streets Anam peered down seemed endless and so very crowded with people scurrying about. The buildings were unlike any he had ever seen. They were built tall and straight, of lumber,a clear substance, and square red stones, and were very unlike the sandstone and cobblestone he was used to.

The cool water felt so very good to his sunbaked skin. The Rasomites were a tough-skinned people, but ten days in the desert was even hard on them. Only Togorasom and Ulyana bore few marks from the scorching heat.

He stared up at the clear substance above his head that allowed him to see the sky. Though the water was refreshingly cool, steam did rise from it and filled the room with a light fog. The air was warm but considerably cooler than the parched desert air he had just left.

All of the Rasomite travelers were here. In one regard, this caused a bit of relief in his tired mind. But, in another regard, he was also apprehensive about his situation as he felt like a prisoner. Besides himself and his people, there were only six young women in this bathing area. They meandered about, dispersing jars of oil and ointment and handing out towels. All of the women were dumb and apparently deaf, as they did not respond to any questions or requests for assistance, but would respond to the wave of an arm or the motion of a hand as they perceived it. Given his preferences, he would remain for a long time in this place, but knew that he would soon have to go to the city leaders and mince words with them.

The actions of Ovey and Nathan on the entryway had Anam baffled. This was a mystery. Obviously, they felt that he was the answer to a prophecy or an omen. The unusual thing about it was not that they were at all awed by the appearance of this unusual looking caravan, as they must have appeared, but they fell into shock at the mention of his name.

One of the serving girls came and poured oil over his back. It made his aching flesh feel instantly better. Anam let his eyes wander across the room and felt pleased at the calm and healing that he knew the women and children must be experiencing. Most of his people were sunk back in physical relaxation, as he was, in one of a dozen or so various-sized hot or cool bathing tubs. A few were farther away, in a special area, soaping and washing their hair. He would get to that soon enough. At this time, he was quite pleased to simply soak in the cool, oily water.

"These must be fed by a mineral spring of some sort," he thought. He began to compose his benediction before the men he assumed to be meeting soon. "Gentlemen, allow me first to express my appreciation for the kindness and hospitality shown us." Then again, he thought better not to ponder the matter. "I will allow myself to be led of God when need arises."

It was, however, time to be finished with relaxing and onto something better. He pulled his naked body from the water and, after wiping himself dry, prepared to put his loincloth on when one of the young women stepped before him with a white canvas bag. Quietly, taking the bag from the mute, he inspected the contents. He smiled at the garments he had been offered. A rainbow-colored shirt. A pair of black pants made of some strange leather that were cut off at the shin. This was a type of vinyl, but he did not know that. A pair of bright blue stockings and pullover moccasins. The garb would make him feel totally foolish. He put on his loincloth, strapped his knife and pouch around his waist, deposited the strange clothing back into the bag and walked away to cleanse his hair.

As he approached the trough that was used for this purpose, one of the mutes rose to aid him. The smaller room he had entered was completely carved out of rock. Warm water tumbled through several spouts in the wall into a stone trough that was about knee-high to him. The water then settled to a low point in the trough and into a hole in the floor. He was very interested in all these things as he had never seen such. The mute lightly placed her hand on Anam's waist and motioned him that he should kneel over the trough. He did so, and she commenced to briskly soak and lather his head with shampoo. After several moments, she rinsed off his hair, smiled at him as he arose, handed him another towel, turned and walked away.

Anam had spoken scarcely a word since he had arrived here. Now, being surrounded by several of the women with imploring looks upon their faces, he opened his mouth and spoke to them.

"Great is the Lord for leading us to this place."

One of the women, Macosena was her name, responded. "Never in my life have I seen such wonders as here. Notice this..." She reached over to a handle above one of the water spouts and turned it. The water from that spout stopped. "The turning of the knob somehow plugs up the flow of water. Very interesting."

"If this amazes you, then you shall surely be amazed at the rest of the city." They turned to see an older woman had entered the room. In spite of her age, she was still quite a good-looking woman. She wore a black robe very similar to Andre's, which bore over the left side of the chest a symbol of the fallen cross. "I am Marta, Andre's concubine. He awaits your presence but felt odd in coming to you and seeing your nakedness. Fresh garments have been prepared for you, but do not feel guilt for turning them away. Your dress is unlike ours, but we accept you by any standard. Take your leisure here or come with me to Andre's home."

"I am prepared to leave," said Anam. He looked about him and said to Elamuna who had just approached, "I suggest that you continue to relax for a bit. I will talk to Andre about finding suitable quarters for us and, especially, food. I shall have Marta return."

Marta spoke again. "I am a priestess of Foramen. Food is being prepared and will presently be made available for you. Unfortunately, there is no one place in this city sector to quarter you altogether. There are areas nearby or, if you are not concerned of being separated, we may find some rooms in this sector. I apologize for our unpreparedness, but we did not expect company by the back gate. Please, accept my excuses."

"Your apologies are not necessary. My people are weary, but they are a very self-sufficient people, so any generosity that you can bestow upon them will be welcome."

"If you are ready, then we can go to Andre."

Anam nodded. She cupped her hand over his elbow and led him back up the same passageway through which they had previously entered.

Once into the passageway, Anam, being freshly washed, felt the coolness of the air around him. He looked the walls over much better than before. It appeared to be totally manmade. A hole had been bore into the earth and then lined on all sides with rough-cut stone, bonded together with firm concrete, much better than any he had seen before. The stone had finally been highly polished so that it was nearly soft to the hand.

He glanced at Marta who continued to escort him by the arm. Anam did not mind the gentle pressure of this comely-looking female. She was a woman in her mid-fifties whose hair had begun to turn white, but was still mostly black. She was much smaller than the Rasomite women to whom he was accustomed; being barely five feet in height. Her face shone with make-up, much like the Atrocene women, but he did not make a negative comparison to her for this fact. He would not make any judgments yet.

Once they had again reached street-level, Anam became like an eager child as he began gazing up and down the busy streets and asking a string of questions.

"What makes the streets so flat?"

"I don't understand your question, my friend," Marta replied.

Anam bent over and rubbed his hand along the surface of the sidewalk.

"Oh," she smiled, "the substance is concrete. It is made of sand and..."

"I know concrete. But the weight of the vehicles and time would cause it to crumble."

"Oh, not really, but on occasion it needs to be patched or resurfaced."

"What is the mirror-like substance so that one can see into people's buildings?"

"This is glass, also made from sand."

"One cannot see through sand." He paused and carefully placed his hand on a window in front of a fruit store."

"There is a process, but I also sense that you are hungry."

"I am very hungry," replied the warrior.

"You shall be the guest of myself and Andre. Your compatriots shall be fed by the servants of the cathedral. Andre has many questions."

"We both have many questions," he said absently as he looked around, thrilled by all the sights. The streets were filled with horse-drawn carts and carriages. There were a wide assortment of people, all were gaily dressed. The women seemed to wear dresses or skirts and high heels. Their hair was either cut short or pulled back in a bun. All wore a certain amount of make-up. They were pretty in their own way, but they appeared to be weak and rather pathetic when compared to the Rasomite women. The men were mostly dressed in dark suits, with or without cravats, or they wore dark-colored work clothes. Their health also seemed to be in a state of disrepair. As he walked the streets, he glanced and, occasionally, stopped to stare through this substance called glass. There were many small shops and each sold a different type of ware. There were shops for furniture, pottery, flowers, bread, and even those that sold nothing but paper.

Marta finally pointed to the cathedral, which was not far from where they stood. It was magnificent. It stretched out for two hundred feet, and the front portion was at least a hundred feet tall. Beyond that was a rounded peak that rose for nearly another hundred feet. It was built of white sandstone with wide marble steps rising to the front. There were twelve archways with columns between each that rose to the roof. Before the building was a wide green lawn that was sprinkled with small patches of brightly-colored flowers. The wide stone walkway that led to the cathedral was prefaced with an archway similar to those of the cathedral, but there was no gate to block entry. In the lawn near the building was a large marble statue of the fallen cross.

Amid all the excitement in Anam's mind was also a certain foreboding that he could not grasp. It concerned his being a savior but went beyond that. Something was very wrong here. It was not the advancement of these people that caused him to fear. It was not their lifestyle. There was, amid all this finery, a dark secret. He did not know what it was.

In spite of all the commotion and traffic behind them, it was quite peaceful walking the last hundred feet to the cathedral. The sidewalks were massive and composed of gravel and concrete. The lawns were very well-tended and trimmed short. There were borders of various colored flowers, all unfamiliar, along the walks. Several sidewalks eventually converged to a large walk area near the cathedral. The marble steps, which led up to the cathedral, spread out for nearly the length of the building. They were short and narrow leading up to the front, but easily scaled in Anam's bare feet. The top of the stairway placed them immediately under the giant sandstone canopy and along one of the columns.

Anam rubbed his hand along the column and slowly lifted his head to its peak. As he looked up, he remembered his God and said a silent prayer for wisdom. He looked back at Marta, who was standing patiently by, and took her by the hand.

"Let us go to your mate," he said.

They turned and walked through the outer portion of the cathedral in the shade. The walls were all of highly-polished marble with intricate-colored carvings cut into the surface of the stone. The rectangular slabs were separated by a thin vein of gold. Everywhere, the predominant theme of artwork was of the fallen cross.

"Later," said Marta, as she reached for the doorway handle of what appeared to be gold, "perhaps you would like to see the servitorium and the sanctuaries. But, presently, Andre awaits you, so I feel you should go directly to him."

They entered a small room with walls of dark, nicely-polished wood. The room bore no ornamentation of furniture except for a small stone table, the surface of which was not more than a foot from the floor. Behind the table was an open-arched doorway that had only a light linen curtain for covering. Squatted behind the table was Andre with two silver wine goblets in his hands, one of which he held out, offering it to Anam."

"Welcome, friend."

Anam took the goblet from the man and sat across from him, cross-legged. They sat thusly for half a minute, staring into each other's eyes as Anam considered how to start the conversation. Anam raised the goblet to his lips and allowed a bit of the cool, dark red liquid to trickle down his throat. He had had water to drink in the saunas and that helped refresh him, but the wine satisfied a deeper thirst, and his tense body immediately responded by relaxing some.

Andre raised his hand, and two servant girls entered the room with baskets of fresh food. There was bread in variety and fresh fruit; apples, bananas, oranges, grapes and such the like which Anam had never seen. There were fresh green onions, carrots, red peppers, and a multitude too great to remember. Also, there were meats. Red goats' meat, fried and broiled fish, sliced chicken, sausages. Of the herbs, Anam ate voraciously, but he did not eat the red meat and only a bit of chicken and fish. Between mouthfuls, they began to probe each other's minds, as their goblets were kept full.

"I see, wherever I go, the sign of the cross, but it is fallen."

"The cross is a sign of the savior who was and who is to be. It is said when he was destroyed, the cross fell."

"So it is said. Is the saying true?"

"It is said he shall return and set the world right. He will vanquish the unrighteous and lead the world out of its misery."

"Is this a saying, or do you expect this to happen in our world?"

"We await his return."

"I was called by your men, Nathan and Ovey, 'Savior'. What of that?"

"I would expect that if a man were the savior, God would have already shown the man this truth. I do not know."

"But they quaked, not at me, but at the name 'Anam'."

"Some of the legends say the savior shall come from the desert; he shall be called 'Anam', which is in our language the same as 'Savior'."

"Tell me again, what do you believe?"

"We raise our praises to God," said Andre with a face growing tired of repeated questions.

"I would expect a holy man to raise praises to none other. I suppose you have your certain words and rituals that are performed to satisfy your cravings for a semblance of religion, but what do you believe in?"

"I have answered your questions. Now, I ask of you the same. What do you believe?"

"I and my people are one. We are the children of God and, for such reason, we therefore love God as our Father. All power of the creation is with the Father. He had the power to create us. He has the power to blank us out in a moment of time. As his true and honest servant, he has anointed me with an added blessing to be able to raise his power and, thereby when he will, to have insight into the minds of men or to destroy the face of the earth. He has called me to travel the face of the earth and redeem his children and, therefore, I have power to judge the integrity of all men."

"Then you know I love God. Your further questions are mute, since you say you can read my mind."

"It is not so easy, my friend, for your words will be the method of entrapment. You have your religion, but I fear, you do not have the power as you deny him by your actions. I fear there are other secrets that must be revealed."

Andre stood up and looked down on Anam with an angry scowl. "You have so soon wore out your welcome. Take your women and your children and your lies and leave this place. Do not speak to the people of Foramen. Do not enter the temples and sanctuaries. Leave the city and leave it quickly."

Anam stood up and dusted off his legs, then turned for the door. "No!" he exclaimed looking over his shoulder. "I will do as my Father asks. I do not know what he will ask. But I do know this. If even as much as the hair of a Rasomite's head be harmed by you, then all of God's wrath shall be incurred against you." With these parting words, Anam quietly opened the door and went back out into the sun.

Standing a few paces from the door with a smile upon her face, was Marta. She was oblivious to the whole interchange which had just taken place.

"Your meal was short, Rasomite."

"The meal was good, but I must beware of who I keep company with."

"I do not understand. Andre is not a rude sort of man."

"There are secrets. Is Andre the chief priest or do I seek another? I know I do."

"Jesepth is the man you seek if it be the high priest you would dine with. He is in the heart of Foramen. However, it being far from here, I shall make haste to get you a coach or wagon. The people will do whatever I ask of them."

"I felt that this be not a small city."

"Jesepth lives in near solitude at the heart of the city, this being several miles from here. Foramen is a very large city, being home to people who number in the millions. This portion, being called Akuwa, is under charge of Andre and also of the governor, Phillip."

"I shall make haste to see Jesepth."

"But gaining audience with Jesepth is not always granted, he being great of years and also in solitude, praying and praising God continually."

"I shall go to him. He shall see me."

Transportation was very organized in the city of Foramen, and it had been simple for Marta to arrange a ride for Anam to the heart of the city. Anam now sat atop an open-air, horse-drawn wagon. The carrier was constructed of a highly-polished wood, and the reflection of the late afternoon sun against the finish was dazzling. It was designed to move six passengers, each with a separate seat supported from the wagon by black-coated wrought iron. There was still plenty of area in back to haul luggage or material and, in fact, there were several empty wire cages on board now. The driver, who sat below Anam, appeared to be in his seventies. He was a tiny man, but for his arms, which were well-developed from driving horses for all these years. Four horses, all black or nearly black, were before them, pulling the wagon. The driver was silent as he had been instructed of Marta to ask no questions, but to deliver his passenger to Jesepth. The payment had apparently been generous as a great gleam came to his eye and a smile to his lips when Marta had given him several pieces of paper, which Anam assumed to represent money. Everything, it seemed, was so different about this place.

The style of the city did not change much as they rode along, except the buildings were closer together and taller as they traveled. After a space of an hour, they suddenly emerged into an expansive garden. There were very few buildings, but there were fountains aplenty. One fountain fired water into the air nearly fifty feet, and its pool was nearly two hundred feet across. In the wake of the downpour were hundreds of brightly-colored ducks and geese. They rode by a rose garden that bore roses nearly the size of a man's head. There were a few small gazebos and one large covered area for music and gatherings. Far off was a temple far grander than the cathedral he had just left. Stretching across the vista for nearly a mile was a fence of marble, which stood perhaps fifteen feet high. Spaced across the top of the fence were pinnacles, one leading into another every foot. The temple beyond spread out for nearly a thousand feet in width and four hundred feet in height. Its design was like the cathedral, except for its massive size.

They reached the gateway, which was open but adequately guarded by several uniformed officers. They did not seem to bear any weapons. After briefly interchanging with one of the guards, who eyed Anam suspiciously, they were allowed to pass on.

Separating them from the cathedral was a wide, shallow pool. Spanning the water was a long wooden bridge that had no railing. As they neared the landing on the other side, the bridge suddenly widened into a sandstone bridge with a railing of stone pillars about three feet in height. It appeared to be under construction. They had reached their destination.

Anam was on the ground before the driver and stood awaiting as an entourage of six men approached him, all of various ages, all wearing the traditional black robe with the now-familiar symbol upon it. They awaited Anam's first words.

"I have traveled far, and I am now awaiting a meeting with the high priest. Let us go."

"Not so very fast, young man," said the eldest among the priests. "The high priest is in prayer, awaiting this evening's ceremony, and it's not possible to see him now. Perhaps on the morrow."

"Nevertheless, my audience with him is of more import than

either his prayer or your ceremony."

The old priest looked at the driver for explanation, who had taken his time climbing down and now stood beside the wagon.

"I do not know the man, sir," he began. "However, we have just now come from Andre who was very insistent that this man see the high priest. He is, it seems, a sojourner from the desert who has traveled far to gain time with His Excellency." Anam smiled inside as the driver stretched the truth a bit, quite a bit.

"Your name, sir."

"Anam."

Upon hearing his name, the youngest priest, who was perhaps twenty-five, nearly passed out. His eyes grew large, sweat formed on his brow, and he nearly toppled over, except the older priests held him up. All of the men, including the driver, were quite visibly shaken by this word. At length, they gathered some composure and the oldest one spoke again.

"You claim to be Anam. From where do you come?"

"As your citizen has said, I have come from across the desert. My hair is still as dry as straw and my flesh is burned, despite your sweet-smelling oils."

"Yes, from the desert, but from where across the desert? Surely, if you claim to be the savior, you know the scriptures."

"I have not been three hours in this city. While here, I have tried to calm my aching flesh. I have drunken wine and eaten fruit. I have walked with Marta and been concerned over the welfare of my people, who all are a godly people, and not once have I laid claim to being a savior or prophet. I know not of what you speak, but each man has called me savior, and I would inquire what this means. Surely I have not said I am savior, but you have, so it would be necessary for you to explain yourself."

The old priest stroked his beard with one hand and motioned the others away with his other hand. When they were at a safe distance and could not here his exchange with Anam, he began to speak.

"There is a legend or a fable that a man called Anam will come from the desert and be a prophet of sorts. It is a story commonly spoken about between school children and some women. We of our faith believe that there is no savior, but you are saved by your acts. It is by your acts that your faith is given substance. Can you understand me for what I mean?"

"I see the truth deeper than you would have it. Andre has already destroyed your idea of a myth and given it hope, for he awaits the savior, though he is not prepared. Your own priest nearly fainted. We of our belief feel that your faith is proven before God and not made justified on earth because of certain rituals as the use of certain words used in rituals are a device of man. I perceive that your faith is weak and that you are a liar. I must see Jesepth."

The face of the priest had begun to turn red with anger. "This is forbidden."

"It is neither in your power to forbid it or to allow it. I keep my peace until I am before Jesepth."

"I demand that you remain in place." The priest turned and strode up the steps to the entryway of the temple.

Anam looked around and muttered under his breath, wondering what these people were. He was confused about being their savior, but if he was a man God had sent to bear light to these people, he could not understand why these priests would oppose him. They should be thankful, or at least open-minded, toward his testimony if they were truly a god-fearing people. He hoped the high priest would be more understanding than the other priests. He looked across the water and realized that a crowd was beginning to form on the other side. The driver had gone across and begun to spread the word.

He heard his name being called by one of the priests and turned about. Several of the priests had formed a line across the top step of the temple.

"Anam," called out one of the priests again, "come before me."

Showing little decorum and his unfelt respect for these men, he bounded up the steps to the one who had called him.

"Are you the one they call Jesepth, the high priest?" he asked.

The priest smiled and shook his head. "Jesepth is in prayer. I am his deputy, Stewart, and I am aware of your confusion, and also your faith. I invite you this evening to the Celebration of Continuance and tomorrow it may be possible to confer with Jesepth. Until then, you are my personal guest and one to be given privilege that only a few have shared, except the priests of Foramen."

"I accept your invitation."

"It is understood that you desire to keep your peace until you gain audience and that is also my desire. I would that you share and witness our rituals so that you can gain understanding, and then we can share in our beliefs so that we may both gain understanding. If you would follow me."

The priest, Stewart, turned and Anam followed him into the temple. The temple they entered was beautiful beyond description. The domed ceiling rose at least three hundred feet above them, and its floor was seven or eight-hundred feet across. In the center of this temple was a raised stage that was large enough for the massive sitting place upon it. The floor was carpeted, and there were no other chairs. The ceiling was arranged in a checkerboard pattern of windows, which allowed the sunlight to enter, and beautifully-painted patterns inbetween. Stewart bent over and removed his sandals and then Anam followed him across the heavily-cushioned floor to a doorway on the far side. They descended a short stairway into a large eating room that had rows of heavy wooden tables and chairs. There was ample seating space for at least fifty men. Several of the seats were already occupied. Stewart turned to Anam.

"There also is a larger room, but this room is adequate for all the priests in Foramen to attend. I would give you an honored seat near the front and, normally, I would be there also, but I feel that you would gain more if we sat in back and could see everything and not be so obvious. Do you agree? It shall be as you wish."

"Any seat shall do well. I only want to witness."

They found two seats together in the back and sat down.

Stewart spoke. "It will still be a bit of time before the ceremony actually begins. This is a time to be in prayer, and there will be much wine." He picked up a large silver pitcher and poured red wine into the crystal goblets. He said a short prayer over his and consumed the entire glass.

"How can I know if I love him? I am not even certain as to what love means. I know the moment I saw him at the city wall, my insides seemed to feel as though they were melting. I don't know why, but I have never felt this way before about a boy."

Elamuna smiled softly and looked at Ulyana with understanding "But how do we know how the boy, Nathan, feels?"

"After I helped him back up and turned him over to other people, our eyes locked and would not turn away except that you called me and I finally followed. Elamuna, I want to see him again."

"I shall help you see him again."

"Nathan, if Phillip were to hear that you were ready to give your heart to some beggar from the desert, he would be furious."

"Mother, you don't even know the girl."

"The much the worse."

"Then the better it would be if you were to meet her. Can I invite her to dinner?"

"No! If the leader of these people were to request a proper audience with your father, we would then meet them. Where is their leader?"

"I am not sure. He dresses like a savage, but he is a religious man and I believe he has gone to the high priest, Jesepth. Must we wait? There is a woman who seems to be her mother, so perhaps you and she can make the proper arrangements."

"It is not my place. You claim he is a religious man, but also these people travel in the desert and wear little clothing. Can anything godly come from the desert? Tell me one thing that would allow me to believe in these dirty travelers."

"The man's name is Anam," said Nathan as he headed out the doorway. He did not see his mother swoon or collapse onto the floor in a fit of tears.

Nathan stared at the back doorway of the temple, which led into the area normally set aside for feasts and celebrations. He hesitated to knock on the door and then pushed the heavy wooden door open to peer inside. It was dark except for a few candles. He crept in. The room was a mess, testifying that the Rasomites had dined there and had moved on. He crossed the room and went out into the sanctuary, which was also but dimly lit. There was no one present, so he stood off to the side, allowing his eyes to adjust to the lack of light. Then he noticed someone lying on the floor on the opposite side of the room. He was cautious about investigating. It could be one of the Rasomite women who was resting and was just too weary to go any further. But it seemed strange she would sleep on the hard floor of the sanctuary. He approached the form and could tell from her clothing that she was not a Rasomite, but a woman wearing a black robe. It could only be Marta.

"Marta," he whispered as he stood over her. "Why do you rest here?" He dropped to his knees and touched her hand to wake her. It was cold and lifeless. His eyes grew large. "Marta!" he shouted as he grabbed her by the shoulders from behind, "What has happened?" He rolled her over onto her back. The woman had been struck in the face several times. Who could have done this awful thing? Then, he knew. The knowledge leapt upon him in a moment.

Earlier, Marta had sent Anam to the high priest and had told many. Andre must have gone mad when he found out. Nathan knew in his heart this was true and he knew what he must do. He was going to find the priest and kill him, for Marta was his father's sister. All other thoughts left him. He knew where to find him also. It would take him a little over an hour to reach the temple of the high priest.

Anam had also drank much wine, as had the men around him, but he did not share in their revelry. He was bored of their all-night drinking party. They had been sitting here for hours, and he now understood Stewart's motives better. The aide to the high priest had decided to get Anam drunk, learn as much about the man as possible, and then induce him to share in the victuals that followed. In spite of the fact that Anam was hungry, he felt certain he would become sick if he ate anything, for he had drunk too much wine. He was about to excuse himself when the high priest, who sat in the front, arose and lifted his arms into the air. Without the need to hear a command, several young boys entered the room carrying platters of what appeared to be goat meat. A platter was placed before each group of about six priests. One platter was placed within reach of Anam. He could not eat the meat, but a good piece of dry bread would taste good right now. Then inspection got the better of him. He picked up a piece of meat to look more closely and the sickening realization crept upon him. The meat belonged to the arm of a man. Anam turned his head and retched. The alcohol left his belly, but he was still sick. These people were cannibals. The Celebration of Continuance? They ate their dead priests? Could that be it? He looked at Stewart, who was ravenously gobbling down an almost raw piece of human flesh, and anger took over his drunken mind. His first thought was to break the man's neck, but he knew he had to stop this insanity. He kicked his chair back and jumped upon the table.

"You are a pack of miserable curs!" he screamed. "Are you all insane?" He shoved the platter off the table to the floor. "What do you think you are? My mind cannot understand. I cannot fathom this disgusting animalism. You are sick and I cannot contemplate forgiveness. I am now going to deliver you to Hell's door itself!"

There was some laughter, some angry comments. The high priest took Anam's attention and prepared to speak. Then, another priest arose. Anam had not seen Andre come in. Andre pointed his forefinger at Anam and made as if ready to speak. He was, however, quite drunken and paused to form his thoughts. Anam stared him in the eye.

"I have heard you before," Anam said. "I will listen no more to your views of a distorted faith. Except that you or any man here deny himself and follow me, he is finished." Anam got off the table and quietly left through the doorway.

Once safely outside, he again looked across the water. There was now a very large crowd gathering, but they still dared not cross the ramp. They had been there all night. Then, one person broke through. After he was free from the crowd, he ran as fleet-footed as a deer. In a flash, he reached the foot of the staircase and bounded up the marble steps three at a time. He saw Anam but attempted to run passed him. Anam put out his hand, and the boy looked into his face. Tears were rolling down Nathan's cheeks, but he could not speak.

"It is finished," said Anam. "There is nothing more that you can do."

"My aunt...Andre...I...I have been looking for him all night."

"Let us go and start over." They walked back down the stairs together and to the beginning of the ramp. Anam turned around and raised his arms into the air. "They are yours, Lord!" he shouted. "It is time to start over."

There was no crack or fissure that began, no rumble or shake from the earth. Suddenly, the entire cathedral turned like ashes and dust and simply collapsed. There was an explosive noise that was heard throughout Foramen, and the city was covered by the dust from the building, but in a moment, except for Anam's and Nathan's headaches, it was over.

Phillip looked out at the gray sky. The rising sun was nearly blotted out by the dust storm and only an eerie glow penetrated the dust. He had seen dust storms before. There were often dust storms from the east and sandstorms from the west. Never before had he seen a dust storm as bad as this or one that behaved this way. This was strange. But what made it seem even more unusual was the fact that there was no wind and there had been no ominous weather changes to indicate a storm. An hour before, he had been taking a stroll through the cathedral courtyard. Now this. Very strange.

He turned to walk away from the window when, suddenly, he heard an explosion that shook the very walls of the house. He hurried back to the window, but nothing had changed. He could not perceive what could possibly be happening. He gazed across the yard. Everything was becoming so dirty. There would need to be a tremendous clean up in his city sector, called Akuwa. Perhaps he should send a runner to one of the other governors to begin organizing a city-wide clean-up. As he stood there, the sky began to clear as suddenly as it had begun to cloud up. The early morning sun was becoming brighter even as he watched. This caused a peace to settle upon him, but he still did not understand. If only Andre were about. He dismissed that thought as he sincerely thought Andre was a fool. How often he had wanted to correct that man. He and all the priests. Priests, indeed. They were no nearer to God than he, and he did not know God at all.

A sudden wave of despair came across him. He longed for the time and knowledge to be a godly man, but there were so many affairs that needed his attention. God was always the least of his priorities. If only someone cared enough for him to take a moment and get into his heart. He was always trying to portray the power-hungry statesman. Always stern. Always busy. Never weak. But in his heart, he was very weak. For though it seemed he had the whole world at his feet, he often felt like nothing really mattered. Then he tried to be alone. He was very lonely. Suddenly, as he stood there pondering these thoughts, tears began welling up in his eyes and he began crying uncontrollably. Unable to bear himself, he fell to his knees and crouched on the floor. He had never felt like this before; lonely, yes. But this was a deep despair.

"Oh God!" he cried out. "Why are you so far from me? Please

help me." He surprised himself as he had never acted like this before. "I am so very tired and weak. I am supposed to be a great leader. The people have put me here to lead. I cannot lead when I feel like this. Help me."

He sat there rolled into a ball in the middle of the room when he felt a hand upon his shoulder. He looked up into the eyes of a beautiful young dark-skinned girl. She was different than any he had ever seen before. Her hair was black as a raven. Her skin was slate-gray. She wore nothing but a cloth around her waist and a small halter top that he recognized as coming from Foramen. For an instant he felt indignation come upon him for being so caught, but awe overcame this emotion. He thought she must be an angel. She spoke.

"God has heard you. I heard you from the outer room. I am not an angel. I am simply a young girl who is in love with your son. However, I think the Lord wanted me to walk into this room at this time. Everyone has gone to see what the dust storm may be all about, so I let myself in. I perceive that you are a man who is dishonest but craves honesty. A man who distrusts, but desires the faith to trust. One who sees power in the world, and has it, but does not know what to do with it. That is because you are driven by what you expect other men want from you. Your house seems strong, but your walls are crumbling. You cannot be strong enough to bear yourself up."

"Then how can I do it? I must be strong."

"You cannot do it unless you surrender yourself to God."

He had felt good for a moment but, now, despair again began to set in.

"I do not even know where God is."

"He is here by us. He wants to be within you. If you ask me to, I shall help you seek him. You called out for him. He has answered. Now, he wants you to decide."

"Help me." He reached toward her, and she knelt before him.

"The spirit of God is here. You must yield yourself to that spirit."

They waited, it seemed, for a long time. Nothing happened. Phillip was prepared to give up, thinking perhaps he was not worthy. Then he began to feel the despair taking him again.

"Father!" Ulyana called out. "I beseech you now to enter into this man's heart. Help him to be strong. Help him to be a shining example of your glory before all people. Give him a reason for life."

Suddenly, Phillip burst out into tears again and his head fell upon her shoulder. Then, he stopped. In a few moments, he picked his head up and spoke slowly. "I feel so peaceful now. Something has overcome me. I do not understand."

"I think that angry demons have been thrown out of your heart. The evil that lurks inside most people has been cast aside, but if you do not daily feed the spirit that has entered therein, you shall be the worse for it."

"Thank you, God."

"I want to continue to be beside you and help you. There are others who also want to help."

They stood up.

"Yes. Yes. Certainly. I think I would feel worse if you were to leave me now. The people of Foramen are also hungry for God."

"They shall be fed."

"They have been led astray for so long. The priests are very much in control. Even though they do not interfere normally with the day to day affairs, they have their presence everywhere. Then again, people are imprisoned because they have rebuked a priest or refused to pay taxes. But the priests do not know God. They behave openly as reserved and philosophical but, within, they are like wolves. They have ceremonies that are ghastly and disgusting, but the people have lost their will to do anything about it."

"If they call upon God, all things are possible through him."

Phillip turned toward the window. "Did you come from the storm? I have told you everything, and I don't even know who you are."

"My name is Ulyana. I come from across the desert where my people have been ravaged by the Atrocenes, whom we have succeeded in conquering."

"Then you travel alone?"

"No. I come with the remnant of the Rasomites seeking peace and a new opportunity to grow and prosper. We are led by a man whom the Lord has spared. His name is Anam."

"Today, truth has arrived in our city. For truly this man Anam is the one we call the prophet. For decades we have waited and now, in my day, I am blessed. Yes, you are nearly an angel. If it be possible, I must see this man."

"He has gone to Jesepth."

"I feel the priests may try to overcome him. They will not be pleased with this prophet."

Before Ulyana could answer, a woman entered the room weeping. It was the mother of Nathan.

"Christa, my wife, what has happened? Why do you cry so?"

"A messenger has just come from the sanctuary. Marta is dead. The belief is that she was bludgeoned to death by Andre because of her support for the visitors."

Phillip embraced her and said, "Many things are happening in the city. I will take that man and cast him into prison."

She spoke on, "I fear, my husband, for Nathan. Some say he went to the sanctuary looking for the girl." She eyed Ulyana. "I feel he found Marta and has gone for Andre. He cannot be found."

"I am the girl," said Ulyana slowly. "I also fear for Nathan. I pray he is brought back to us quickly." Tears started to form in her eyes as she remembered the commitment she had made in the desert – to never love a boy.

"You precious child," said the woman, "you truly do care for him."

"I am not sure what I should feel like to be in love, but my heart has gone after him, and he is so soon removed."

"Don't fret, my friend," said Phillip. "We must be strong. I think he will be here very soon."

Anna dusted off the window ledge and leaned against the glass in an attempt to see if Ovey was coming.

"Where could that man be?" she said aloud. "I get so disgusted when he wanders off and doesn't come home. One minute, he asks if there is any more tobacco about and, the next minute, he is gone. No 'goodbye, dear' or nothing. Just wanders off and comes back when he feels like it."

She wadded her dust rag into a ball and threw it among an untidy collection of items on the floor.

"Look at this mess. Why can't that man put anything away?"

She got on her knees and started sweeping tobacco ashes back into the overturned ashtray with her hand, wiping the soot on her apron and then started rearranging the books and papers into a neater pile. Finally, she spread her dust rag out and filled it up with food wrappers, apple cores, an empty tobacco tin, a pair of old shoelaces and more. She finally gave up in disgust and left the entire area alone.

"Worse than a little boy." The woman went back to the window. "I do wish he would come back. It's been nearly a full day since he left. He's never done this before, but he has come creeping home in the wee hours of the morning. I hope nothing has gone wrong."

Anna was a short, stocky woman. Her arms and legs were as tough as old cow leather from working so many years, hauling ash and coal for others. Her back was still strong, though it had a stoop to it. It had been some time since she had bathed, so there was an ungainly repulsive aroma about her. Not that it mattered as she didn't associate with anyone, except her husband, and she was seldom home while he was there.

"Where could that man be?" Shaking her head and puffing air in exasperation, she sat down on the only chair in the room and soon fell into a light sleep. However, her sleep was soon interrupted when Ovey walked in.

"Who's there? What? Oh, you." She stood up and looked him in the eye.

Ovey stood speechless, with his mouth partly open, as though he were in a mild state of shock. He had been up all night before he'd met the Rasomites at the gate and had trailed Anam to the temple of the high priest, where he'd seen the destruction. He had heard Anam as he began speaking to the people gathered there and had stayed for some time, listening to him speak of truth and of the living God, but more people were showing up, and he was finally too far back to be able to hear plainly. Then, wiser, but still confused, he had come home to tell his wife.

"So, speak up plainly, man. Where have you been off to this time?"

"I have been listening to a man."

"Well, that's more than you'll give me," she snapped back and turned to go.

"No," he said quietly and placed his hand on her arm. She looked at him with a bit of deference because it had been some time since he had touched her. "Sit down, Anna. I need to talk to you."

She sat back in the chair slowly. "Yesterday, I saw a man

come from across the desert. Now, I feel I have seen God." She looked at him totally absorbed in what he was saying. "It is no fairy tale or such nonsense. The prophet has come. I am sure. He has come, and we were not ready. Remember the poem? It's often repeated. Remember the lines, 'and he came unto them who were mighty, and they were not where they should be, so he took their lives and their wealth and their souls and cast them into the sea.' And also, 'and he looked around and saw the weak and the lost, and they would not either so their souls were also tossed. "Why weren't we ready?" he finally shouted at her.

"Who has come?" asked Anna.

"The prophet called Anam."

She nodded and smiled, "What less could we expect? Is life no more than the drudgery of carrying ash for those more fortunate than yourself? What did he say?"

"He said that God wants to live inside of us and that he is a living God. He said that we can be forgiven our wrongs."

"The words will anger the priests," she said, raising her eyebrows.

"I don't know if there are any priests. Did you see the dust storm?" Ovey pointed towards the window. "It was no dust storm. Before he began to speak, he turned toward the temple of the high priest, spoke a few words, and turned back again. The entire building collapsed to the ground as though it were nothing. There was a tremendous noise and, then, the dust billowed up into the sky. We could see nothing for several minutes. I believe that all or nearly all of the priests were in there when it happened."

"He spoke and the building collapsed?" she said in disbelief. "Ovey, such a thing cannot happen. It cannot be explained except perhaps he had placed explosives in the building or done some mighty work to pull out the columns."

"I say he spoke and the building collapsed. If you could hear the words of this man, you too would believe."

"Do you believe?" asked Anna.

"I am afraid. Everything has changed. What will happen next?"

As if to answer his question and aid his wife in her unbelief, there was suddenly a commotion in the street. In a few minutes they had both gone outside to see what could be happening. They saw several people moving hurriedly along the street, so Anna stopped a man and asked him what was happening.

"There is a woman, a woman with gray skin, and she speaks of God."

"But," said Anna, "women are not allowed to speak publicly of God. It is only for men."

"So the priests say. But then, maybe, if this woman doesn't do it, then no one else shall, either. The priests surely don't speak of God, except in some vague way in the sanctuary. Come along and see what is happening." He moved on.

Ovey took Anna by the arm. "Come, I'll show you what I was talking about."

They soon reached the end of the street where the four corners met. On the opposite side was a veranda that was attached to a hotel. On the stairway of the veranda was a young woman, and she did indeed have gray skin as the man had said. However, from this distance, Anna and Ovey could not plainly hear what she was saying.

The woman was Crazon, one of the Rasomite women. Anna could hear that she was speaking about God, but she wanted to hear more. Excusing herself, she tried to move forward and the crowd parted because they did not want to be near the foul-smelling woman. Soon, however, Ovey was trapped in the crowd behind. But now, she could hear.

"I say to you, my children," said Crazon. She had one hand partly raised with her palm up. Her eyes were closed. She had a sweet voice, and Anna liked listening to her. "I love you. I love every one of you. There is no one less in my kingdom. I love them all the same. Only, come unto me so you can accept my love." She stopped for a moment and dropped her hand to her side. "Why do they not come to me? They cannot bear their burdens. They live only with grief and loneliness. They toil and build and, yet, they have nothing. I can give them more. I give you life. I give you love. I give you health. I give you companionship. Nothing is beyond me. Will no one come forth?"

Crazon opened her eyes and looked at the crowd. There were nearly two hundred people before her, and it was not yet six o'clock in the morning. She looked across the crowd, not really seeing them, but then her eyes fell upon Anna. The people near her turned to see what had drawn the Rasomite's attention. Anna was dumbfounded.

Crazon reached her hand out and said, "Come to me, my

child."

Someone said, "The old woman is twice her age, or more, and she says, 'my child'."

"Who is that old woman?" asked another.

A well-dressed man raised himself to his toes and said to those near him, "That is Anna. She has been employed by me for years. But this young woman does not know how bitter the old woman is, or she would not call her forth."

Anna slowly stepped forward, not taking her eyes off the woman until she was standing beside her. Then, she felt a bit foolish being before all these people.

"What is your name?" Crazon quietly asked her.

"Anna," she mumbled, staring at her feet.

"Anna, do you believe in God?"

"Yes, there is a God," she said, not turning her head.

"Do you trust him?"

"What do you mean?" asked Anna as she did not understand. She looked at Crazon.

"Do you believe in God?" she asked her emphasizing every word.

Anna was about to cry. "I want to believe, but I'm just an old fool."

"God loves you anyway," Crazon said with a smile and placed one arm around Anna's shoulder. It was then that Anna realized that she was considerably shorter than this young woman. "I want you to trust me," she said as she placed her fingertips on Anna's cheek.

"I trust you."

Crazon placed her free hand above Anna's head. "Touch my hand with the top of your head." Anna looked up at her hand. It was just out of reach from her head.

"You don't understand," said Anna, shaking her head and shoulders. "I am a working woman, and I have a bow to my back because I have carried a load all of my life."

"God's load is light. Trust me."

"I trust you and I want to believe you, but when I try to stand up straight, it hurts too much. But I will try." She closed her eyes and strained to stand up straighter, but could not.

"Anna. Anna. No. Trust God. Look." Crazon took both her hands and symbolically acted as though she were removing a load from Anna's back. Then she turned her around to face her and nearly yelled, "Anna! Stand up!" Without thinking, Anna leaned back to look into Crazon's face and then realized that she had straightened her back. She rolled her eyes around and a silly smile came to her lips.

"I...I...I can..."

"I know. I told you that you could. Now it is early, but I am hungry. I want to have breakfast with you and your husband. Now, go. I will speak to the people, and you can go prepare yourself. Soon, I will follow you."

Still awed, Anna walked down the steps and the crowd again parted for her but, this time, from respect. Ovey was waiting and eagerly took her by the hand.

"I'm so excited," he told her. "I saw and heard everything. She's coming to spend time with us. I feel so honored. Now, I wish that God would make me want to get a job so I could be a help to you."

Anna tightened her hand on him. "I don't know, Ovey. I know God is in us but, perhaps, there are some miracles that even he cannot cause to pass." She laughed and had a sparkle in her eye. Ovey had not heard her laugh for a long time, so he laughed too.

After Anam had dispersed the crowd, though several people still lingered, he desired to get to know the boy, Nathan, better. They also wanted to return to Nathan's part of the city. All the city was quite familiar to Nathan because of his daily runs. He knew not only the major byways, but also the side streets and alleys that often were less trafficked and, therefore, more easily traveled on foot.

"I shall show you the best route, but it will still take two hours to walk the distance. I have run this route many times."

"Then, perhaps, we should run it today."

Nathan looked up at the man who was solid muscle from head to foot, doubtful that such a large man could run at a very good speed. "However, you have already run this route once today and, perhaps, you are too tired."

"All of this you have said and done this morning, concerning God, and you can do more?" Nathan asked.

"I can do more," said Anam, smiling. "I am no lame cripple

that I can't get about."

"I have spent a thousand hours or more running these city streets and, see my thighs, they are quite developed. However, your body ripples with great strength and to attain that strength would require all of one's time. How is it that you have become so wise and yet so strong? How were you trained?"

"I was not trained, except as a youth. I was turned in the right direction, that of God. I give all the thanks to God, and he has dealt with me thusly."

"I would like to know your God as you do."

"I sense a bit of covetousness in your heart. Only because you know God does not mean that he will treat you as he has treated me. Do you still want to know God?"

"I do. I feel that I could bring much peace to this city. I have been around the town and know the broken hearts of many people. Will you help me with these people?"

"Even as we speak, much has already begun. Do you know that if I knew the route, I could probably best you in a race?"

"Oh, I see now that you want a race. As we come around this corner," he pointed to the end of the street where one must run right or left, "it is a straight run along a quiet street for nearly two miles. But, when we reach the overpass it is best to wait until there is no traffic because the way is so narrow. Let us run from here to the foot of the overpass. Go!" the boy shouted.

Anam was not ready for so soon a command, so the boy was several feet ahead of the man for the first half-mile. Soon, however, the man who had run with wild horses and deer passed the boy. The air was still dusty from the storm, as were the streets, but it was a cool morning and the wind felt good going through Anam's hair. Though the run was intended to be for fun and to keep the two tired runners alert, who had yet to get any sleep from the night before, it soon became very competitive. They had spectators, as well. Many people along the way who were cleaning their doorsteps knew Nathan and were surprised to see this large man running ahead of him. There were very few in the city who could outrun the boy, and the number became fewer every year. At last, they reached the foot of the overpass and it was quite clear that Anam was the winner. They sat on a concrete abutment from the bridge and tried to gain their breath. They also were sweating profusely. Finally, Nathan spoke.

"It is not far from here." He stopped to breath. "We can walk or we can hitch a ride from one of the market wagons."

"How far is it if we should run the rest of the distance?" asked Anam who also took time for heavy breathing.

"Too far," he answered, looking at Anam in disbelief and then glancing absently down the street.

Anam surveyed the overpass by which they were sitting. There was a steady stream of traffic emerging from this end, mostly consisting of wagons and carts pulled by horses or oxen. There was no foot traffic. The bridge was about a hundred feet long, spanning a canal, and was built of concrete with thick walls placed only far enough apart to allow one-way traffic, and even that with a very tight fit. There was a growing line of wagons forming on their end of the bridge.

As they watched, a dozen wagons pass by from the other side, the lead driver on their side stood up, waving his arms to the drivers across the bridge, and yelled out "Whoa there!" The traffic coming from the other end stopped, and the rest of the traffic on the bridge soon passed by such that the caravan could start from the side where Anam and Nathan patiently waited.

"Come on," said Nathan. They got down from their seat and climbed into an empty wagon. "See, this is an illegal bridge. The governors are allowed to control their own city sectors and are also allowed to build foot bridges between the sectors. Each part of the city is surrounded by a canal or bordered by the city wall. However, the priests control all the market traffic over the bridges, and the drivers must pay a toll or taxes. This overpass was authorized as a foot path and was so constructed. However, at the end, the clever architects who had conspired revealed their bridge and it was just wide enough to allow a wagon to pass and so they do. This is the only bridge in Foramen where a driver does not have to pay toll or procure a pass. As a further snub to the priests, when it is possible to ride, no one walks on this bridge. It is also the shortest route back home."

"I see many drivers," said Anam, "and it makes me think that these priests lacked a few followers."

"The priests' hold on the city was never as tight as they would have liked to believe. Mostly, people just paid their tithes and other charges and went about their business. I think there will be much happiness when people discover that God is so much more than was thought. However, there are people in jail for no good cause, and that will have to be fixed."

"Perhaps, there will be happiness," said Anam thoughtfully. "But, also, people do not like to change."

They had reached the other end of the overpass and climbed down off the wagon, waving goodbye and thanking the driver. There were here, gathered about, a number of people talking amongst themselves, but loud enough for all to hear."

"It has never been so in all of history before. Why should it be so today?" one asked.

"I do not know," said another. "I only know what I saw."

"Tell us again what happened," said a younger man.

"I saw a young gray-skinned woman speak to a little one who could not see and she suddenly began laughing and saying, 'I can see! I can see!'."

"Where did this take place?"

"In the courtyard of Governor Andullo, only a few minutes ago."

"Tell us about this woman. Where did she come from? Who is she?"

"I do not know. I believe she is not alone for she said, 'I go unto my sisters and return'. She said that the Spirit of God lives inside of us. We can only be free by obeying that spirit. That we must all love God and each other."

"You speak as a fool. God is in us? How can God be in us?"

"I do not know. In the clouds or somewhere if there even is a God."

"Tell us again about the girl," asked the young man.

"I have already told you twice before. Why do you want to hear it again?"

Anam and Nathan had stood by overhearing this conversation, unnoticed by the men despite Anam's appearance. They were about to speak when, suddenly, a man on a horse ran across the bridge, shouting as he passed, "The temple of the high priest has been destroyed! Repent, all, for the end is near!" And he rode on.

"What, what is this?" said one of the men. "The temple, destroyed? The priests dead? What kind of day is this? I must be with my family." He turned to leave, faced Anam and his mouth fell open. He fell to his knees. "Forgive me, angel of God. I am a good man. I provide for my family as best I can. I do not curse or drink much. Forgive me." The other men stood idly by, not knowing what to do, though they were also amazed at the appearance of this stranger.

Anam put his hand on the man's shoulder. "Do you want to be forgiven or do you do this only out of fear, believing this is the last hour?"

"I do not know. I am afraid."

"If you trust God and fear nothing, God will be with you. Do you want to believe?"

His eyes did not stray from Anam's as the tears began flowing. He took several deep breaths and began sobbing as he dropped his head. "I am a sinful man, my Lord. I have deceived my partner in business. I have been slack in my trade and unfair to my customers. I have been callous toward my neighbors, yea, even my family. I have treated my wife unlovingly and without thought and abused my children beyond the need of discipline. I am unworthy to enter God's grace, but I want to believe." He looked back into Anam's eyes, trying to control his crying.

"Today, salvation is brought to you and your house. Go and tell your wife and your children of the things that have transpired here today." Anam helped him to his feet. The man continued to gaze at him as though ready to burst into tears again.

He turned to the one who had doubted God. Anam continued, "A fool has spoken here. You have spoken as a fool. God is not only in the clouds, nor only in your heart. He is everywhere. But, herein is the difference. The clouds behave as God has created them. Can you speak as boldly for your heart? I think it best that you go and leave these other people alone."

"But, but, who is God, anyway?" muttered the man, looking around at the others. "I don't believe there is a God, at all, and any who blindly fall under the spell are fools."

"It is better to be a fool for God than to be a fool for oneself."

"I am not afraid of your tricky tongue, foreigner. I have lived in this city all of my life and have met all types of vagabonds and wanderers who puff themselves up."

"Is it worse to be a wanderer and act righteously than to stay in one place and act like a fool?"

"There you go again, trying to turn my own words upon me stranger. From where have you traveled? What do you call yourself?"

He was tempted to tell him that his name was Anam, only to see the effect on the man, but thought better of it. He turned to the young man. "Do you also doubt God?"

The man was instantly overcome with embarrassment as his face flashed red. "Umm. I don't know, sir. I've never given it much thought."

The older man juxtaposed himself between the two. "Now, look here. We were having a talk, see, and we were not finished."

Anam caught his eyes with a cold stare. "Our talk and your salvation appear to be over, my friend. If you are in a hurry to condemn your soul to hell by your unbelief, do not be so hasty with the souls of your friends."

"I don't know what to say," said the older man. "I'm sorry. I only meant...that is, I wanted to show a friendly gesture."

"It would be a friendly gesture to fall on your face before God and ask for repentance or, at least, not to stand in your brother's way."

The older man backed off. The younger had turned to walk away. Anam called to him. "Have you turned your back on God?"

The young man was by now twenty paces off and turned back. "I am not ready, my Lord. That is, there are some things that I have to do first."

"In a moment, you may die. First you should ask for salvation."

"I'm just not ready, yet," said the young man, shaking his head nervously, almost in tears. He turned and hurried away.

"There are many," said Anam, "who are good and admit to salvation, but are never ready."

Nathan touched his arm. "Are the good also condemned? Can the bad be saved but the good must die? I do not understand."

"There is much that will not be understood this side of salvation, my friend. The bad prosper and the good live in filth. The man with an evil heart lives to an old age and the good die young. Why are these things? I cannot say except that you must seek salvation."

Anam looked around and all of the men, except the one who had believed, had departed. "Go to your wife and tell her what has happened."

He took Nathan's hand. "Let us go."

Ulyana and Christa, the mother of Nathan, sat alone in her bedchamber. Phillip had been called by the Captain of the Guard to explain what was happening in the city and to stop any uprising.

"Do you have a mother, child?" asked the woman.

"When I was little, almost too small to remember, my mother and elder sisters were killed in an Atrocene raid. I survived because they did not see me."

"And your father?"

"I never knew my father. Word came of his death on the day I was born. Since my mother died, I have been raised by a friend of my mother's. Her name is Elamuna."

"She has done an excellent job. But my, what a horrible life. Have you ever lived in peace?"

Ulyana sat quietly for a moment as she thought back of countless Atrocene attacks and her peoples' training for the next conflict. "I'm not sure if a Rasomite was meant to live in peace, for I have not seen it." She sat quietly again. "I'm so tired of running. We are supposed to be a holy people."

"You shall run no more. If this man, Anam, would allow it, you can stay here in Foramen. The people need one such as you, and you need us."

"I spoke rashly to your husband for I made a vow to stay with him and teach him about my God. I should have asked."

"Phillip will understand if you must leave, but let us not dwell on things beyond our power. I have heard of these Atrocenes and their warlike ways. In fact, there are Atrocenes living right here in Foramen." Ulyana looked at her with doubt. "I am telling the truth. Even in an evil place, there may be good. It would seem that a few of these people have ventured across the desert and arrived here to escape the evil of their own kind. There are things lacking in our city but, at least, we live in peace. At least, in the city walls, we live in peace."

"I don't understand."

"Beyond the city walls is a land that is as bounteous in its gifts and beauty as it is in its evil. There are monsters out there."

"I do not believe in monsters. Tell me more."

"No. These are not monsters as we think. There are, however, evil creatures and an untamed land with savage animals and savage men. Bands of robbers and cannibals and other such things. We travel beyond the wall only as far as is needed to find produce and to hunt to feed this city. It is a generous land, but every year we must send our harvesters out further, and every year fewer of them return. There is no army or other force to protect them from marauding animals." She had a faraway look in her eye.

"Yes. Is there someone close to you who has gone out?"

"Before Phillip, there was another man. He was a captain in the city guard, and they took turns protecting the harvesters when they went forth. One day, they were attacked by a disgusting group of men. Many of our brave young men were killed or captured. They don't know what happened to Eric but, as they fled, he was calling out for the others to come back and help him. We were to be married soon, but eventually I had to give up. But my love life, I am sure, bores you. Let us prepare some breakfast and wait for the men to return."

"There is nothing at all about you that bores me and, if it seems right, I would be proud to call you 'mother'." They wrapped their arms around each other and sat for a moment. "Why do you care for me?" she finally asked.

"I'm not sure. You are a wonderful girl and I enjoy your company. Perhaps I have just sat in this house too long and become bored. You are like a ray of sunshine. Something new. But more than that. I think I see in you a little of myself and, yet, something exciting. I hope you can stay with us."

There was a noise in the outer entryway and she knew the sound of Nathan at the door.

"Mother!" he called. "We have a guest for breakfast!"

Both females excitedly bounded for the bedroom door. Ulyana was the first to see Nathan. They both stood a few feet apart, smiling at each other.

"We were afraid for you," she said. Anam entered. "Anam! Then you have been together. We were afraid for both of you. Strange things are happening in the city. Their lives have been turned around."

Christa entered the room.

"Mother," said Nathan. "This is Anam, The man of whom I spoke. You would not believe the things I have seen today."

"I know," she said. "Marta is dead. We thought you had gone to the temple. There was a terrible storm."

"Then you do not know," said Nathan. "The temple of the high priest has been destroyed, and all the priests with it. The Rasomite women and children have gone out to spread the good news about God."

"What good news?" she asked.

"The news that God lives and we are free."

"Damn it!" he screamed. "Damn this man and his people! Why have we been cursed with this further calamity? Were things not bad enough? The customs and tithes have suffered. The people make a mockery in their disobedience. Now this. And what can we do to stop him? The people are even now standing out there and agreeing in public that he is the man, the prophet they await."

Gathered in this darkened basement room were half a dozen men, wearing the familiar robe and amulet of the priests. They had pulled their hoods over their heads in the half-light created by the lantern on the table so that only their disturbed faces could be seen, except for the glitter of the fallen cross. They were angry and determined men, but, they were also afraid. Their greatest fear lie in that of the Rasomites, by whose presence they felt doomed. But, now, they also feared the people. Already, there were some reports that priests had been stoned to death or hung by the people determined to rid their city of every trace of these men. The temple had been destroyed for only one day. It was known that many priests and their concubines and followers were being hidden by a few who sympathized with their stand, and some had barricaded themselves in deserted basements and waited as did these men.

"As I see it, the only choice is to find some common clothes and escape from the city."

"Then what? We face the barbarians in the hill country."

"Well, we cannot stay here."

"We are hungry. Soon, we will run out of clean water. Even if they do not find us we shall begin to perish in a day or two."

"I say that this evening, under cover of darkness, we leave here and attempt to leave the city, then, flee to the hill country. Better to face the unknown than to remain here and face certain death."

"There is no other way."

"There is one other way," said one. He drew all the others' attention. "If we are able to capture one of these Rasomites, we could hold that person as a hostage."

"For what good? To buy a few more hours and, then, draw more anger. I say we leave the city."

"This is my home. I will never leave. I would rather die at home than to run and die at the hand of some thief in the mountains. I say we seek a hostage. Who supports me?"

He looked around at each face and saw only fear and desperation.

"Are we not all priests of the Most High One? Are we not eligible to be victorious? Why must we dumbly submit to this desert savage? I say we gain the upper hand and not run like a pack of rats. If no one supports me, I shall go alone, but it would be better to be a team. Come on now, who shall support me?"

And still no one spoke up. "Then, I will do it myself. I hope you all die horrible deaths. When darkness approaches, I will be gone." He got up from the table and went into the darkness of one of the corners.

"Then, for the rest of us, we shall leave the city tonight."

"I have never gone through the feelings that I have now. I have always been afraid to care for a young man, because I knew his fate would be death."

"I do not understand," said Nathan to Ulyana. They were walking through his father's garden, which had been cleaned up and revitalized since the dust storm.

"Do you see any men with us?" she asked him with an imploring look on her face. "Except for Anam, who has God's grace, they are all dead. Neither are there many children. Why would one give birth only to supply fuel for Kiwatuan's furnace?" She was shouting and suddenly broke down into tears. Nathan held her close.

"Oh, Ulyana. You have no need to fear the Atrocenes anymore. Anam has said that you and Elamuna will stay with us and teach us about your God. We are eager. I think your only loss now will be saying goodbye when your people leave. I will be with you. Someday, I pray, you will be my wife. I love you."

She looked into his eyes and a smile started to come to her lips. "I have waited since birth for a time like this. I never dared believe it would be real."

"It is real. Already, Father has begun to refreshen the sanctuary for you and Elamuna. It is now that it becomes a sanctuary. Before, it was only a name."

"I love my God above all things but, right now, for me, you are my sanctuary. I love you, Nathan."

Darkness had taken hold of the city, though many lamps still burned as people talked far into the night of the things which were continuing to happen. Most of the people had taken to this new concept of God. There were more happy faces now than had ever been seen in Foramen before. There were, however, some very angry people as well as many more who had not been borne into this new faith, yet.

Ulyana sat alone in her sleeping quarters in the new sanctuary. She had never lived in such a beautiful place. Her large canopy bed was the centerpiece of a room filled with gifts given to her mostly by Nathan and his family and, also, by many others. Many of the gift-givers she had never even met. She lay there in that place between sleep and awake when one begins to remember and to wonder.

But she was not alone in this place, for hiding in the next room was an old, angry priest who only awaited his opportunity. The original idea had been to capture this young girl and use her as a pawn, but he could not conceive of what he would do with her. He had decided to kill her and flee the city. That would be his revenge.

Finally, Ulyana stopped stirring and fell to sleep. Nervously, the old man crept out from his covering behind the curtains. He reached into one pocket to feel of his amulet, which had been placed there to facilitate his sneaking about in the dark. No one could see him in his black robe as he crept about in the night. He placed his hand in the other pocket and closed his fingers about the dagger. An evil grin revealed his teeth in the dark as he approached Ulyana. He brought the dagger over his head and, just as he came down with it, the girl opened her eyes and screamed. He stabbed her in the chest. He brought the knife up as she struggled to roll out of the bed. He came down again and the knife entered her back. She shook a few times and stopped moving. The old priest's eyes glowed like an evil fire.

Nathan screamed and sat up in bed. He sat, looking at the wall for a moment, trying to remember where he was and what was happening. His body was shaking and he was soaked with sweat. He realized it was merely a dream, though, his eyes were filled with tears.

"No!" he screamed. "I must see her." He quickly pulled on his running shorts that had been dropped by the bed and ran through the open window.

The sanctuary was very close. In fact, from Nathan's room, the light of Ulyana's room could be seen reflecting against the birch trees near her window. When Nathan entered the sanctuary, all eyes turned toward him. There were all of the servants and Elamuna sitting about on the floor. She had been teaching them and also giving them some instructions.

"Nathan!" she said in alarm, "What is wrong? You look so excited."

"Where," he breathed heavily, "is Ulyana?"

"She has already retired to her room. She is probably asleep. Why?"

Ulyana's room was removed from the main room of the sanctuary and up a small flight of stone steps. Nathan quickly bounded up the steps and pushed open the door. Ulyana sat up in bed.

"Nathan, why do you look so upset? What is the matter?"

He picked up a length of wood that had been left lying in the hall by the workmen. It took a moment to adjust to the room, since he had not been there before, and it appeared different than in his dream but, then, he saw the curtains move in the next room. In a flash, he was there but not in time. The priest, fearful of capture, had plunged the dagger intended for Ulyana into his own heart. He lay dead in a pool of blood on the floor.

By now, Elamuna and several of the others had come upon the scene.

"Who is he?" asked Elamuna.

"He is the murderer of Ulyana," said Nathan.

"But," corrected Ulyana, "I am here, whole and alive and in good health. I did not know he was there, but he never touched me."

Nathan sat on the bed next to her and looked her over intently, then he dropped his head in thought. Finally, he spoke, "I do not completely understand, but just now I had a dream. I dreamt of a place much like this. I saw you lying in your bed, sleeping, and then this priest came out from behind the curtain. You saw him and screamed. He stabbed you in the chest and then here." He placed his hand on her back. "Then, I saw his face. It was this man's face, but his eyes were like fire. Then, I awoke and came quickly. The priest's amulet is in his pocket."

One of the serving girls spoke. "They never remove the amulet. They even sleep and bathe with it on."

"The amulet is in his pocket," he repeated.

Elamuna extracted the amulet from the dead man's robe and spoke. "When Anam first came here, before he went to see Jesepth, he called down a curse on anyone who would harm a Rasomite, even so much as a hair on one's head. God has shown you these things in a dream before they were allowed to be completed. You responded as God knew you would."

"You saved my life," said Ulyana. "I don't know what to say."

"Don't thank me," said Nathan. "Give the glory to God. He has saved your life by trusting me with this dream. He knew how I felt about you and that I would respond. I thank God for bringing you here."

Chapter 7
The Butcher

"I don't care how you do it! Just do it!" the man called 'The Butcher' raged. "Bring me one of their women. If it pleases me, she shall be mine or, if not, then we shall all make sport of her."

"You do not understand," pleaded the other, named Vance. "They are lovely as angels and fierce as raging bulls. Already, two of our best men have been severely injured by one, and she being barely a child. This is a foolish enterprise. The men say we should lay low until after they pass through."

"The men are turning into whimpering dogs! They are supposed to be men of battle, not whining dogs. I have seen them come back from their quests shaken and defeated."

"These are mighty women, sir. I feel that the very sword of Kiwatuan is carried before them."

"Have you seen their idols?" he said, furrowing his brow.

"No, but some have seen them bearing a cross."

"A cross?" asked the fire—haired leader. "A cross is the symbol the stupid priests of Foramen use. I am confused. These priests have no power. I really am confused, but not on one matter. Bring me one of their women! Now go!"

"Yes, sir. We shall do our best."

"Send me Artero."

The ruddy-faced man sat back on his cot as the other left. He lived in a small, dry cave. It was a very simple dwelling, adorned with many artifacts of his marauding. He rested his feet on a trunk full of gold and silver coins that had been bartered with the residents of Foramen in return for safe passage to hunt. Hanging on the wall near him was a coat of mail made of iron, adorned with precious diamonds which he had fashioned from the ransoms he had demanded from the city for the return of their citizens. An armament of swords and knives were also on display. All of this was bought at the price of much blood. A small fire near the mouth of the cave supplied some light and also provided an obstruction to intruders. He got up and went to the fire to look out. A young man was coming up the path towards him.

"Artero!" he called. "Come in."

"I have spoken to Vance about this thing you want to do," he said as he entered. "What is the matter with you?"

"How dare you speak to me like that."

"You know I am not a silent person," said Artero. "I have no need to be. Now, tell me plainly what you want of this affair."

Artero was a fair-haired young man and was good to look upon.

"I want a woman. Is that hard to understand? These women are beautiful and strong. One of them would be very good for me. You understand because you have Mothana."

"Don't talk like a fool. Mothana has me. I do her bidding. But, if you wish, I will go to her with a message."

"Tell her to bring one of these women to me."

"That is not a message. It is a demand. I will talk to Mothana and see what she will do. She does not know these people, so we cannot work on them, but I will ask her to lend strength to your men and make them wise to develop a plan, if she will. I will go and talk to Vance, then return to Mothana."

Artero climbed over the fire and left the leader alone.

"Then," he said, "if Mothana will work one of her charms for us, perhaps we shall be victorious."

"This is foolish. Why are we perched in a tree like a bunch of parrots?"

"Shut up, fool!" snapped Vance.

Vance and three other men from the thieves' camp were sitting on the bough of a tree. Every morning, they had watched one of the young girls go this way at the same time to get water from the nearby river. Now they had a net made of sturdy burlap ready to drop on the unsuspecting girl. In the brush nearby, they had five properly muzzled horses to make a hasty and silent retreat. The knowledge that Mothana had given them her blessings had bolstered their courage enough to attempt the capture of a Rasomite woman.

Vance had kept his attention steadfast to the bushes at the end of the meadow wherein stood the tree and was both pleased and slightly dismayed when she appeared. Fear began to take him but, as he remembered the appreciation he would receive, his concentration was renewed. When the girl was beneath them, she stopped, sensing something was wrong. It was too late. The net and four men fell to the ground, simultaneously and in silence. But the girl had no intention of being silent. Her first notion was to pull the knife from her belt, but it was quite useless trapped as she was. She opened her mouth to scream, but nothing came out as Vance struck her solidly across the side of her head and she lost consciousness.

Quickly, they pulled her from under the net and carried her to the horses. Her horse was quite ready for a load. This was the steed of Vance's own leader. They tied her securely to the back of the animal and prepared to mount their own. There was no time.

The first man fell to the ground and screamed his last after having most of his face torn off. The others turned and stood, dumbfounded, before one of the largest brown bears they had ever seen. The creature was easily ten feet tall. One of the men jumped onto his horse, but the giant snatched him from the steed and crushed him to death. His screams lasted for only a moment. Vance and the other man stood facing the beast, blades drawn. They had not been prepared for a battle. The only blades they had brought were their knives to cut the cords of the net as they had intended to travel unencumbered. They had never conceived of running into this monster.

As the startled horses ran off in different directions Vance yelled to his partner, "Run! Run into the forest and find a tree. Perhaps he is too large to climb."

Both men left in opposite directions. Vance knew the bear could climb. He had never seen a brown bear that could not climb. He had other ideas. The bear could not swim and was most likely leery of the water. If he could get into the water and even get waist deep, the animal would probably leave him alone. The river was very close but, before Vance reached the edge, he could hear the awful screams of his friend. It was not too late for Vance. He was nearly across the river when he heard the roar of the bear and turned. The giant was standing in water barely two feet deep, having a fit. It was still terrifying to see the brute less than a hundred feet away frantically waving his forepaws over his head and roaring.

Vance breathed a sigh of relief, however, as his feet were once again upon solid ground. When he was safely up on the bank, he turned and saw the great bear slowly lumbering away. He fell to his knees, kissed the ground, and rested. Soon he heard a rustle in the bushes and nervously looked up, expecting to see the bear. The first sight was several pairs of legs which caused him to breathe a sigh of relief, but then he remembered where he was and looked into the eyes of Artero.

Artero stood over him, smiling, which relaxed Vance, but then he noticed all the drawn blades.

"My friend, Vance. My very good friend," said Artero. "You are in the wrong place."

Shaking, Vance quickly explained the bear and the deaths of his comrades.

"These things," responded Artero, "are of no concern to us. The agreement is that you will not cross the river or else you are ours."

"No. No, please. I give myself to your mercy. Spare me," cried Vance. "I can be of some use to you."

"Then you shall be spared," said Artero. Vance smiled. "However, your head is ours."

"No!" screamed Vance. He jumped up to run back to the river, but a spear met the back of his skull. As he fell to the ground, the spear came free and he attempted to crawl away. One of Artero's men was upon him with a hatchet and made short work of severing his neck.

Artero was once again in the thieves' camp. With him were two of his men and a horse-drawn cart.

"Oh, my comrade, this is a sad day for us!" called out Artero.

The man called Butcher, leader of the thieves, had scrambled out of his cave when he had heard that the headhunters were coming. He now stood among his men.

"What has happened? Why have you brought these people here?" he demanded, pointing at the escorts.

"This is," he pointed at the cart upon which was a wooden box, "our dear friend, Vance."

Butcher was shocked and suddenly filled with sadness. "How

could this happen? I sent him on a simple mission to find a girl."

"I believe he was attacked by a bear. This is what he told us before he died. You know there are bears in the woods. He was not armed to defend himself from evil creatures that lurk in the forest."

"This was my best man. One of the few that I could trust. How could this have happened?"

"My men are here to help you bury him," said Artero. "We have already constructed and nailed shut a coffin to show our respects."

"I must see him first."

"No. That is not wise as he is in such terrible condition."

"If it were possible for you to speak to him before he died, he is good enough. I have seen worse. Now, open the casket." He directed several of his men to start the work.

"Then we must be going. I cannot bear to look at this again." He turned to leave, but the casket was already opened.

One of Butcher's men looked in, contorted his face from the sight and yelled to the others, "Stop them, for they are murderers!"

Artero stopped, as did the others, and turned. "You know that Mothana watches over me. If you dare harm me, she will never stop hunting you down. Besides, you have given me safe passage to come to this side of the river. Vance came to us without permission, so we did what we desired. We are without guilt."

"It's true that you never suffer from guilt," said Butcher, "but you are deserving of much guilt. Tell Mothana, that wicked witch, that you have safe passage, but you never asked us if they could come here." He pointed at the other two men. "Kill them!"

Before the two could move, the thieves were upon them and, out of anger for their dead friend, hacked the two into pieces.

"Now, get out of here and tell your witch what your treachery has done."

Artero looked him in the eye and said, "You shall suffer for this." He turned and walked away, leaving his dead comrades and horse and cart behind.

Sarare, for that was the young girl's name who was Vance's intended victim, had eventually managed to wrestle herself free of the rope that bound her to the horse. She had spent several hours in the woods deciding if she should return to the Rasomites or if she should go on. Her decision was to remount the horse and let it go where it would. Very soon, the animal was back in the camp of the thieves, looking for her master. The horse was barely aware of the young girl astride her and, as soon as Sarare entered the camp and saw nearly a hundred dirty men, she felt certain she had made a mistake.

A ripple of excitement seemed to sweep across the camp as the men began to take notice of the voluptuous young girl barely clad in a rawhide brassiere and loincloth. When the horse reached the foot of the path to the leader's cave, she came to a halt. None of the men had stirred since her arrival but, now, lust gripped them and they moved forward.

Just before one of them grabbed her leg, she screamed and this stopped him for a moment. He gazed up at her with a toothless smile and grabbed her. "You have nearly a hundred men to satisfy here, so there is no time to waste," he laughed.

He pulled her from the horse and threw her to the ground. Instinctively, she reached out for a stone and bashed him in the face as he approached.

"You are a wild one," he laughed as blood crept down his forehead into his eyes. "This will be a pleasure." That was just before he doubled over in pain as her bare foot met the crotch of his pants.

She leapt to her feet with a branch of wood in her right hand. It would have been hopeless, however, for she was surrounded by a pack of at least twenty men. Suddenly, another man appeared on the scene and stood beside her. He was obviously one of them, but the look in his eyes seemed to plead with the girl that he would help her. The other men, grumbling, began to back off and walk away.

"You are also one of these scalawags. I am afraid, but your eyes show tenderness."

He opened his mouth to speak, but only stuttered.

"I have said that I am afraid," Sarare continued. "Why then, should you be the one at a loss for speech?"

"I...I love you."

"Oh no!" she moaned.

Anam looked at the netting, which had been brought back, and buried his head in his hands again. "Where could she have gone?" he wondered aloud. "Where could they have taken her?"

The thieves' camp was very well concealed and, though he had sent several out looking, most of them had returned with no information. The trap had been found as had the three dead men. The paths of the horses had been lost in the brush.

The Rasomites had formed a camp among the rocks and brush about a mile from where Sarare had disappeared. In the five days they had been here, they had had several skirmishes with both the thieves and the headhunters, as well as attacks from bear and wolves. They had remained unscathed, until this episode, and now Anam was upset. He was sitting upon a rock slightly apart from the others, whom he had sent away. All, that is, except for one woman, Paluqua, who had recently been attending him. He looked up at her.

"I do not understand their disobedience. I have said that no one will leave the camp, except in pairs and adequately armed for any defense. Now I see that they routinely leave by themselves to run their errands."

"You are right in thinking them wrong, Master. I also am wrong, as I knew of their meanderings."

"But why?" Anam half-smiled and shook his head. "I am only concerned for their safety. Why don't they listen to me? Now I can only pray that Sarare is safe and that we will soon have her back with us."

"Does it seem strange to you, Master?"

"What is that?"

"The protection that the Lord has offered us and the unity we are beginning to experience. Remember your curse that you spoke in Foramen."

"I remember and hope that God continues to hold us close. However, that is no reason they should continually tempt the Lord."

Suya, Ean and Macosena sat on an uprooted stump of a tree, enjoying a drink of cold water not far from the place where Sarare had been taken. She had been given charge over the girl, Suya, and the boy, Ean, both of whom were only about eight years of age. As they finished their drink, Macosena spoke.

"Let us do this. But we must continue to be very careful and not take chances." She handed the water flask to Ean. "Take the flask down to the river and see as you go if there be any sign." Ean started to protest. "Hush. Walk from here down the path to the river and fill the flask. I will go the long way around near where they took Sarare, and I will meet you at the river."

"So many have already looked," complained Ean. "I am tired. I want to go home."

Macosena stood up. "The Rasomites do not have a home. Go quickly and be very careful."

The children stood up and, without speaking, walked off towards the river. Macosena took a deep breath and ran towards the brush, away from the path.

When Ean and Suya reached the river and its clearing, Ean knelt down and filled the flask.

"I want to go home," he said grouchily. "I'm tired."

"Me too," said Suya, looking around. "It's starting to get dark."

As they stood there in the twilight, they heard a crackle in the bushes.

"What was that?" yelled Ean.

"Macosena," whispered Suya. "Is that you?"

Instead of their mother figure, a horse slowly put her head into the open.

"It's a horsey," they both exclaimed.

"Come here, baby," beckoned Suya. "We won't hurt you."

The animal was lost and thirsty and had been waiting for dark to go back to the river. It seemed that the horse would naturally get its water by day, but the Rasomites had been too much of a disturbance for the young animal, so it waited every day until nearly dark. It had not expected to find these little creatures waiting for it. She trotted out to the two and they covered the tired little animal with love and affection.

"Let's go for a ride, Ean."

"I don't think so," he said, making a face. "Let's wait."

"Help me on then. I just want to sit and wait."

It was easy to help her mount the mare, and the young animal didn't seem to mind at all.

"It's real nice up here, Ean. Why don't you come up, too? She won't mind."

"Maybe another time," he said, letting go of its mane and

sitting on the ground. "Where's mother?" he complained.

Suddenly, Macosena burst out of the brush and, not realizing the children had found company, caused the frightened horse to bolt and run.

"Suya," screamed Macosena, "stop her!"

"I can't," she yelled back, too frightened to look, as the horse ran along the river in the near-dark.

"Then hold on tight," she said quietly as she took Ean's hand and started after her.

Suya had never before been on the back of a horse because the Atrocenes controlled all the domestic horses in her homeland and the wild horses were such giants. After a few hundred paces, the animal slowed down to a trot and turned away from the river onto a path rising into the rocky cliffs above. When it finally reached the treacherous points, it slowed down considerably and carefully picked its way over the rocks. At this higher elevation, it was no longer dark and Suya began to enjoy this ride. Enjoying it, that is, until she looked back and saw how steep the incline was they were climbing. It appeared to be straight down, thus causing her to cling even tighter to the neck of the horse.

She was also suffering indecision as to whether to continue this ride or if she could get off. There was hope in her that Macosena and Ean were following her and would eventually catch up. If she got off the horse, however, she would be alone on this cliff and was afraid of the wild animals. On the other hand, there was no way of knowing what danger the horse might take her into. Still, the animal might take her to Sarare, so she could be reunited with the Rasomites. Perhaps, it was God himself who had planned it this way, she thought.

After a slow ascension of several hundred feet, they came to the top. Suya dared not let go of the horse and look at the valley below but, instead, kept her tight grip on its neck. The horse came to a stop and lifted her head, sniffing the air and then started running again down a path into the woods below. It came to a stop once inside the line of trees and Suya sat up. She could see the wisps of smoke being broken up by the branches and knew they had arrived somewhere. She did not want to go any farther and slipped off the side of the horse. It was now dark and Suya wondered how she had gotten herself into this mess.

"Dear Lord," she prayed, "I don't know what's going on. I'm

scared, and cold, and it's very dark here. I know you are here, so that will make it all right, I hope. Please, have Macosena and Ean find me and take me home."

The horse, after losing its rider, continued on into the thieves' camp, and she followed it until she could see the tents and huts of the thieves. There were people moving around, but it was too dark to see them clearly. When the horse appeared, several figures moved toward the animal who welcomed their presence.

"Hey!" one yelled. "It's Vance's horse. She finally came home."

There was also a lot more murmuring, but she couldn't understand what was being said, so she began to creep closer until she was just out of the ring of light created by the fire. By this time, the men had led the horse away and she was alone, she thought. How she wanted to get by the fire and warm up.

"If you try to run, I will kill you!" came a gruff voice from behind her. "Don't turn around or move quickly. Just stand up and walk forward."

As soon as she was in the light, several other of the men were attracted to this new intruder. To Suya's young eyes, they looked like the trash of the Atrocenes. They were all dressed in rags and chopped-up clothing. Most had scraggly beards. They were all thin and haggard-looking. Even now, Suya knew she could outrun them and escape. There were only four men before her and they had not sounded an alarm.

"Better go get the boss. The devil only knows how many more of these people are going to come wandering in here," said the eldest of them.

One of the men departed further into the camp. Suya was prepared to run when the oldest of the men spoke again.

"Don't worry, little girl." He sat down on the ground by the fire. "Come here and get warm." He looked up at the man who had first spotted her. "Will you get out of here with that foolish spear before I break it over your head?" Both of the other men departed into the darkness.

Suya had been watching this man closely and was beginning to trust him. She sat on the ground near him by the fire and wrapped her little arms around her cold and naked legs. He was an old man compared to the other three. He had long white hair and a scraggly beard. His eyes seemed to sparkle in the firelight and, though his face was thin and tired, his smile seemed genuine.

"You're a pretty one," he said. "My name is Ernest, but just call me Ernie. I bet you came looking for your friend, Sarare." When Suya heard her name she sat up straight and looked him in the face. "Yea, I figured as much. How did you trick poor old Vance's horse into bringing you up here? That's how you come this way, isn't it? Is there more of them following you?"

Suya thought of Macosena and Ean and started to speak, but stopped.

"That's okay. You ain't gotta tell me nothing. But, if you want, I'll be your friend. You're going to need a friend in this ugly place." His talk was disturbed by the return of the messenger and several other men. "Aww. Now they've gone and spoiled everything."

"He wants to see her," said the man Ernie had sent. "Let's go."

"I'll only go if Ernie goes with me," Suya said as she stood up. "I want to see Sarare."

"Who are you to be making demands upon me, little girl?"

Ernie stood up and took her hand. "Better be quiet, Sebastian, or the bears'll get ya." Fear had spread among the men after what had happened to the kidnapping party. "We're going to see Sarare and the boss."

A look of disdain crossed the younger man's face, but he moved and let them pass.

Once into the darkness, away from the light of the fire, Suya could more easily distinguish the camp. They walked passed the tents and oddly constructed huts that these men called home and walked up the path toward the cave.

"They think I'm just an old fool," said Ernie as he guided her along, "but I've been around long enough to know which folk I ought to be acquainted with. When that girl, Sarare, looked me in the eyes, I could see the love of God there. Besides, I know what happened to poor old Vance and the others when they crossed her path. No, ma'am. I intend to be around a bit longer. Hey!" he called as they reached the entrance. "You got company."

A man's face appeared at the doorway and he nodded his head, indicating they should enter. It was the boss, the Butcher. As soon as they entered, Suya ran to Sarare and they threw their arms around each other.

"Oh, baby," said Sarare. "Why did you come here? Are you alone?"

"We have been looking for you and then a horse brought me here. Are you all right?"

"I'm fine. They are treating me well. I just want to go home is all."

"They won't let you?" asked Suya inquiringly at the two men.

"I want her," said the younger man.

"But she cannot give herself," said Suya.

The man turned away with a disgusted look on his face.

"I don't know what to do," said Sarare. "This man wants me and is willing to go talk to Anam about it."

"But do you want him?"

"No," she answered and lowered her face. "I just don't want a fight. I want peace. They say tomorrow we can go, and I just figured it was easier to do it that way and avoid a fight."

"You didn't answer her other question!" snapped the leader as he swung around. "Are you alone?"

"I am never alone!" Suya snapped back at him.

"Better be a might more civil, boss," said Ernie. "You don't want to be upsetting these good people."

"What have they done to you?" Suya asked Sarare.

"Nothing. Nothing at all. He just keeps saying he loves me and he wants me. I think he's sick in the head, but he hasn't touched me."

"Did you bring anybody with you?" asked the man again.

"I don't know," she answered. "Maybe the whole Rasomite nation is out there waiting for me. Why don't you let us go? I haven't got to tell you anything."

"Listen, you little..." he came at her with one hand up, but Ernie grabbed his arm.

"Don't be a fool! Why can't you settle down? You're usually so cautious about everything. Has lust started tearing apart your mind? Why don't you get some sleep?"

"I...I don't know," he said. "All right." He looked around the cave.

"Not here. Let the girls have this place tonight. I'll stay out by the doorway. You just go away and get some sleep so you can think straight."

"Yea. I suppose." He picked up a bedroll of blankets and headed for the doorway, taking a last long look at Sarare as he went out.

Sarare dropped her head. "What am I into here, anyway?"

Suya and Sarare clung to each other and pulled some blankets over themselves. Ernie threw the last two pieces of firewood on the dying fire and stared at the girls for a moment. Nothing came to his mind that seemed an appropriate thing to say. He went out but knew he would return.

Macosena chastised Ean, "if we get too far behind them, we are going to lose the scent of the horse and we may never find your Suya."

"But, I'm tired," grumbled Ean as he stumbled over another stone in the dark. "I want to sleep."

"I told you that you can sleep. I'll put you in a safe place, but you'll be out here alone."

"I'm afraid."

"Nothing will harm you," pleaded the woman. "You can sleep and, after I get Suya, we'll come back for you."

"I will stay here."

All along the cliffside were several small hollowed-out manmade caves just large enough to fit one body in a sitting position. They appeared to be used as a defense toward the valley. Though it was dark now, Macosena knew that the valley was spread out before them for miles. The caves were empty and one of them made a very safe place to burrow Ean away for an hour or two until she could find Suya and, hopefully, Sarare. The path was much used and because the horse had made the effort to climb it, she knew wherever the horse had gone, it was not far off. After Ean was safely tucked away and they had said a short prayer, she took off again up the path, moving much faster now.

As soon as she was over the summit, the dim glare of the lighted campfires met her eyes coming from the thicket below. She knew she had been led to the camp of the thieves. Even though she had not met any of these men yet, the stories of encounters were going through the Rasomite camp. They were an ugly lot, but seemed to be excellent fighters. She was not afraid of a fight, but was not prepared to take on the entire camp. At first she thought her only hope lie in her dark-colored skin and her prayer that she could steal into the camp, remove the two girls, and escape. She was not, however, very confident. Suddenly, a better plan seemed to take place in her mind and, though it seemed foolhardy, she took advantage of this impression. She walked through the woods into the light of the fire. Just before the light was upon her, she began to call out. "Suya! Sarare! Macosena is here to help. Hello! Can you hear me? Oh, Suya, Sarare!"

In a moment, she was surrounded by a dozen weapon-bearing men who were obviously terrified by this bold and unorthodox entrance.

"Good evening, boys. I am sent to rescue two young girls who seem to have lost their way. I have every reason to believe they are here, and it would be a lot easier for you if you would simply turn them over to me so we could depart in peace." She looked over the faces of the men, who still could not believe the cockiness of this woman. She continued, "I do hope that you won't do anything foolish and cause trouble for yourselves." No one moved. "As you wish." She looked up toward the sky. "Well, my Lord, it appears it is time for you to take over. What calamity can we bring down on these fools? Perhaps fire from the sky or, maybe, the place could be overrun by vicious wild animals as I and the girls make our escape."

"That's enough!" said Sebastian as he pushed his way through the crowd. "There will be no God-given destruction here, for we will not stand in your path. We are not fools." He pointed to one of the men and told him to go find their leader. "We do, however, have a situation that is not easy to resolve."

"Speak on," said Macosena impatiently.

"It seems our leader has fallen in love with your Sarare. He does not want her to leave, and he wants to entreat your leader for a marriage."

"Now I know that you are all fools. Anam would never consent to a marriage under these circumstances. There is no problem for us. The problem is yours. I will take the girls and leave your foul-minded leader to pine away." She looked down, shook her head in disbelief, and returned her glare to Sebastian. "I cannot believe that Sarare has done anything to prompt this situation. This is quite a leader you have. How many men have been sent to their deaths in his vain attempt to kidnap one of our children? How much danger do you think he has placed you all in by keeping her here against her will? I do not want to be a problem for you, but I feel it best that we leave now before anything does happen. And you say, 'we are not fools'."

They were interrupted by the reappearance of the messenger and the man called Butcher.

Macosena immediately confronted him. "Are you the man responsible for kidnapping the children? Who do you think you are?"

He was not at all put off by her directness, but countered with a long, cold stare. Then he turned to Sebastian. "Why have you allowed this person to enter this area? How dare she affront me with this insult." He looked back at her. "I am no pervert, but I have become very fond of your girl, Sarare. I do deeply desire that she stay with me. I have not and shall never do her any harm."

"I have no interest in fulfilling your lustful desires! Bring me the girls. I have grown impatient."

"The little one may leave freely. In the morning, we shall come with the girl and speak to the man she calls Anam. Is he not your leader? I do not deal with women."

At that moment, three figures appeared out of the darkness. Ernie walked into the light with both the girls following him. Macosena breathed a sigh of relief as the girls ran to her and threw their arms around her, smothering her face with kisses. The woman looked into the eyes of the man who so wanted the young girl.

"For many years," she began, "young and beautiful Rasomite girls have been used to satisfy the sexual fantasies of indecent, immoral men of war. When I recall some of the disgusts that I myself had vision of, I become sick to my stomach. Never again will I allow one of our women to be exposed to man's sickness like this. I will fight until I die, but God is on my side. Do we fight or will you stand aside and allow us to leave?"

After anger left the man's face and despair had clouded upon him, he released a puff of air into his moustache and said simply, "let them go." He turned and walked away with his men following, leaving only Ernie behind.

"I know that you are people of God, and I know that you are very angry now. I beg of you not to curse us. We shall be of no further hindrance to you. During the brief time I have known these two girls, I have seen how close your people are and so, I have felt love also. There is no love in this place and now that you take this love away, we shall never be the same. But still, go in peace." He turned and started into the darkness.

"Ernie!" called Suya. He turned back "Will we see you again?" He only smiled and turned again into the darkness.

Artero had assembled several able-bodied men that were available with Mothana's permission, and they now stood before her. Mothana's beauty alone was enough to captivate any man. Her long blonde hair hung down to the middle of her back. The darkness of her eyes and the warmth and innocence they seemed to generate welcomed one to come in. The soft cream-colored skin made a man eager to be held in her arms and become part of that voluptuous body. She wore a small crown of gold on her head and a bracelet consisting of a strand of gold that encircled her right arm several times. Her wrap consisted only of a transparent silk skirt. But even beyond her beauty was the great spiritual power men felt she commanded. With her curses or her blessings that were bestowed upon any man she would feel deserving of, great things could usually be done.

She had established a reputation for telling men's fortunes, and it would usually come to pass. For, while a man was in awe of her beauty, she would learn of his strengths and weaknesses and also his fantasies. No god was hers, for she was worshipped as God. There were enough followers that would do her bidding that those she could not beguile would either be forced to obey by her tribe or they would be put to death. Even Artero, who knew more of her than any man, was her captive.

The village consisted of three dozen large thatched huts arranged in several concentric circles, with the hut she shared with Artero in the center. Each hut served to house about fifteen people, which included at least two men, with their wives and children. The village was very difficult to penetrate, as there would always be six or more men or women roaming the forest around the area, besides the wild wolves and bears that were often fed and were tame enough to trust as neighbors to these headhunters.

Arranged about the village were twelve poles upon which were perched the heads of those foolish enough to come near. The headhunters never went on raids, but there was a circle bordered on three sides by the river that was certain death to any who entered it. The heads served no real spiritual significance but were mainly used to keep intruders away.

The men that Artero had gathered were about forty in number and were now prepared for their goddess to order them into battle against their neighbors. The village was in total silence.

Mothana closed her eyes and tipped back her head. "I am God!" she shouted. "Who am I?"

In unison the men chanted, "You are the creator. You are life."

"Artero!" she called. He left the place he was standing with the others and ran to her, falling on his knees and bowing his head.

"Goddess," he said quietly.

She looked down at him. "Tell us what they said."

"I cannot," he said looking up, "but, because you say so, I must. Make me strong."

"It is yours. Speak."

"The first time, he said he wanted a blessing from you to satisfy his lusts. The second time, he called you a witch."

"And who am I?"

"God!" he shouted.

"And what must happen?"

"A man who would ask for a blessing of one he calls a witch must die. A man who calls God a witch must die."

"I, who have created all things, must also come as a destroyer and the commander of such. Go and kill him and any who would defend him."

Artero stood up and looked into Mothana's eyes. "My princess and my god, I obey you."

She turned around and picked up from a rock on the ground an arrow which she handed carefully to Artero. "I have worked a charm on this arrow. It shall harm no man but this evil worker and anyone so foolish as to touch the tip of it. Use this by stealth to destroy this lustful person, and I shall reward you with my love."

Artero's face broke out into a broad grin, and his body seemed to pulsate as he shook from the satisfaction he knew would be forthcoming.

"It is as you say!" He turned and raised the arrow over his head. "They are doomed," he shouted, "because God has taken away her grace. The war has begun."

This had not been a prosperous hunting trip at all. Several of the men, on occasion, would band together and go in search of food. If they were quite fortunate, the thieves would feast on a buck or wild ox. When fortune did not come their way, the meal would consist of rabbit or some fowl. On this day, the forest was nearly barren and, when they did come upon some possible provision, their aim was not good at all. Eventually, just before dusk, they were forced to give up. They had spent most of their arrows and had absolutely nothing to show for it. Grumbling and disillusioned, they prepared to return to camp before dark, but as they packed away the last of their hunting supplies, with no warning a rain of arrows tore through the air. After the first volley, only three of the men remained unhurt and struggled to prepare their bows and seek their unseen enemy. They did release several arrows and begin to help the wounded, but then the second volley appeared. In a moment, every man lay either dead or wounded and unable to defend themselves. The headhunters appeared and beheaded two of the men, killed the survivors, and fled. Within five minutes, the battle was begun and completed.

When the hunting party never returned the first night, little thought was given to it. The assumption was made that they were staying the night in the woods and would return the following morning. The following day, concern for their comrades began and Sebastian decided they would organize a second hunting party to go after the first and also to find provisions, as supplies were very low. The leader had not left his cave since the night Sarare had gone, two evenings before, and neither had anyone interrupted him.

Having no idea where the first party could have gone, they set off on the most used trails but, after two hours of hiking, they had seen little game and no trace of their comrades.

"I sense," said one of the men, "some danger. I do not think we are alone in these woods. Never have I seen the trees so barren of birds or so little trace of the larger beasts."

"Aye," said Sebastian. "This is also my thought and probably also of the others. Perhaps, these people have decided to make revenge."

"Or worse," said another man. "Perhaps, their God himself has reached out to us in vengeance..."

"I do not think," said the first, "we have committed a deed against these people or God sufficient to justify any vengeance from them. When that woman came, we easily turned the children over to her. I think there is another evil out here."

"Perhaps," said Sebastian. "But then, we do not know these people or their ways. We are enemies of no one else."

"There are the headhunters of Mothana's village. Artero vowed to get even for our killing his two men."

There was silence as the men looked into the thick green covering around them and were certain they were being watched.

"There is evil here," whispered Sebastian. "We must get into the open."

Everyone grew very nervous as they picked up their packs and started down the path toward the valley. The foliage was so dense here that their eyes could not penetrate to see the death that awaited them.

"This is not our way," said Sebastian. "I am afraid of no man or beast. If it be the devil or God who would destroy us, we have no hope. But if it be a living thing, we must fight."

They reached a small clearing and without instruction, the men suddenly fanned out across the area and hid as best they could to prepare for a fight. However, several minutes later, nothing had happened and the surrounding forest remained quiet.

One of the men near Sebastian whispered that they should make a run for it back to camp.

"I do not run from a battle. I am prepared to die, but I will face my future," said Sebastian.

"I intend," said the other, "to have a future. Therefore, I flee." In a moment, he had run into the forest. After the rustle of leaves, there was no further sign of that man so they, supposing he was safe, began to come together to prepare for their return home. They had not seen, however, that only moments into the brush, he was miserably slaughtered by the unseen headhunters.

They began laughing and carrying on about being so foolishly concerned about nothing. They quickly made the decision to return home where they expected the previous expedition had already arrived.

As they reached the peak of their joviality and began to pass the flask of whiskey, the comradery was suddenly destroyed. The first arrow tore into the side of one of the men who let out a shriek of agony. The second shaft pierced the flask that was being held by another man. He quickly threw the empty container aside and fell to the ground to pick up his weapons. There was no time. The hunters were hopelessly outnumbered. The few who survived the attack ran into the forest to escape, only to reach the hands of their foes and a worse death.

The headhunters came through and slaughtered any who remained. One wounded man, however, had managed to crawl into a crevice beneath an uprooted tree trunk and remain unseen. After it became quiet again, Sebastian pulled himself, bleeding, from his hiding place. Twice, he had been struck. One speeding shaft had tore a gash across his cheek. The wound did not concern him. The blood quickly dried and the pain subsided. The wound that was causing his agony was an arrow that had entered the inside of his left forearm and had nearly pierced the skin on the other side. It was impossible to remove the shaft. Amazingly, the broadhead had not cut the artery. He lay his arm on a large stone and, taking his knife, sawed at the shaft as quietly as he could until he could break it off about three inches from his arm. He then took several pieces of cloth from his dead companions and wrapped the wound as best as he could, so the shaft would be immobile. Finally, he began a slow lope back to camp, always keeping an ear open to noises in the forest.

Wherever Sebastian could find a hiding place for a moment, he would stop to catch his breath. His immediate fear was, of course, for his own life. However, his greater fear was for the rest of his band as they might be in grave danger. He could not think clearly because of his pain, the loss of blood, and the fear of being followed. When he began to see familiar things on the path, he felt relieved and wanted to call out for help but was so very tired, he could not. When he entered the camp, everyone crowded around him to find out what had happened. They first saw the bloody gash on his face, and it was not until they were nearly upon him that any could see the wound on his left arm.

One of them, named Peter, was something of a doctor and immediately went to work extracting the wooden shaft. By this time, Sebastian's arm was nearly paralyzed, but Peter assured him the damage would heal. He would not lose his arm, as he feared. After removing the cloth wrapping, Peter poured a syrup over the front side of the arm, which caused it to go numb. Then he and some helpers tied Sebastian's arm quickly to a post and, taking a very sharp knife, cut a hole where the arrow had nearly come through. It was then easy to grasp the broadhead and pull it out. Then, he took more of the syrup and poured it directly into the wound. They cleaned it out very well with hot water, covered it with a salve, and rewrapped it with clean cloth.

All through this time, they had been giving him several cups of strong wine so he had begun to be intoxicated. He was finally asked what had happened.

"Artero has killed us. Artero and his dirty bunch of murderers. I escaped. Somehow. I'm sure the rest are all dead. They took some heads." Sebastian could not hold up any longer and broke into tears, so he could do nothing but babble.

It was not fear that overtook them. It was anger. For years, they had managed to live across the river from these headhunters with very few problems, until now. The thieves were not as organized or as stealthy as the headhunters. But the headhunters were outnumbered and were also hampered by their women and children. Quickly, it was decided they would stage an all-out attack on their enemy's home. They would leave no man behind because, if the headhunters launched a similar attack, it would not be safe in this place.

Their original idea had been a wild assault on the village, but it was feared an alarm would be sounded, and it would make it impossible to take them unaware. Instead, they sent six men ahead to eliminate any guards on the west side, which would also make it difficult to see them against the afternoon sun. The main group would follow them after two or three minutes. Ernie had taken a few of the older men, who were unable to fight, as well as Sebastian and Butcher, apart.

After allowing a space of time to elapse, the main thrust of the thieves went up the shallow slope and were delighted to be met silently by their victorious comrades who had killed two women posted as guards. This testified that the men of the village were not present, ensuring them of an easy victory. They would burn the village, kill the women and children, capture Mothana and wait for the men to return. Then, they would destroy them when they went into a panic.

From the edge of the forest to the first row of huts was about one hundred feet, and there were several women going about their business as they waited for their men. Many of the children were also present. A rain of arrows showered down upon the unsuspecting group. In the first thrust, because of the distance, only six women and a few of the little ones were struck down. The men made a running attack. The line in front fell to their knees about halfway and released another torrent from their bows. The villagers were still not prepared. They had never suspected anything like this would happen.

The attackers moved forward and approached the first row of huts. Then, a second group, who followed them, lit their firebrands and began setting grass huts aflame. Several of the women were now fighting back, but they were little match for the men who had them outnumbered. The main concern of the women was to remove the children to safety. As the men moved into the village, lust began overtaking them. It was not so much the lack of women that had driven them to this as a hatred of these people who had helped murder their comrades. In a matter of a few minutes, six of the homes had been set afire, and at least thirty of the villagers were dead or severely injured. The men knew that they were victorious.

Suddenly, a shower of a different type of arrow fell from the sky. The men of the village had returned and the thieves were taken totally unaware. The battle became hand to hand fighting as hatchets and knives tore into human flesh.

Amid the foray, Artero managed to find Mothana, and they escaped into the forest.

"Paluqua, it is time for us to move on," said Anam as he took a drink of water from the cup she had brought him. "However, first I want to go out and scout a bit and see what direction it would be best to move in. I would have you tell the others we shall leave upon my return in an hour or two."

Togorasom was sitting on the ground nearby. He looked up at Anam and back at the ground in prayer.

"You will go unaccompanied?" she asked.

Anam nodded.

"I shall tell the women to be prepared. I want you to be very cautious, for there are many animals in the woods that prey upon men," she urged him.

"There is no wolf or bear that I cannot outsmart or outrun," he said with a smile. "But, yes, I shall be very careful."

Togorasom looked up at Anam and said, "Don't go, Father. I

do not know what, but there is an awful danger out there."

Anam looked at him imploringly. "I do not understand. What danger? Am I not God's anointed? What can happen to me?"

"I do not know," answered Togorasom with a frown. "I am afraid there is danger. Probably, you will not heed a mere child, anyway. So go, but be very careful."

Anam sat beside him. "You are more than a child. If you tell me what to do, then I shall try to understand."

"I do not know. I only know that there is an animal so wise that mere arrows cannot stop it and you shall not be able to flee."

"Now, I must go so I can see what manner of creature this is that is so dangerous. Can Satan create an animal that will destroy me?"

"Let us pray not," said Paluqua.

"You shall not be destroyed," said Togorasom. "Only, be careful."

"I shall be fine," he said as he stood up. "I shall go in the direction of the river and go away from the mountains. I will not be gone long." He placed his hand on Togorasom's shoulder. "Goodbye!"

With that, he checked his quiver of arrows and knife sheaf, picked up his bow, and was gone.

Moving along at a slow jog, which he could easily maintain all day, in a few minutes he had reached the top of the hill and headed down towards the river. He stopped in a clearing where he could see the water a few hundred yards away and then moved on, traveling diagonally through the shrubbery until he was at the water's edge. Here, he rested for a minute, taking a drink of water. Then, as he was prepared to move on downstream, he heard the laughter of a woman's voice in the distance. He cautiously moved back into the shrubbery and headed in the direction of the voice.

As he walked downstream, the sound of the woman's voice became clearer, and he reached a point where the river curved in a u-shape and created a quiet pool that had been formed over many years. Wading in this quiet pool was the most beautiful woman Anam had ever seen. Her blonde hair fell over her shoulders below her breasts. She was quite naked, standing in water that lapped at her thighs. No flaw met his eyes. Her flesh was firm and muscular, but soft in all the right places. Anam ached to be close to her.

Instead of walking around to the pool, he removed his

weapons and silently climbed down into the water and paddled underneath until he knew he was near her. When he shot up out of the water, he was merely three feet in front of her. He blinked hard, twice, to get the water from his eyes and then looked into hers. She had the face of an angel. Her dreamy blue eyes locked into his and showed no surprise or displeasure from his sudden appearance.

She looked him up and down, admiring his dark grey flesh. He quickly took her golden-tanned body into his eyes again and then looked back at her face. A pleasant smile crossed her lips, and she extended her hand toward him. He took it, and they walked to shore where she led him to a bed of leaves and motioned for him to lie down.

He started to speak, but she put her fingertip to his lips to silence him. He clasped her hand with both of his and began kissing it as he continued to gaze into her eyes. She gently coaxed him to the ground and, taking one of his hands, she placed it just above her knee as she silently nodded her head. The blood was pumping hard into Anam's heart as he slowly moved his hand up her leg.

Suddenly, the picture of a young boy in prayer flashed into his mind. Finally, he spoke in a whisper. "Who are you?"

She smiled and slowly looked away. "I am your heart's desire. I am your moment of passion. You have found me alone and helpless, and now I am yours." She looked back into his eyes, pleadingly. "Only, please, I beg of you, do not hurt me. I only want to satisfy your every fantasy."

"I could never harm a precious beauty like you. You are, to me, like a beautiful gem I have found on the beach. Your beauty surpasses the lilies in the spring and the stars on a cool summer night. You have stirred within me a great warmth that the water from all the seas could not cool."

"Then, let me be your lover," she said firmly. "Take me."

"I have never loved a woman, but one who was my wife."

"No eyes can see us here. Only your eyes and mine can gaze in eager anticipation of delight. I want to delight in your love."

"One sees all," he said, raising his eyebrows. "Even the Lord, my God."

"Forget God for now and, if I cannot satisfy you enough, you can repent in the morning."

Anam closed his eyes and rested his forehead in his hand.

"This is not the time for silent meditation," she said, taking his hand in hers and kissing each fingertip. "You have the most beautiful body of any man I have ever seen. Please, share it with me."

He stood up. "I cannot. Though you are the most lovely woman I have ever seen, you are obviously too preoccupied with its sensuality and not with those better things."

"And you are a fool. The God that you pretend to worship is but an active imagination." She stood up. "You had best flee before I destroy you with the power I have."

"I know that power. It is the power of lies and delusions. It is the power of sin and death!" he shouted at her. "Your body is wondrous and is merely the decoration for the evil within. You have no power but your tricks and your charms. Repent and be saved, or die, and then you may try to charm your real master."

Anam heard a noise from the bushes but, as he turned, he realized it was too late. Artero released an arrow, and it sunk deep into Anam's arm. He wrenched the shaft from his flesh as blood began streaming from the wound. He vainly looked around for his weapons as his head clouded with drugs and he fell at her feet.

"Do I kill him?" Artero asked as he pulled out a hatchet.

"Don't be a fool. I have slept on the ground in the dirt last night and, now, I'll be no witness to your murdering. Help me drag him to the tree and we can tie him up before he comes around. If we can tie him sure enough, the wolves shall finish him off when they sense the smell of blood."

"This one will continue to be a problem. I say we destroy him."

"Who am I?" she demanded.

He looked away from her. "I am sorry, princess. Forgive me. You are my god. I was only afraid of him."

"Fear me! Now tie him up!" she ordered as she picked up her wrap and walked away.

The man was big, but Artero managed to pull him by his feet to a large tree and tie him very securely. Then, when he was certain that Mothana had gone, he placed a piece of shale under Anam's head, picked up his hatchet, and held it over his head. Silently and quickly, he brought the blade down toward Anam's forehead, but just before it struck, he heard Mothana call him and, glancing away, he missed. The metal blade shattered against the piece of shale. Artero starred at his worthless weapon in disbelief. Mothana called again.

"I curse you, man of God. We shall meet again."

Anam was quite conscious of all these actions, though his eyes hurt so bad he kept them closed and he was quite unable to move. Several hours passed and, at about noon, he heard a rustle in the bushes near him. He tried to turn his head but still was unable to move. There was silence, and then he heard heavy breathing near him. He felt the rope that had been tied around him go taut and then snap as it broke. A large, hairy arm encircled his waist, and he was hoisted into the air. Beneath him, he could see the brown fur of a large animal's back. It was not clear as his eyesight was blurry. Though he tried hard to remain conscious and discern what was happening, he passed out as they entered the water.

"Gonna rain, sure as I'm alive," offered Ernie. "We'd better get our duds together and move into the forest for cover."

He looked around at the six other men there at the campfire. Sebastian sat next to him. His face was red, and sweat was on his brow. Ernie knew he had a high fever from the wound. There was little that anyone could do but offer him wet rags to keep cool. They had to keep him alive. With their real leader still in shock, Sebastian was the only other choice. Beside Sebastian was Butcher. This man, who had been named 'The Butcher', by his enemies and renamed Butcher by his comrades, sat there with his arms wrapped around his waist. His feet were pulled up so he formed a little ball. The man shook as occasional sobbing came from deep in his chest. The four other men, being old and crippled, could only get about slowly or with help.

A cool wind hit Ernie's neck, causing him to get up and start carrying their blankets and bundles into the thicket in an effort to escape the inevitable thunder shower. It was becoming dark from the overcast and, in the distance, began a beautiful display of lightning. Once all of the supplies were safe, he got first their leader up and into cover and then started to help the old men. Sebastian got up and headed into the cover just as the skies unleashed their fury. As soon as they were all safely moved, Ernie returned to ensure that nothing had been left behind that would be destroyed by the rain. The fire was dead.

Suddenly, as if from nowhere, a large, hovering beast appeared before him. In fright and awe, he looked up at the powerful creature. He had never before been this close to a brown bear that was still free to move about. His first thought was that the animal had wandered this way by mistake because of the sudden change in weather. Then, he saw the man. The great bear put the man carefully on the ground before Ernie and, while bending over to look into Ernie's face, the old man's fear left him. If the bear chose to destroy him at this point in time, fear was not a good defense.

Ernie looked into the bear's eyes and saw a little hint of intelligence. This act was clearly not the beast's decision but from something greater. The animal turned and lumbered off on all fours into the rain without as much as a glance over his shoulder and was gone.

Ernie got down on his knees and inspected the man before him. There was no doubt in his mind that this was the man that Suya and Sarare had talked of. They had said that he had no fear. That he was constantly protected by God. That his body was strong and without fault. Now, he lay here on the ground in the rain, unconscious and bleeding, by this miserable old man, one of the least of his people.

"Where is your God now?" he said aloud, and then he remembered the bear. A new awe entered Ernie's mind. He had never known anyone to be protected like that. The bears were either skittish of man or they turned upon them in great anger. "Then, you are protected," he said, "but why were you brought to me? I am of no help. Nevertheless, I shall do what I am able to do."

Anam was too large to be moved, so Ernie, leaving him where he was, pounded two sticks into the ground near his shoulders. He then took a large flap of cloth and erected it over the sticks to form a lean-to, which was held down with several cobblestones. At least this much kept the wind and rain from him. The old man propped Anam's head up with a bundle of clothes. He could think of nothing else to do.

"I don't think you're gonna make it, fella. You just came to the wrong place for help," he said to the unhearing man. "Besides, this was a bad day. Most of my people are dead. Nobody left but a bunch of weak old men that ain't good for much." Ernie wiped a mixture of tears and rain from his eyes. Then, he chuckled. "Sorta reminds me of a story a young teenage girl was telling me about you. Wonder what it was that made you folks keep on going. Wish I could have that much faith. Ain't ever had much faith in much. Never knew my folks. Never could love a woman and make it last more than two nights. Reckon the best thing that ever happened to me was meeting that young girl, and then she went away."

He stared off into the rain in silence, then looked back at Anam. "I just can't do it!" he shouted. "I don't understand. The only gods I know are Kiwatuan and that make-believe one the priests in Foramen prate on about, and then they go and do what they want to. Seems like Sarare said her god was in her heart. That's what I want." He clutched his chest. "I want my god right here inside of me, so he can help me whenever I need him. And, maybe, he can help me get my head screwed on straight. Wish you could talk to me and tell me some stuff. You'd know what I ought to do. She said if I prayed and meant it, then I could have her god. I don't understand." He leaped up and threw his arms in the air. "God, aren't you listening to me, or are you as pig-headed as I am?" He fell in a heap on the ground into the mud. His body jerked a few times as he stifled his crying.

Then he stopped and sat up. "Okay. I'm gonna try this thing. She said if I prayed and believed, then it would happen. God," he yelled, "make the rain stop!" Nothing happened as the downpour continued. "Hmph. Just like I figured, it wouldn't stop. Maybe, that's too big for ya. How about if you just make it so I stop crying and feeling sorry for myself like a little kid." He waited. "Well, I ain't crying no more, so that's something. Now I'm gonna pray for him." He looked sympathetically at the man under the blanket. "Dear God, make it so at least me and him can pull through this storm together." He lowered his head. "I know I ain't ever done much right, but I'm willing to start right now if you'll help me along. Let's just take care of one day at a time." Before he went any farther, he passed into a deep sleep.

Ernie looked up at Sebastian. The rain had stopped but the air was still very damp. The sun was near the horizon, which indicated that he had slept several hours. He looked into Sebastian's blank face and waited for a comment.

"We wondered why you never came back, but no one had the strength to go after you."

"How do you feel?" Ernie asked him as he stood up and reached to inspect Sebastian's arm.

"I'm much better. The fever passed in spite of the weather, but," he said, moving back, "it still hurts awful. So, don't touch it. I'll check it out in a little bit. Who's that?" he asked pointing at the still unconscious man lying on the ground.

"Who d'ya think he is. It's that guy those young girls were talking about. I forget his name."

"Don't tell me a story, old man. I heard you out here hollering to God in the rain. I didn't know that he was here." He looked around. "How'd he get here, anyway?"

"A giant bear brought him to me. Carried him right over his shoulder like a sack of potatoes."

Sebastian broke out in laughter. "That's great. Now, tell me. How'd he get here?" He realized that Ernie was not laughing. "C'mon, Ernie. Bears don't do that. Besides being afraid of men, they can't walk upright and carry a load like that."

"A big brown bear walked in here and put him on the ground, looked me right in the eye, and left!" Ernie shouted indignantly. "And if you don't believe me, I don't care."

"All right. All right. Settle down. If you say so, it's okay with me. What are we going to do with him? He needs help."

"Well, I can't help him. He must have got one of the headhunter's arrows in his arm. It's a pretty bad wound, but I've seen worse. It must have had one of that witch's drugs in it, or something."

Sebastian pulled the wet blanket back and got down to look at Anam's arm. "Well, if the headhunters are shooting at him, then he can't be all bad." He sat back and shook his head. "Ernie, what are we going to do? Everything's messed up now. We can't make it out here with just us. We'll all die before winter sets in. There ain't any hope."

"Look," said Ernie, pointing toward the horizon. "A rainbow. That's a sign, you know."

"Yea," said Sebastian, getting up and heading back toward the shelter of the trees. "It's a sign that it rained and now the whole world's a sloppy mess." He turned back to Ernie. "What are we going to do?"

"Let's see if we can bring him around, patch him up, and get him home," he said, nodding toward Anam. "Maybe, his people will be so thankful that they will help us out."

"I ain't no poverty case," Sebastian retorted.

"Well, then great," he sneered. "You come up with something better!"

"Okay." He closed his eyes in thought. "I'll come up with something."

"Well, we can't just leave him lay here any longer. We've got some clean bandages, so why don't you go down and get some water, and then we'll clean and rewrap both yours and his wounds."

A few minutes later, Sebastian returned with several leather flasks full of water. Ernie had rummaged around and found clean wraps, so they set about cleaning up Anam's wound first. Except for a few moans while they were working, he did not respond.

"Now it's your turn," said Ernie. "Let's see if you can cooperate half as much as him and not be a big baby about this."

"Oh, shut up, nurse. Just fix me up." Sebastian lay down on the ground and extended his arm to his friend.

"You do the shutting up or I'll just cut off the fool thing."

Further up the river, the Rasomites had become very impatient. Paluqua had ordered them to pack and be prepared to leave, arranging themselves in companies, and they had done so. That had been a long time ago. After about four hours of waiting, she had organized a party to go in search of Anam. They had discovered the place where Artero had tied him up. They had also found Anam's weapons and Artero's broken hatchet. However, when they attempted to follow the bear's trail, they could not, as the rain had covered all trace. After several hours of walking in the rain, they decided to stay under cover until the weather cleared. Paluqua sent one of the women back to tell them of their progress and to help Togorasom find Anam in prayer. That left her with Crazon and Zoana.

God had been gracious with Crazon, for he had given her the gift of being able to see into a person's heart and appease their troubles. Also, Zoana was quick-witted and could easily see her way through a crisis. She feared nothing. Paluqua sat in the mist under the trees, praying and weeping for the man she cared more about than life itself.

"I have discovered something," said Crazon to Zoana as she listened to Paluqua. "Though we all revere Anam and respect him for what he is, something different has happened to Paluqua."

Zoana looked into Paluqua's face, which was taut and covered with tears and anguished over the disappearance of their leader. "She feels very strongly for him, I know. I can see her grief."

"Do you not hear her words, though, she prays for herself and Anam? She asks for Anam to be brought back to her and us. She asks to be near to this man, so she can feel his strength again. She also says she wants to share her secrets with him. Do you not see that the woman is in love?" Zoana looked at her in surprise. "Anam has many gifts. God has blessed him with both mental and physical strength. Though he has been called 'savior' and 'anointed', he is still humble toward God. He can call down fury and healing. But to understand the heart of a woman, our glorious leader is a fool." Zoana almost laughed out loud. "He spends all of his time with God and wrapped up in his thoughts and caring for us and doesn't even see what is going on around him. What are we going to do with him?"

"I say we go after him, bring him home, and marry him off to someone who loves him." She looked at Palaqua. "Let's get out of here." She stood up. "I've been thinking. If one of these bears carried him off, it could not have been the bear's decision to do so. It was God. The bear has taken him to people. He didn't bring him to us. It was the headhunter's arrow that brought him down. He took him, I'm sure, to those men who had the girls. Let us hope that man Sarare spoke of, Ernie, is tending Anam's wound right now."

Crazon had also gotten up and gone to the opening of the thicket. "Zoana." She was smiling. "Look, the rain has stopped and the sun has come out. Let's go. Paluqua! Look, the weather has changed. We can go for Anam."

As soon as they were in the open, it was easy to see the campfire several hundred yards upstream. Eagerly, the three women headed toward it, but also with caution.

"There, that's much better," said Ernie. "We'll just keep the filth out of that hole for a few days and, I think, you'll be all better." He inspected the wrap to make certain it was secure. "Also, thanks for being a big boy."

"Oh, shut up," said Sebastian.

While they had attended to the injuries, the rest of the men had wandered into the sunshine. Then, they realized they had visitors.

"We mean you no harm," yelled Crazon, who was ahead of the others. "We seek him." She pointed at Anam as she clamored over the rocks towards him.

For a moment, they were all silent, and then Sebastian spoke. "We have no weapons. Do what you will. We cannot stop you."

Paluqua fell beside Anam and immediately laid hands on him and began praying for him.

"Oh, Lord, forgive him for his error and deliver him back to us. Pity us, Father. If not for the sakes of all Rasomites and mankind, then only because I love him. But not my will, but thine." Anam stirred. She looked up at the others with tears in her eyes. "He's going to be all right. Oh, praise God."

Throughout all this activity, the man called Butcher had sat by, quietly watching, unable to respond. But then, something else caught his attention. Artero and Mothana had also appeared.

"All this has happened," screamed Artero, "because you would not worship her!" He directed his speech to the confused man sitting alone. "This is for you." As he spoke, he released the arrow that Mothana had earlier given him. But Zoana was faster because she had seen what was coming. As the arrow passed by, her powerful arm shot forth, and her hand caught the arrow in flight.

"Not this man, but you, devil worshipper!" she yelled. Artero started backing up in terror, but the arrow entered his heart before he could resist. The poison was so powerful, he died instantly.

Mothana had been very sure of herself and had stood by with her arms crossed over her chest, feet apart. But the moment Artero hit the ground she turned and ran into the forest. She knew she would be pursued, but she did not realize her pursuer would be no human. God's giant servant had one more mission to do before he could return home to his kind.

Zoana looked back and forth between Ernie and Sebastian. "Who is he?" she asked of the man whose life she had just spared.

"This is our leader. He has been like this since we returned Sarare to you people," answered Ernie.

Zoana stared at him and scornfully shook her head. "This is your leader. Can a female have that much effect on a man?"

"Listen, woman," spoke Sebastian loudly and pointing at Anam. "Our boss has saved us through many hazards. He is quick-witted and sneaky as a fox. It is indeed a shame that this has happened, but he has not allowed himself to fall into a witch's trap as your leader. Your leader who is now near death. Both of these men need help and we are no doctors. Shall we find fault or do we go after help?"

"I am sorry," she said. "I was not thinking. Yes, let us certainly return home."

Paluqua, still sitting, turned around from where she sat praying for Anam. "He has been very strongly drugged. It will wear off, but only after many days. I agree, let us band ourselves together and return to camp where it is safer. Are you willing?" she asked, looking at Sebastian.

"Well, I can't think of nothing else to do," he answered. "I suppose we can do that."

"I think it's an excellent idea," said Ernie.

"It's about two or three miles from here," said Crazon, who had been inspecting their new allies. "It will take us too long to travel with a group like this and Anam unconscious. Zoana, you will return ahead and send help back. It should only take a couple of hours. We will stay here."

"One step better, Crazon," said Zoana. "Everyone is ready to move out anyway. There is a lot of room here. Whoever is ready shall go. The rest may come in the morning." She looked at the horizon where the sun was just beginning to set. "By the time one returns, it may be dark. Do you suppose," she looked at Ernie, "there be any more of his type out there?" She pointed at the body of Artero.

"I don't know," he said as he closed his eyes in thought. He looked at her. "Do this. The headhunters are not aware of our number or of his condition," he pointed at his leader. "They may suppose us to be rallying for a counter attack. Cross the river at this point. If there be any of their bloody number left, they would not cross the river but would retreat back into the forest with which they are familiar. The other side should be safe. I feel very sorry for anybody who crosses you." There was a smile on his face. "You should go quickly before it is too dark to return."

She nodded her head as a farewell and was gone.

"I was going to ask her," said Ernie, as he dropped his head a bit sadly, "to ask Sarare and Suya to come quickly."

"Don't worry," said Paluqua, "when they hear that Anam is here, the whole nation will rise up quickly."

"Ernie," said Sebastian. "Very soon, we are going to have

many guests. I suppose it would be well if we were able to feed them with some of our victuals that we hid. What do you say?"

"It will take many arms to carry enough for this crew. We are few. But, perhaps, we can offer enough to slacken their hunger." He looked at Crazon. "Buried in a hole near here is enough dried storage to satisfy our appetites for many days. With your help, we can begin to bring it here and prepare it for eating."

"Your generosity seems odd to me for a bunch of thieves," replied Crazon.

"Never mind that," said Sebastian, "we are going to feed you."

It was decided that Sebastian, with his bad arm, would remain to watch camp and tend the fire. Paluqua, Crazon, and Ernie headed further upriver. It was only a five minute walk to the shelter that had been formed where two large trees had fallen side by side over a crevice. The foliage was more than sufficient to hide the entrance to most casual observers. Inside, in a small area, were stacked dozens of leather pouches and bags, each with a variety of dried fruits and meats. There were also several kegs of wine. In separate earthen containers were also sticks of dried bread. Ernie explained.

"When the decision was made to attack the headhunters, we also decided to temporarily abandon home. It took only a few minutes to stock this for an emergency if they had mounted a counter attack. Most of this food originally came from Foramen."

"I wonder," asked Paluqua, raising her eyebrows and looking at him questionably, "how it came into your hands?"

"It is probably best now not to discuss our past. The supplies are here to be used or not."

"Never mind," said Paluqua. "We do, however, have a small problem. The Rasomites are not allowed to eat meat, except sometimes that of fishes and birds."

"I don't understand," Ernie said, shaking his head.

"It is a pledge," interjected Crazon. "It is no matter, for there is much. We will suffice and, on the morrow, perhaps we can go fishing."

"Let us go back," said Ernie, "with as much as we are able, because soon it will be dark. All of this is for you, if you wish."

In a few minutes, the women had burdened themselves down with several pouches of food. Ernie had strapped a keg of wine to his back, and the trio headed back downriver. They were pleased, upon their return, to find that Sebastian had started to gather more dry branches for firewood.

"Any change?" Paluqua asked Sebastian of Anam.

"Nothing. He simply sleeps soundly, it seems. I am pleased to see you thought to bring back one of the kegs with you. They shall be very dry when they arrive here." He picked up a drinking cup. "It would be best to test it and make sure it hasn't gone bad."

Crazon gently took the cup away from him, leaving him with a startled look upon his face.

"That is a wonderful idea," she said. Ernie pulled the cork from the keg and helped to fill the cup. She took a long draught. "It must be very cool in that shelter, for the wine is as cool as spring water and its taste is superb. I'm only teasing," she said, laughing as she returned the cup to the still startled man. "I hope this all means that we can become very good friends."

"Ya know," spoke up one of the old men finally. "I guess nothing ever stays the same forever. I've been living out here all of my life. Figured it would never change. The whole thing closes up and changes in a day. The old die and the young come and start over. I ought to be depressed, but I know that city," he pointed toward Foramen, "will cover this whole territory. Farms will spring up. They'll probably sell tickets to see the old stuff. Sorry, my name's Zack, Zachery. It just makes me feel good to see you pretty young women carrying on. Even though, I know, you'll be leaving. Tell me something. Do you turn the world upside down everywhere you go?"

"Crazon!" called Paluqua. "Sebastian, what did you do with the slain headhunter's body?" She was standing upon the outcropping of rocks where Artero's body had fallen.

"Not me," he said. He joined her. "The camp has been very quiet since you left for the food." He looked about nervously and then added. "I'm worried. I cannot help but think the headhunters snuck back in here and retrieved the body when I was gathering firewood."

"There are no headhunters or other dangers here, or one of us would sense it," said Paluqua. "I do not understand. I had thought we would bury him."

"Maybe, it was that bear again," said Ernie.

"Weren't no bear or nuthin'," mumbled Zachery. "We been sittin' here the whole time. We'd of seen that brute."

"Maybe, he wasn't dead at all," suggested Ernie, "and just got up and stumbled away."

"I say he was dead," said Sebastian, "because I rolled him over once while you were gone."

Crazon had been standing near the fire with her hand on her forehead, deep in thought. She spoke and, though it was her voice, it was as though she was not forming the words. "Beware, oh child of God who has destroyed this man. As I am God, I warn you to beware this one whose ground is cursed. Though he walks with men, his life is not still in him. He has been delivered to the very hand of Satan to go out to the world and destroy this one. He will not arise now, but will return at a time and place when she is not prepared. But I shall remain in you."

They were all silent for a moment and, finally, Sebastian asked what this could mean.

"It is the word of God," said Paluqua. "Artero will try to destroy Zoana. I've never known anything to happen like this. Satan must have had a lot of pleasure with these people. Let us pray."

They all gathered together and said a prayer of deliverance for Zoana but knew in their hearts that she was still in peril. It was not as if an angry man was after her, but Satan himself wanted to destroy her.

"We have one great strength and that remains the curse upon any who harm a Rasomite," said Paluqua.

"Nonsense," said Sebastian, spitting on the ground. "How can you curse Satan. He is already cursed and could care less. Better keep your eye on that lady."

"Hush," said Crazon. "Listen."

"I can't hear anything," said Ernie, looking around the clearing in the near-dark of a nearly completed sunset. Suddenly, he stood upright in surprise for before him was a crowd of Rasomite children. They moved out of the way as Zoana appeared on a large black horse. She beamed with pride at her silent invasion as she dismounted and headed for Crazon.

"We traveled quickly and silently. Even the evening animals were not aware of our presence. Not yet have we lost our touch." Crazon tearfully embraced her. "Our parting was not so long ago. Is this a pleasant welcome?"

"Things are not pleasant, Zoana," said Crazon with her head

bowed. She looked into her friend's questioning face. "Artero, the headhunter, is about."

"But, I thought..."

"Wait," said Crazon firmly, putting her hand on Zoana's shoulder. "The man who died is now on the loose. God gave us a word. Satan himself has taken over this person and seeks to kill you." Zoana's mouth fell open and she shook her head in disbelief.

"How can this be," she said, "that Satan can walk with men? I wish Anam were able to help."

While they had been speaking, the Rasomite people had moved in and taken over the camp. Zachery and the other old men sat quietly, watching all the activity. Sebastian was surrounded by four women to whom he was trying to explain why his arm was wrapped. Ernie attempted to stand off to the side, looking hopefully for a familiar face. Anam, naturally, was the center of activity.

Several women, having already been informed of his condition, immediately began prayer and the laying on of hands. As they prayed, there was an obvious stirring in Anam. First, his hands began moving and then his lips as though he were about to speak. Suddenly, his eyes opened up and he looked about with great satisfaction upon his surroundings. He ran his hands up and down his body, grasping his flesh to prepare himself for standing up.

Paluqua had, when she saw him moving, sat down next to him. She was the first person he noticed.

"Paluqua, my helper, I have been in a deep sleep and have dreamed a dream. With you, I must share it. First, will you be mine to marry?" Everyone close heard what Anam had told her, and she was instantly embarrassed. "I already know what you will say. I want to tell you this, while I wait for you to say 'yes'. I had a vision, a dream. In my dream, there was a beautiful little house on the seashore. Beyond the house was a garden filled with flowers and all sorts of lovely plants. I also saw many kingdoms. There were castles, and cities, and tents, and mountain caves. These are our children's kingdoms and they covered, it seemed, the whole earth. Now, you can say 'yes!'."

Paluqua closed her eyes and started laughing quietly. She looked again at Anam. "Yes."

As Anam continued to expound on his dream, one man had sat quietly off to the side in silence. Sarare had looked for her former captor when she first arrived, but had gotten sidetracked when Suya had called her over to show her that she had found Ernie. There were many hugs and smiles. Suya promised Ernie that she would tell him all about her God before they fell asleep that night and Sarare offered to help. As they stood talking, her eyes suddenly fell upon that man whom she had sought.

He sat by himself on a stone within the protective shrubbery. She ran to him, fell on her knees, and looked into his eyes.

"I thought," she began, "that you might become depressed. Do you not know that my God, your God, does not wish it so? He wants you to be of a sound mind. He also wants you to become pure and be forgiven your past wrongs. My Lord wants to dwell in your heart. I know now that the war you have fought with mankind was not because of your strength, but because of your weakness. You wanted to cover up your lack of confidence by behaving like a savage. When your heart was broken, you had nothing left." She closed her eyes. "I wish you could hear me," she spoke quietly as he was unresponsive.

"I can hear you," he said. "I feel so empty. I don't know what to do. My whole world has been destroyed. Even if I wanted to, I couldn't put it back together. If I could, it would still be so empty. My feelings for you have changed. I still want you. I want to know about your God. I think I love you. But it's different than before."

"Will you do something for me?"

"I would do anything for you."

"Will you pray that God gives you a sound mind such that you can decide what way, not you, but he should have you go?"

"I will if you will help me with something." Tears were forming in his eyes.

"You are a great leader and you shed tears? I know what you want, and I shall teach you to pray and to love my God."

The remainder of the evening was spent in prayer and feasting. One of the women prayed for Sebastian, and he was instantly healed of his wound. Though his body was delivered, his mind remained skeptical. Since Ernie gave his heart to God and was so open to the Rasomites, Anam decided he should proceed with them.

Early the next morning, the two leaders had a meeting.

"I have thought and prayed and tried to rationalize in my mind a relationship between you and the young girl, Sarare," began

Anam. "She has also entreated me to allow you more time. I believe your heart is melting and that you would like to come to know God, but I cannot give away the girl without knowing she will be well. Besides the curse. If it did not go well, then your own life could be in peril."

"I am trying to understand. I have learned a lot of your God already. She told me of your lives and the tragedies that brought you here. Also of your deliverance. I believe all this. Why won't you trust me?"

Anam stared at the other man sternly. "God has placed each of these children under my care." He looked around at the women and children that were his. "I cannot let one of these out of the fold, except that I know that it will be for the glory of God. Though you are willing to hear the story of our pilgrimage and you want to believe, you are not yet convicted. Do you see that man?" He pointed at Ernie, who had started a game of tag with the children. "He has already developed a strong love for these people. That man is convicted. What is your name?"

The other man dropped his head. "I have names. Butcher is the one I go by."

"When you were a boy, your father gave you a name."

"Yea," he looked up angrily, "I had a name. I used to be called Eric."

"You were a captain in the city guard."

"How did you know?" Eric asked, staring blankly at Anam.

"Because God has put me together with people who used to love you. Now I know what you must do. If you are to be convicted of God, then you must do what I say."

Eric nodded. "I have nothing left here." He shook his head. "I will do what you say."

"You must return to Foramen, immediately. You must go to the man who will soon be the city governor. His name is Phillip. Tell him that I have sent you. You must organize the people so that they can harvest and live safely in this area."

"But in other places, near here, there are also other gangs of robbers and savages."

"That is the reason I am asking you to return with Sebastian and the older men. You and Sebastian know what must be done. You know the territory. Will you do this?"

Eric closed his eyes and covered his face with his hand to

prepare his argument. "When I was captured here," he began, "I had to learn to live like an animal. I had to become ruthless and unforgiving. I could not return to Foramen because I knew it was ugly. The priests ran everything. The people just kept to their own business. I hated it. I swore I would never go back. But now, all that has changed. They have God and, maybe, a revival, but they will still hate me. I have many crimes and they will want to put me to death."

"If you go to Phillip, he shall love you and allow you to redeem yourself. It is the only way you can make things right. Trust me."

With reluctance in his voice, Eric finally consented to return to Foramen. "But what will happen to Sarare?" he asked.

"She will go with us and someday will meet a strong, faithful man to marry. Wouldn't you want her to have the best?"

Eric nodded silently. "After we eat, I shall head out with the others to go home. I hope all goes well with you."

Anam watched him go to Sebastian and discuss their imminent departure. He felt a female hand brush his arm and turned to Sarare.

"It will not be easy for him at first." She said watching Eric. "But it is best that he go, for the people of Foramen will need the help. And what of us?" She looked up at Anam. "Where do we go next?"

"Where can we go but to look for that place the Lord has prepared for us? A place for you and your brothers and sisters to dwell in peace. We shall cross the mountains and let God show us the way."

Chapter 8
Aris-Akana

Galincia took another leaf from the Spongy plant, a bush the leaves of which were always full of water, even here in the desert. Though the taste was very bitter, he needed some moisture in his mouth, if only to slacken the dry cough he had. However, chewing on Spongy leaves was not going to fill his belly or mend his wounds. He had tried to look over his shoulder at the still-open lash marks on his back and wished he had even a scrap of cloth to hide it from the sun. He could see the dried blood on his shoulders, but the pain was too intense to turn his head to gaze at his back. He shivered from the mere thought of the pain and humiliation he had suffered as he remembered being driven from Aris-Akana.

Galincia was the second-highest ranking priest of the religion of the Mozanas. As long as his uncle, Mordi, was in prison, Galincia was in charge. There was very little to be in charge of for, unfortunately, the great cathedral was nearly empty, save for a few devoted servants and, until yesterday, himself. The torches were never lit because there was no more money to sustain those types of amenities.

Galincia had sat in the cathedral, maintaining silence long enough. He had prayed diligently for the deliverance of the wicked and lustful King Goranus and his family, as well as the population of Aris-Akana. But, daily, they sank lower into their deviant practices.

He remembered only a couple of years before how things had been so much better. It all changed with the arrival of the prince. Recently, God had increased Galincia's determination to bridle his tongue no longer and speak out against the filth. His Lord told him he would, in the end, be victorious. At first, it was merely unheeded shouts from the cathedral entrance. Yesterday, he had become angry and decided to deal directly with the King.

He had strutted past the palace guards, who had laughed at his anger and condemnations, and found King Goranus in his garden with two young women who fled naked when they saw the young priest.

"You are a dirty dog," he had shouted as the fat man wiped scented oil from his naked body, truly unabashed by the priest's name-calling but nonetheless upset that his little party had been so rudely interrupted.

"And you are a fool," said Goranus. "Why do you waste your time calling out to your imaginary God and prating on about sin? Sin is only as a man defines it. My god is Akaka and you refuse to worship it so, in my eyes, you are a sinner. I have been patient and understanding with you..." Galincia tried angrily to interrupt. "Shut up!" shouted Goranus, "or you shall die now. You are a fool. Why cannot you see sensuousness is real and pleasant, while your prayer and fasting is more than a waste of good time?" Goranus snapped his fingers and several young women came to wipe his oily flesh down with cool, damp towels as it was the heat of the day. Galincia shook with anger.

"Goranus," he replied quietly, stifling his bitterness. "I know you shall never believe in the god of the Mozanas. You are too conceited. But, look about this fair and once-prosperous city. The people are turned to their own lusts. Their great productivity has been stifled by this darkness. Sickness of not only the mind, but also the body, is beginning to appear among the once-healthy Akanians. I fear an epidemic is about to follow. Many are already sick and some dead. They are polluting each other. If not for their eternal salvation, then, I urge you for their health and prosperity to cause them to repent and control themselves. Of what good are they to be in death or sickness to either God or Akaka?"

"There is some worldly logic to your argument. However, it is better to be pleased with life and suffer and die than to never have found enjoyment," replied the King.

"Will you be so sure when they lay your aching, rotten bones in your bed, never to arise?"

"I will have my memories. Now, leave. I have promised Pholipi a bit of enjoyment."

Galincia's eyes grew huge and, for a moment, he had been speechless. "No, King, not with your own son. I forbid it."

"In the first place, he is merely my adopted son. In the second place, you are in no position to forbid anything. Now, get out of here!" the King had ordered.

Several guards had then ran into the garden and proceeded to remove the priest.

"You shall rot in Hell!" Galincia had screamed when he last saw the King.

The guards had approached the top of the stairway and thrown Galincia down the twenty steps to the street below. Galincia had slowly gotten up and began dusting himself off as he continued to mumble to himself and cast curses toward the palace. He had waved his fist over his head and had screamed, "I condemn you all to Hell, you scum of the earth!"

Someone kicked him from behind, and he turned as the angry crowd began beating upon him and calling him disgusting names. Somehow, he had found himself with his hands tied together and looped over a pole, and the crowd backed off. He was not prepared for what had happened next. Something snapped in the air behind him and grazed his back. He received the second lash before he felt the sting of the whip. The crowd was applauding but, while he was fully conscious, he continued his railings and curses. Finally, he had no more strength and closed his eyes as their whip continued to beat against him.

He found himself lying on the ground and tried to get up. He had risen to his knees but had not the strength to stand. The crowd had regathered around him and continued to shout and yell, but it was like a great buzz in his ears, for he understood nothing.

He looked up to see if there would be even one friendly face, but his eyes filled with sweat and tears, and all seemed a blur. His face became wet. Someone had spat on him. He cleared his face with the palm of his hand and could see clearly the nasty expressions of his tormentors. The crowd parted and Pholipi came into view. The young man said something about cleaning Galincia's wounds, and the priest had hoped for a reprieve. The prince struck Galincia in the chest with his knee, and he fell over sideways. Galincia tried to pull himself up and suddenly realized his entire body was becoming wet. He thought someone was washing him and looked up at Pholipi. The prince finished urinating on the priest and turned and walked away.

The people had loaded him on a horse and driven him from the city. He had awakened the following morning in the place where he sat now, several miles from, but still in view of Aris-Akana.

"My Lord and my God," he began. "Is the entire city and all I know turned over to deprivation and folly? And what will happen to those few huddled folks who have clung to faith because they knew I was there and Mordi was still alive? What of my uncle? Will they torture him?"

He stopped and, in his attempt to swallow, started choking because his throat was so dry. Finally, he began again. "I have failed," he said, trying not to sink into self-pity and cry. "What is there left that I can do? I have not even the strength left to go back to the city. I have barely the strength to speak." He put his hand to his chest and then realized he had a broken rib. He winced from the pain. Dropping his head with his eyes closed, he sat in silence and misery for a long time. It was not possible to think clearly, but his mind rambled on about his despair over his own situation and the loss of his home. "I suppose," he finally said aloud, "I shall sit here until I die. Forgive me for my weakness, my self-pity, and the spiritual death of Aris-Akana."

He sat, feeling as though at this moment he would die but, after several minutes, he again opened his eyes and plucked another Spongy leaf, placing it in his mouth.

The years in the mountains had been prosperous for Anam and his family. Paluqua had first borne him the triplet sons by the names of Oranea, Bonifa, and Darophil. Then, she had blessed him with a baby girl, Comeana. The boys had, for a long time, been toddling on their own. It gave everyone great pleasure to watch them at play. They were all strong and healthy and grew quickly. The babies thought it was wonderful being mothered by so many women and older children.

Anam had hoped to stay at least a few more months in the otherwise uninhabited mountains. The peace they had known during these times had been the first peace many of the young people had ever really known. It had allowed them time to praise God without fear. They had spent time training with their bows and knives and challenging each other. However, the greatest blessing had been that not only had Anam began a family, but several of the young men and women were now married, and some of the girls were now carrying babies. Anam closed his eyes and laughed out loud.

Paluqua sat, breastfeeding Comeana, leaning against Anam's mighty arm. When he laughed, she snuggled closer and lay her head back against his shoulder. She looked at Ernie, who was prancing about playing his pipe and acting silly to entertain the boys. The little ones giggled and clapped their hands as the bearded old man pretended to fall.

"Ouch," he said, acting hurt. "I'm a poor, old man and now I've gotten hurt. Won't you help me?" He looked at the boys questioningly. They all clambered around him and reached out as though to lay hands on him for healing but, instead, started tickling him. He laughed and continued his play.

"Ernie," said Paluqua. "Play something mellow on your pipe to help Comeana go to sleep and, perhaps, the boys need rest also."

Ernie extracted himself from his playmates and pointing at each of them, told them to sit quietly. They instantly obeyed and sat wide-eyed, waiting for his sweet music. He sat upon a small boulder, closed his eyes and, without speaking, commended his music to God. Then, he slowly put his pipe to his lips and played a sweet tune as he watched the eyes of the girl and then each of the boys drift close. The effect was almost instantaneous and, within two or three minutes, all of the children were fast asleep.

He played on a bit to ensure they would sleep for a while. Then he stopped, took a deep breath, and whispered, "I think I have played myself to sleep. I do believe it's a good time for an old man to take some rest."

He quietly got up, arranged the boys on the carpet of grass where they lay, covered them with a fur in case a summer breeze picked up and, after smiling at the parents, turned and walked away to his little tent.

"Except for you, my darling," she said, "I love that wonderful man more than any other man I have ever known."

"As you have told me often," he answered, "and I continue to agree. He is like a grandfather to many of these. I needed this time to speak with you."

"First, my husband," she said, "let me lay her down." Paluqua got up and placed Comeana in a cocoon-like wrap of blankets. She adjusted her brassiere and sat at Anam's feet, resting her hands and chin on his knee. "Now, you have all of my attention."

"I know that you, and all of these, love it here and that we have been blessed while here." He closed his eyes trying to think of the best words for his news.

"My husband," said Paluqua, "we do love it here. But we all know that sitting here in this mountain hideaway is not our destiny. Now that we begin to have families, there shall never be a good time to leave, but I and all these others are devoted to you. When you say it is time to leave, we will simply pack up and go. We have a world to tame, and we are still the Shamra. We must chase the devil until we die. Has God told you it is time?"

"Most precious," said Anam as he touched her cheek softly with the palm of his hand. "You make leading too easy. God has indeed spoken, but not to me. Last evening, Togorasom came to me and told me he had had a dream. He saw a dove flying over the plains, and everyone obeyed this dove. But, then, a hawk came with many birds, and they tried to kill the dove. But God spared him. Then, a flock of brave eagles came and utterly destroyed the hawk, and the wild birds and their bones and feathers were picked upon by rats and vermin. The prophet asked me what this could mean. I am not sure but, as I told him, I believe a dove is in trouble and we are, as the eagles in the dream, to vanquish his tormentors. We are near no town but I believe, if we leave soon, the Lord will direct us where to go and we shall be there in time to save this dove. It is noontime. I told Togorasom to spread the word at noontime that we would leave at dusk and travel by the full moon."

They sat quietly for a few minutes and finally a young, sandy-haired boy appeared. Togorasom noticed the sleeping children and said quietly, "I have done as you asked. They asked many questions for which I had few answers. However, I had no challenge convincing them that God wants us to go. Many of them are resting now and will pack in a while so we can leave at nightfall. With your permission, Father, I would like to relax a while as well."

"You have done well, my son." Anam placed his hand on the boy's head and smiled. "Go and rest. We will leave by nightfall."

"I pray, my Father, we will not be too late." The young prophet turned and walked into a cranny among the rocks and rolled up into a ball. His grey complexion blended into the stone around him and Anam watched him settle down to sleep.

"The children are asleep and the camp is peaceful, my wife. I want to make love with you."

She smiled and nodded her head. "I had hoped that you would suggest that. It could be some time before we have another opportunity."

The old man stared at the bleeding stump that had been his right hand. He trembled and held up his arm close to his chest and wished the pain would stop. Garanus had promised that, on the next day, he would lose his other hand or perhaps a foot, until the fifth day when he would have him beheaded. If only God would grant him the strength to last that long. Then, it would all be over. But he was still afraid for the people.

Mordi heard the keys of the jailer and looked up to see the feeding boy slink quietly in with his head down, place a platter of food on the little wooden bed stand, and depart. As he tried to get up from the mat he had been sitting on, he suddenly felt very light-headed and nearly collapsed. He was able to get to the bed before falling. He had lost a great deal of blood, in spite of the tourniquet and the searing of his flesh. Mordi lay on his back with his mind swirling for several minutes. He was not certain he could stand the pressure for the five days, but he knew he would never be subject to Goranus. The King had told him to deny his God and worship Akaka, which was a set of things he could never do.

Mordi sat up and looked at the food. Since he had been imprisoned, the cathedral servants had been diligent to prepare a generous platter of food each day, and the King either did not know or did not mind that he ate well. Each day, they sent him a variety of good things, and it was the only reminder that there could be good things in the world. He began with the pieces of sliced fruit. The muscles in his throat and the rest of his body were too tight to begin with crackers or bread. Then, he realized that something was missing.

Every day, the platter also contained a small cloth napkin. That was his message that things were well with Galincia, his nephew. There was no napkin. Something was wrong. Mordi's mind raced. Perhaps, a servant had forgotten to include it. Perhaps, it had been removed by the guard. Could Galincia also be in prison? He must talk to one of the servants. Mordi held his forehead in his hand. What could he do? He slowly got up and walked to the doorway, peering out the tiny window. He heard no sounds and did not see the fat old guard that would be on duty now. Then, he saw the boy sitting in the corner on the floor with his head down. Mordi made a small noise to attract his attention and the boy looked up. Nervously, he got up and came near the doorway. Mordi had never spoken to the boy before, as he lived in fear of retribution, but now he was desperate.

"What has happened?" he whispered.

The boy's eyes grew huge as he thought of what to say. Finally, "Galincia has been driven from the city. It is feared by the silent ones he is dead."

When he spoke of the silent ones, Mordi understood. They were the ones who did not agree with the perverted lifestyles or the reign of terror, but were too afraid to speak out. Mordi trembled. With Galincia out of the way and himself in prison, there would be no one for the people to turn to.

"You must get a message to the servants. Tell them that they shall be victorious."

"But what," whispered the boy, "are we to do? We are powerless."

"If you believe in God with all your heart, you are never powerless."

They heard a noise of the guard coming back, and the boy fled. Mordi knew he must get out of this place. He looked around the tiny, underground room. There were no windows. The door was of heavy wood and bolted securely. He fell to his knees and reached out to God for an answer.

Galincia jumped and surprised himself. Had he been sleeping or dying? The strength was not even in him to open his eyes. He could barely hold his head up. The Spongy leaf plant was providing some protection in, this, the latter part of the day. Every inch of his flesh was sunburned red, except for his buttocks, which had not left the spot where he sat cross-legged. In spite of the heat, he shivered. It was a deathlike chill that came from deep inside. His arms were clung about his chest and, with great concentration, he was able to open his fingers and let them fall to his lap.

"Why, dear Lord?" he thought. "What did we ever do that was so evil that the Mozanas should perish like this?" What would become of the Akanians? He begged for pity on the people who had not fallen into perversions and hoped they would suffer through. Perhaps, those with depraved minds would all fall under the plague and the good ones would be spared. "What of my uncle? Does he live? Does he know what has befallen me?" He shivered again. "Take me home, Lord. There is nothing else that I can do here. I have suffered for you and been shamed. Not one would raise a finger to help. But, perhaps, someone has reached out in prayer. There is no strength left in me. Let me pass now. Forgive me for falling short of your glory. I only wish I had been victorious."

"We have power," said Arthur, the young servant. "Mordi, the priest, said we do. For we have God."

"Has he helped us as of yet?" asked his friend. "Look at us. Look at what is going on."

"But," said the boy. He thought for a moment. "Have you really reached out to God? Have you surrendered to Him?"

"Have you?" asked the second boy.

"No," he said quietly. "But perhaps if we do, I mean all of us, we can come out of this. I'm sure we can. If we have God on our side, how can we be defeated?"

"You did not see Galincia as they drove him out of the city," said his first friend. "A bloody mess. And I don't think we shall ever see him again. We do not have the strength to suffer like he did."

"I don't know," said Arthur, "but can we forever live as we are? Hiding in the alleys? Afraid to speak?"

"It's better than dying," said the first friend. "Besides, we are only three boys. If we were the whole city, or the city were to rise up, we could be heard. But we are only three boys. What can we do?"

"We can free Mordi, the priest," replied Arthur. The other two exchanged nervous glances.

"Can we do that? How can we do that?"

"I have an idea. You know that I am trusted to take food and water to him each afternoon from the cathedral. If we do this properly, this will work. The daytime guard is an old, fat man. He curses and spits on me and he's stupid. If you will help me, then we can overcome him and save this priest's life. Perhaps, with Mordi as a rallying point, we can prove that God will give us power."

"And if they catch us?"

"Then we shall die young, I suppose, instead of having to wait. What do you say?"

The three boys looked nervously at each other. Arthur extended his right hand and the others clasped it and exchanged firm grins of agreement.

"What, are you back again today, you little ass?" barked the guard at Arthur.

"I have returned for the tray and cup," he answered quietly with his head down. "They wanted me to return it to the cathedral."

The guard spit a ball of tobacco juice onto the floor. "Waste of my time. Get out of here!"

"Please, let me get the things, that my trip not be wasted," he begged.

"Oh, all right. Then go and leave me alone." He pulled out his key ring to open the door to Mordi's cell. Arthur clutched the dagger that was hidden within his shirt as the guard turned. As soon as the door was pushed open, he jumped onto the man's back and dragged the blade across the man's neck. The man released one long groan as he fell to the floor. His arms and legs pulled into a ball and he stopped moving. He was dead.

Arthur dropped the knife and stared at the man in horror and confusion. Then, remembering his mission, he turned to the room to rescue the priest. Mordi was not there. In great fear and confusion, he ran from the room into the hallway and back up the narrow staircase to the large entryway above. He stopped for a moment to calm his beating heart and rapid breathing. Then, he tried to head for the exit. As soon as he entered the area, he heard a sound in an adjoining room, so he stopped to glance in.

Mordi was standing in the middle of the room with his left arm tied to a post. Another guard and the prince, Pholipi, stood by him. The guard was holding a large ax. The prince was telling the priest to repent and worship his golden wolf, Akaka.

"Wouldn't it be wiser, old man," said Pholipi, "to at least pretend to be obedient? That's all you have to do. Just say a few words to satisfy Goranus' arrogance and you can go free. I don't want to maim you again. Of what good are you with no hands?"

"I will never turn against God," Mordi answered. "I shall never worship your stupid golden wolf."

"What's the point, priest?" asked Pholipi. "What good is it? All you must do is to go through the motions and you can go back to your lonely cathedral."

"Where is my nephew?"

"Huh?"

"You have scourged my nephew, a prophet of God, worthy of your praise. What have you done with him?"

"How did you know? Who told you?"

Afraid to betray the boy, Mordi at first remained silent, but finally spoke up. "A messenger of God came to me."

"I am not being condemned or questioned here," said Pholipi nervously. "Guard, let's have done with this." He backed off.

Before the guard had a chance to commit his dirty deed, the three boys overtook the room. Two of the boys were armed with Arthur's and the dead guard's knives.

"Okay," said Arthur slowly, standing between his friends, "untie the priest."

The guard hoisted the ax over Mordi's head. "I think," he said, "you should stop this foolishness and drop those knives. Or this man will be dead."

"If you kill Mordi, I know his soul will be joined to God. Besides, your King wants him alive. If you kill him, I swear, you will die instantly. My friends have lived in the streets. They know how to throw these knives. Are you prepared to face God's anger? Again, I say, put down the ax and untie the priest."

"You'll never get out of this prison, you little fool."

"I am becoming impatient," said Arthur. He glanced quickly at his friends. "Kill them!" Both boys drew back their arms to throw.

"No!" yelled Pholipi. "I'm not going to die. Untie the old man, you idiot. Who do you think you are to put my life on the line? Move quickly."

In a few seconds, the three boys and the priest were out in the afternoon sun. Immediately, the half-dozen armed guards who were stationed on the grounds were alert.

"Don't anyone move!" yelled Arthur, with the knife at the priest's neck, "or the old man dies."

The guards looked at the boys and the priest, whom many still held in reverence, and then at each other in confusion. The four of them ran out the open gate and quickly disappeared into the surrounding slums.

"Stop them!" screamed Pholipi as he burst through the door and started stomping his feet on the ground impatiently. The guards watched him. "What are you looking at, you stupid idiots? Go after them."

But the priest and his rescuers had disappeared into the city.

"Tell me," said Mordi to Arthur, holding one of the knives, "do you know how to use this thing?"

One of the boys started laughing. "Except for helping my mom slice food for cooking, I've never really touched a knife."

The other boy held his hand out. There was a small deep cut bleeding from one finger. "I cut myself from holding that stupid knife so tightly."

Mordi covered his face with his good hand. "I don't believe this. Why did you do this?"

"Because," said Arthur with tears filling his eyes. "You are a priest of God and, perhaps, our only hope." Mordi hugged him.

"God bless you all. I have never seen so much faith or bravery in children your age. You are the real hope of Aris-Akana."

Galincia felt something touch his forehead.

"He's alive," said Crazon. "Only barely. God give us the strength to save this one."

Anam had left the others behind, two days before, as they were moving so slowly. He sped ahead with Crazon, Zoana and Togorasom. Now, they only wished they had left sooner. Crazon took a few drops of water and moistened Galincia's lips.

"Can you hear me, man?" asked Anam on his knees next to the young priest. "We are here to help you."

"What can we do?" asked Zoana.

Anam stood up and looked around.

Zoana continued. "The man is going fast. We have little water and no supplies." She closed her eyes and touched his forehead with her fingertips. "Dear Lord, we have found your dove. Teach us what we can do. Reach into this poor shepherd's body, right now, and cleanse him and heal him. All things are possible through you, Father."

"We need water to clean him. He needs shade from the sun. He needs some type of nourishment," said Anam, gazing off into the distance. "There is a city near here. We will take him there."

"That is the city which has scourged him," said Togorasom. "Nevertheless, we must go there. This man is their priest, and they need to see him be victorious."

When the group arrived in the city, the residents watched them closely and were silent. They had never seen people with grey-colored flesh and were not prepared for the priest's return on the back of a large man with two beautiful women and a young boy. Mostly, they were terrified.

The Rasomites approached the doorway of the first home of great size they saw and, without speaking, moved passed the well-dressed man and woman who met them. The two women immediately saw a lovely quilt, neatly folded, lying on a trunk. They quickly cleared the table and spread the quilt upon it.

"What is the meaning of this intrusion?" asked the man, placing his hands on the quilt to remove it.

Togorasom tapped the man on the arm. "I think you had best either go away and be quiet or be willing to help."

"And who are you, little one?" he asked.

"I am a prophet of God. Would you go get a bowl of cool water, please? Oh yes, and some sponges or soft washing towels."

The man's eyes grew large and he went to the kitchen sink, where he began to fill a large earthen bowl with water.

Anam had lain Galincia on the table. Now, the man's wife came forward.

"You are making a mess of my home," she said, looking around at the group. "I demand that you leave immediately."

Anam looked down at the woman, as he was much greater in stature than she. "Do you have any very weak wine or, perhaps, a bit of goat's milk?" She looked into his face, opening and closing her mouth several times without speaking.

"I said..." he started again.

"I know, I heard you," she said nervously. "I have both, which do you prefer?"

"It's not for me, madame, but for your priest."

She looked at the bloody, sunburned, dehydrated man on the table and looked back at Anam. "I thought he was dead. I'm sorry."

Galincia moved his hand just enough to touch hers. She drew

back as though bitten by a snake. "I...I'll get a little wine in a cup," she said, backing away.

By this time, a very large crowd of people had begun to gather in front of the house. It was a mixed group. Some were yelling to remove Galincia from the city. Some were excited for his return. Most stood in silence to see what would happen next.

The owner of the home and the two Rasomite women began to carefully wash down Galincia's body.

"There is nothing else we can do here, my son," said Anam to Togorasom. "It's time we went to the people who are responsible for this. Let us go and hope they shall be willing to repent of this act."

Togorasom shook his head. "They shall not. But I should like to meet this King who is so eager to make Hell on earth."

"No, really. That's fine, Arthur."

The priest lay his head back on the pillow the boy had propped up for him against the wall.

"I wish I had more for you," replied Arthur.

"Oh, my lad. You've fed me, provided drink, and washed me. You've tended my wound and given me a pillow for my head. What more could you do?"

"I would, if I could, have you free."

"By the way," Mordi asked as he furrowed his brow, "whatever happened to the guard who was watching my cell?"

Arthur reluctantly spoke. "I think, just yet, I'm not quite able to talk about that."

They were hiding in an abandoned basement of a printing shop. All of the windows were shuttered, and there was a heavy bar over the doorway that led to the street. Some light was provided through the cracks in the flooring above them, and there was one hole in the wall about the size of a fist, which provided a perfect view of the main street.

The other two boys had gone out to see what Garanus' reaction would be to this escape. They had found a water pump near the building, and a friend of Arthur's had offered food upon his request without asking what trouble he was in.

"How is your, ah...?" Arthur pointed at Mordi's stub of an arm, not certain what to call it.

"Well, the pain has subsided and the bleeding has stopped. I had lost a great deal of blood, but I am regaining my strength. I shall always be grateful to you for a daring rescue."

Arthur flushed. "Well, actually, it was pretty stupid. But we had to do something real fast."

"So you risked your own lives?"

They heard a noise at the door and both silently held their breath.

"Arthur, quickly, let us in," one of his friends whispered. "We have great news."

Quickly, the doorway was opened, flooding the room with light and quickly closed. Both of the boys began at the same time.

"One at a time, please," Arthur whispered. "Gregor."

"We thought how we could find news the fastest, so we went to the 'Scallywag Shot' and swept floors."

"That bawdy house is the most disgusting drinking place in the city," interrupted Mordi.

"Aye, the worst filth of Goranus' troops drink and fight there," answered Gregor. "As was our line of thought."

"We fled for our lives," said Piper, the other boy.

"Let me finish. So, we found that the King is extremely angry and has issued a decree that every young boy in the city shall be brought before himself and Pholipi to be judged and either released with a mark or killed as they see fit."

"Because of me," said Mordi, getting to his feet. "I shall go to that old devil, and that will be the end of it."

"Oh, no. No. Please sit. There's more," said Piper. "As we were coming back, we heard an awful excitement erupting. At first, we thought an awful thing could be happening. A great man and a small boy appeared and were headed toward the palace."

"And they had grey skin," interjected Gregor.

"Yes. But the people were saying many things about this man. Some cheered and others fell to their knees and wept. They also say," said Piper, quietly dropping his head and then looking back at Mordi, "Galincia has come back. But he is dead. I'm sorry."

Mordi leaned back against the wall and was very quiet for a long time. The boys sat by, being very silent as they allowed the priest to shed tears. Finally, he spoke up. "The man who is going to Goranus. What of him? How is he called?"

"I don't know," said Gregor, trying to remember. "Things were happening so fast and we were afraid."

"He is a big man with grey skin," said Piper. "I think they called him Anam, or something like that. I'm not sure."

The priest bolted to his feet. "The savior, Anam, has come to us. Oh, praise God. Hallelujah!"

"Anam?" the boys said to each other.

"Who is Anam?" asked Arthur.

"Oh, some said he was a fairy story. Just made up. But there is a tale in old Mozana about a man coming from the desert with a powerful army, and his name is Anam. We must find him."

"I think we must wait," said Gregor, "for he is gone to Goranus. But, if we go to Galincia, I am sure that this Anam shall come back."

"I am old and impatient, but you are correct. Let us go to Galincia first."

"By the living God, I condemn you and your house for your crimes you have brought against the people of this city and the folly you have brought down upon them," screamed Anam from the courtyard to Goranus, who watched with amusement from the balcony above. "Before this sin is chased away, many shall die. They shall die in the darkness you have given them."

"You entertain me, man. Say on."

As Anam spoke, he and Togorasom were being surrounded by several of the king's archers, both on the balcony, which encircled most of the courtyard, and below the balcony. Each man fell into formation about three paces from the other. All wore mail and stood with their bows strung and ready to fire.

"I urge you to repent of this. You are a leader. You, of all men, should know that people look upon you as one who is skilled and wise. But, instead, you have turned upon your own lusts. Even now, you can go back. But why is it that you cannot see? Are you so blind?"

Goranus shook his fat, greasy body. "You make me laugh," he said as he walked down the stairway. "Why this craving for righteousness? What is right? I am King, so I am the one who says what is right. I beat and drove one fool into the desert to die, and you shall soon join his ugly soul."

"Galincia, who you say you killed, is alive and living in the city. Mordi, who you say is your prisoner, is free. The people are yelling praise for God. Despite all this, you are still an idiot."

Goranus stood before the man and boy.

"How dare you call me an idiot. The old fool shall be found. The young fool is of little concern to me. In a few moments, you will both be turned into pincushions. Then, we shall hear what the people shout. They shall shout, 'good riddance'. Do you have any thought-provoking comments to make before I have you killed?" He looked Anam in the eye.

Togorasom looked up at Anam and then at the King. "I say you should cower in fear, beg forgiveness and warn your archers to do the same."

Goranus looked at the boy. "I don't deal with children." He waved his arm around at the men poised for firing. There were nearly a hundred. "Is the child insane? Does he not see death staring at him?"

"Can I assume you will not repent?" asked Anam. Goranus did not move. Anam looked up at the sky and back to the ground. "Dear Lord," he said quietly, "what fools. We can do nothing for them. I commend them unto you." He looked at the boy. "Let us go."

Goranus had walked back under the shelter of the veranda among the archers and now raised his hand as he prepared to raise his voice and order them to stay, but his voice was drowned out by the great roar of the sound of the balcony and part of the walls of the palace giving way. In a few seconds, the action was done. The King's men of war were either scrambling about helplessly from shock or were lying buried under tons of concrete and stone, dead or near death. Goranus ran about the yard frantically pulling at his troops in an attempt to organize them. When he realized the futility of his activity, he prepared to turn again on the man and boy, but they were gone.

Struggling over the debris, Goranus was able to reach the gates of the palace. He did not know if he was seeking escape or if he was after revenge toward this man of God. He left the palace frustrated, dirty and angry. He did not expect Anam to be waiting for him.

"Oh, you foolish man," said Anam when Goranus approached him. "You have so often been afforded the opportunity to repent and change your ways. Today, you shall learn of God's vengeance for those who do not follow the Lord. Today, you shall fall under the plague, and your own son shall murder you. For your only son is not yours, at all, but the child of Satan." Anam and Togorasom turned and walked away, leaving the King shaking in fear and unable to even speak. He ran back into the palace in terror.

Once inside the dusty hallways adjoining the garden, he crumbled in despair and fell to the floor. He wept for several minutes without interruption. When the balcony had given way, everyone had fled that area into other parts of the building. However, eventually Goranus sensed that someone was watching him. He looked up.

"You fat, old fool," said Pholipi. "Did you expect that you could live this life forever with no consequences? You have spread death and sickness throughout Aris-Akana and, now, you are a failure. You should have set aside one good act against the day of judgment."

"But one act. Yes, my son," he wept. "One act. When you came to me alone and hurt, I took you in."

"This act was your gravest error. Now, you are dead."

"No. No, my son. Help me, and we shall reign together." The King was so fat, he could not even struggle to rise from the floor where he had curled up. "Help me, my child." Goranus smiled weakly.

"You are a fat, old pig." Pholipi picked up a very large piece of broken block lying on the floor and hoisted it over his head.

Goranus screamed, but only for a moment. The block fell upon his head, cracked his skull, and he died instantly.

"Zoana!" The Rasomite warrior opened her eyes and looked around to see who had called her. It was very dark in the bedroom where she sat guard over the still barely-alive young priest. Also, it was very hot in this room. The wealthy family, who were the owners of the house, had given themselves wholly to God after spending the day with the Rasomite women.

When the old priest and his three young friends had appeared and witnessed his great love for this nearly-dead man of God, the couple were moved further to obey God and had dedicated everything they owned to the Rasomites and the Mozanas, as much as was needed. They had moved Galincia into this patio bedroom, because it was much more suitable to the situation. The adjoining garden was lovely. There was more room for gatherings and visitors.

Zoana cleared the sweat from her brow and looked around the room. Besides Galincia's presence were also Mordi and Arthur. Arthur's friends had finally gone home, but Arthur had vowed to remain at Mordi's side forever. The priest and his young friend were both sound asleep. Zoana was certain she had been awake. Her eyes were heavy and the heat added to her fatigue, but she would not sleep on duty. The woman stood up and moved closer to Galincia. She wondered if he had spoken. The man's forehead was still warm and air still left his lungs. He lived but was not conscious.

"Zoana," came the call again. The voice seemed audible but was more sensed by her mind than heard by her ears. She pushed open the garden doors and felt the cool relief of the late night air. It might have been better to stay outside than in the hot room. Nothing in the garden moved. Zoana twisted her head around to stretch her neck in an effort to shake off the tiredness. What time was it? Crazon would soon be relieving her and would stay until dawn.

She felt a cold chill all over her body. It was not caused by the night air. Her hand grasped the handle of the dagger slung to her waist as her eyes carefully scanned the garden. To the normal eye, the garden would appear only as darkness, except for those things close by. However, she applied all of her perception and was able to see everything in the area quite clearly. Nothing moved. Quietly, she moved along the garden path that encircled most of the house. Perhaps, she should go back and warn the others, or at least awaken the old priest. But, perhaps, she only imagined the voice. She kept moving.

Then she saw a person in the darkness near one of the garden gates. It was an elderly Rasomite woman.

"Zoana, my darling," she said. "They told me you were here, and I did not believe them. It has been so long." The woman moved forward a few steps but, when she saw how nervous the younger woman acted, she stopped. "Don't you remember me?" she asked with a smile.

"I seem to remember, but it seems so odd. I cannot remember who you are." Laughing and crying at the same time, the older woman held out her hands. "I am old and silly. Of course you don't remember me. I am Asafa, your mother. You do remember? Please, remember. I know you were only a baby, not quite two."

"Mama, Mother!" said Zoana as tears started to fill her eyes. "I can hardly believe it," she said as she ran to the old woman and embraced her. "I thought you were dead. I thought they had killed you."

"They would have killed me. They beat us. They raped us. Every foul manner of thing was committed against us. Then, they made one mistake and we were able to escape. We were pursued and so, we continued to run. Until we came here. No one knew us here. We were just strange women. They left us alone. There were four of us who arrived, but the others have passed on. I believe I have lived for this day. Today is the happiest day of my life."

"Zoana!" called a voice from the house. It was Anam.

"I must return. I am a Rasomite warrior, and I am also guarding the young priest. Come with me."

The two women turned and headed back on the garden path. When they reached the doorway, Zoana entered the room first and saw Anam standing at the foot of the bed with an angry scowl on his face. She had never seen him before seem so upset with her.

"Do not be angry," said Zoana, spirits high. "I heard someone in the garden so I investigated. At first, I was not certain what should be done. However, everything is fine. I am very pleased this night for I am reunited with my mother, Asafa." She motioned her hand toward the garden. However, no one entered. No one was there. "Mother!" called Zoana. She stepped outside and glanced around.

"Is there someone in the garden?" asked Anam patiently. "Where are they?"

"Really, my Lord. I heard a voice calling me from the garden. I went out and found an old Rasomite woman. I can barely remember her as I was only a tiny child when I lost her. The Atrocenes took her away. She says that she escaped to this city."

Anam walked to the doorway and looked into the garden. "Come here," he said. They walked across the brick patio to the path she had followed. "Look." He pointed at the sandy walkway. Before dark, the groundskeepers had cleaned up the garden and their last act had been to rake out all of the paths. The marks of the rake tines could still be easily seen on the path. "There is one set of bare feet leading out and one set returning. Would there not be two sets coming back? Did the woman follow you this far?"

In dismay, Zoana both nodded and then, shook her head. "I do not understand. The old woman followed me all the way to here," she said, moving back to the door.

Anam held her and then looked into her tear-filled eyes. "Are you tired? It is not at all like you to allow your mind to play tricks on you. I think you should rest."

Mordi had come out onto the patio and looked out into the darkness. Zoana sat on a bench connected to the outside wall of the patio.

"I will stay here in case she returns," she said. "I cannot go away now."

"I understand," said Anam. "But I want you to rest. I will sit in the room with Mordi over the young priest."

"There is one thing that bothers me," said Mordi. "I am a very old man. I have lived in Aris-Akana for over seventy years. I believe I have seen just about everyone. Until I met you, I never knew a Rasomite. There are no other Rasomite people in this city."

"I saw my mother!" retorted Zoana. "I spoke with her. I embraced her. We mingled our tears of joy."

"Zoana," said Anam. "I want you to control yourself. I know you are no fool. Don't let emotions get in the way of your logic."

"But I saw her. I spoke with her."

"Lie down on the bench and try to get some sleep. I probably could not convince you to sleep elsewhere. I shall be watching you very closely."

Anam and Mordi went back inside and, eventually, Zoana fell to sleep.

"Zoana. I have come back."

The young Rasomite woman opened her eyes and picked up her head to see Asafa standing by her.

"Mother. Mother, where did you go?"

"I remembered the old man was here and, as glad as my heart was for you, I had no interest in mincing words with him."

"You mean Mordi, the priest? He seems good. We have spoken at length. We have differences of belief, but much common ground, and one God."

Zoana got up as they moved about the patio.

"I still say," said Asafa, "to be very careful with these

Mozanas. I don't like them."

"Let us not argue of differences of religion. I praise God for bringing us together."

"Every day, I rotted in that Atrocene pig sty, and I always fell on my knees and begged God. On the day I cursed him, we were free."

"However, perhaps," said Zoana, "God forgave you that day and remembered your fatigue and your bitterness and mostly your prayers and delivered you away."

Asafa scowled. "I doubt it. The day I was free, I gave up on worship and spent my time enjoying life."

"Then, my mother, we have a serious problem. I can never give up on my God. He is my salvation. Even in death, he is my redeemer."

"Foolishness. And what has it gotten you?"

"Without faith, I would doubtless have never ventured near this city and been with you."

"If the Rasomites didn't believe the slop about being a chosen people, they would not have the problems that are dealt to them. But, enough of this. Let's not argue. So much like mother and daughter." The old woman laughed. "Do you have children?"

Zoana laughed. "Mother, as I said, I am a Rasomite warrior. Besides, except for Anam, all the men are gone."

"All of the men are dead? Even old Mebiktu?"

"We buried Mebiktu in the desert two years ago. He had a beautiful death."

"Will you stop that, woman. This is old religious nonsense," said Asafa, bitterly. "I want you to stop it."

"I am sorry if speaking of Mebiktu's death offended you, but it was clear that God was present."

"So, are there any more of you? I mean, are there others left?"

"The rest are on their way here. The women and children."

"It's a shame there are no babies," said Asafa, thoughtfully. "I would like to play Gramma."

"Some of the young girls will soon bear children, and Paluqua has four little ones. She is the wife of Anam."

"So, she is a better woman than you?"

"I don't understand."

"This Paluqua, is she your better because she has progeny or your worse because she's not one of these great warriors?"

"I have not seen you for all these many years. Why must you belittle me with everything I stand for?"

"I had hoped you would have had a good life and become somebody."

"I am somebody. I am one of the best Rasomite warriors and, perhaps someday, will be commander of the Shamra."

"Shamra?"

"That is us. We are the Shamra. Not only in flesh, but also in spirit. Ours is a battle against Satan, both in the flesh and in the spirit."

"Here we go. You are boring me. Do you know anything else?"

Zoana held Asafa close to her. "You act so much like a mother. I'd have hoped for more. We are going to have problems, but you are still my mother and I dearly want to love you."

"Then, you'll have to start putting away all the nonsense, dear."

"Zoana. Zoana, wake up, please."

She sat up and shook her head. Anam was on his knees before her. She had been asleep. The whole episode had been a dream.

"Anam," she said, trying not to cry. "I have been dreaming. I still do not understand what is happening. It was so real. I was standing right here with my mother when you awoke me."

"I hesitated to wake you, but I knew you were having a very troubled sleep. What is wrong?"

"I can't say just yet. I'm very confused." She stood up. "I'm going inside to sleep. It makes me nervous out here."

"What makes you nervous?"

"My mother has said many bad things about our feelings and our people. But I cannot agree."

"You are being tempted." He kissed her on the cheek. "I will be ready to listen when you are ready to talk. Crazon also is understanding. You can talk with her."

"Thank you." She started walking inside and dropped her head a little as a sign of her despair. "I thought," she said when she was out of Anam's hearing, "I was doing so well. But, right now, I feel like a failure. And why do I feel so bitter about life?"

She found the bed that had been offered to her earlier, lay down, and almost instantly fell asleep. It seemed like only a few minutes had passed by when she heard a voice call her, "Zoana." Pretending to be sound in sleep, she did not move or open her eyes.

"I know you are awake." She recognized Crazon's voice and sat up, staring her good friend in the face.

"I am glad you came to me," she answered, "but I needed the sleep. Did Anam send you?"

"Of course not. I came of my own volition."

"I am glad."

"You are glad," laughed Crazon. "I came to put you to work. Paluqua and the others are expected to arrive in a few hours. I want you to finish my watch so I can get some rest and be suitably cleaned-up before they arrive."

"But didn't Anam tell you about my dreams and my mother?" Zoana could hardly believe her best friend wanted to take such an advantage of her.

"Anam said nothing about any of your problems," snapped Crazon. "I want you to finish my watch. I care for neither your mother nor your dreams. Please, get up." She turned and walked from the room.

Zoana was angry. Her head hurt. It was difficult to keep her eyes open. However, Crazon would not put a demand upon her like this for no reason, so she would get up and help her friend. Still, a good explanation was in order. She looked out into the hall and could see the window at the far end. It was just beginning to be daylight. She had managed to get at least four hours of sleep and had often been able to go for a long time on less. Why, then, was she so weary now? She entered the large garden bedroom. Crazon and the young priest were the only two present, and the Rasomite stood up and smiled when Zoana came in.

"I'm so glad you came. Did you sleep well?"

"What do you care? I'm not pleased at all and, no, I did not get enough sleep!"

"What is wrong, sister?" Crazon asked as she approached her.

"I'm angry! That's all!" Zoana was shouting. When she realized Crazon was walking towards her, she swung around to avoid her and struck her head against the metal door. The concussion nearly knocked her out. She started to fall to her knees but grabbed at the door on the way down to pull herself back up. Crazon's hand was supporting her. "Leave me alone!" she yelled, almost in tears. "Just leave me be." She fled from the room. Crazon started to follow her, but decided against it because of her duty.

Zoana ran from the house. The noise would only arouse Anam

and the others who would be very willing to extend their sympathy and healing hands. She didn't want it. She wanted to be alone. She ran out to the street and veered off into an alley. After jumping a fence, she fell to the ground out of sight from her supposed pursuers. She looked around and realized that she was on another not-so-busy street. It was, in fact, deserted at the time. She closed her eyes.

"I'm confused. I'm tired. My head hurts. No one cares."

Suddenly, there was an answer. "You are, I perceive, a stranger to Aris-Akana." Zoana opened her eyes and jumped back so quickly she nearly upset the old picket fence. She leapt to her feet with her dagger drawn.

Pholipi stood before her with no weapon and unable to defend himself. "Caution, stranger. Who are you?"

"You know who I am, Son of Satan. Get away!"

"If I leave," he said quietly, "I must call the authorities and have them throw you in prison. You are a Rasomite woman? You are the one I seek."

"Go away," she said again. "I know who you are."

"I am Pholipi."

"You are a liar. You are Artero. You have sought me to destroy me."

The man before her bore an amazing likeness to the once-dead headhunter. She was sure it could be no other.

"I think," he said slowly, "you are confused. Mine is a kind hand. I mean you no harm."

"You are a liar!" she yelled. "You are not a man. You are Satan."

"I have not been good. I want to change. I mean to extend the hand of fellowship."

"How can you lie?"

He showed that his patience was wearing thin. "Look, woman. The King is dead. I rolled out of my bed early this morning to find you and the young priest, Galincia."

The similarity of Pholipi to Artero was too uncanny. The fear of trying to barter and reason with a man who might be Satan was incomprehensible to Zoana. She was afraid. She tried to think quickly in what way she should react. She wondered if he really sensed her fear. Perhaps, he could even read her mind.

"You are very beautiful," he said. "I do not mean this as one who merely ogles, but as a compliment to your femininity." It had been a long time since a man had told her she was physically attractive. "I wish you'd put your blade away. It really does make me nervous. Especially as I am quite unarmed. I think you are disoriented and tired. Please, relax. I won't hurt you."

It had been a long time since Crazon had made her prophesy concerning Artero. It had not been forgotten completely, but it had not occupied all her thoughts. The two peaceful years had lent a great calm to the people. Also, she was tired. She had only seen the headhunter for a few seconds before he had died and, then, he had disappeared. Some people had suggested several possibilities of the whereabouts of the body and the meaning of the prophesy as to allay her fear.

Now, this handsome young man stood before her. He was wearing a cream-colored tunic that fell to his knees and leather sandals on his feet. If this was the prince of Aris-Akana, she was at least impressed by his simple clothing. There was no mark or crown or emblem that would indicate his rank. His long, blond hair fell almost to his shoulders. The young man's bright blue eyes seemed to create in her a longing to know this man better before condemning him. She sheathed her dagger.

"I'm sorry I acted so quickly. I am a warrior and, often, we must first judge and then ask questions. Have you always lived in this city?"

"I was born to Goranus' first wife twenty-four years ago in the palace. I am not a traveler and have never been more than a day or two away from home. Can we, therefore, be friends?" He extended his right hand.

Zoana shook her head slightly. "Let us go very slow. I am not quite ready for friendship. Be patient."

"I have, then, done what I set out to do. The King, who has destroyed this city, was killed yesterday when a piece of the palace wall, that your gallant young leader destroyed, fell on his head. A fitting end. Today is a new day for Aris-Akana. I shall try to lead them as best I can. I must return home. I do hope that it is possible we spend a great deal of time together. I believe when you learn I shall never try to deceive you, we can be friends. I like you." He turned to leave.

"Wait," she said. "One question." He turned back. "An old woman came to me earlier. She was a Rasomite woman, therefore, she also had flesh the same color as mine. Are there other Rasomites in this city?"

"Several years ago, a group of refugees came to us. They arrived at the palace and sought Goranus' attention." Anger started to cover his face, but then he relaxed. "There were about thirty of them altogether, among whom were four women, colored like you. If Goranus had had his way, they would have been tormented again as much as they had before. The people went away, but they kept returning. Finally, some of the Akanians took them in. I was only a baby at the time, but my step-mother explained these things." He looked Zoana in the face and smiled. "Why do you ask? I'm not sure if any of these women would still be alive."

She hesitated and tried to speak as a tear formed in one eye and a smile crossed her face. "One woman does live. She came to me in the night. Later, I think, I dreamed of her, but I'm not sure it was a dream." Pholipi nodded. "She's my mother. Her name is Asafa."

Pholipi's mouth opened in awe and then he smiled. "I am so happy for you. Now, I must go." He turned again.

"Wait. Another question." He looked over his shoulder at her. "The old priest, Mordi, said there were no Rasomites in this city. Why would he say that?"

"I must leave, but I leave you with one thought. Don't trust the Mozanas." He walked away.

Zoana leaned calmly back against the fence and watched the prince until he was out of sight. Then, she took a deep breath, climbed back over the fence, and returned to the house. However, she kept the blue-eyed prince and his words to herself.

"I just need to go for a walk. I've got a lot of things on my mind. Besides, we've been sitting in this house for too long," Zoana reasoned with Crazon and Anam.

"You are right," said Crazon patiently and looking at Anam. "However, perhaps I should go with you. It is a big city and, also, I would like a break."

"With your permission, Anam, I would like to go alone," Zoana asked.

"Will you be safe?" he asked.

"I shall be fine. I admit my purpose. I want to seek my mother.

Either I saw her and spoke with her last night or I imagined the entire thing. If I do not do this thing, I will remember it for the rest of my life."

"Then go. Keep in touch, because I know you shall not return until your curiosity is satisfied. If you do not return soon, send a messenger. Everyone knows where Galincia is lain. God be with you." Anam held her close and then kissed her on the forehead. She exchanged caresses with everyone in the house and, lastly, went to Galincia and softly kissed him on the cheek.

When Zoana left the house, she was feeling very good about herself. Her high-spirits were groundless. She had just told the first lie of her adult life. She felt that her reasoning was clear, as she was certain the others would not understand. Zoana headed for the palace.

"Mordi, come quickly," called Arthur. "It's Galincia. Anam says to come quickly."

The old priest had been walking about the garden in the front of the house and marveling at the good selection of plants that had adapted so well to the dry heat. He had seen Zoana leave a few minutes before and had not interrupted her departure. Either she had not seen him among the bushes or she had not cared. He had a bad feeling about her leaving but finally shrugged it off as just being sensible to the fact she would not find her mother.

When Arthur ran out from the house with his announcement, Mordi knew instantly that the worst had happened. Galincia was dead. He ran the first few paces but then realized its senselessness. There was nothing more that could be done.

When they entered the room, everyone else from the house was already there. Anam sat on the edge of the bed, holding Galincia's hand. Several people had arrived that morning from the temple and so the room was quite full. The weeping and wailing was overpowering. The people moved apart to allow the old priest to move forward. He placed his hand on Anam's shoulder and waited for him to open his eyes.

After several minutes, Anam arose, looked the old priest in the eye, and said, "Clear the room. It is important that everyone leave the room now. God has told me that this man's work is not done, but that he shall lead a revival. I must know more."

He looked around the room at the distraught gathering and said loudly, "Quickly, it is important that everyone leave. I believe that this man will live again."

A hush fell over the room as most of the people exchanged looks of awe. However, they were obedient. The priest was the last one out.

He looked back at Anam. "Not in the entire history of Aris-Akana has one risen from the dead. But I know, if God has told you, then it is so." He turned and left, closing the door behind him.

Anam felt himself passing through what was like a heavy fog, although it was not damp. In the mist, he sensed the presence of another and then was able to lay his eyes on him. The young priest was whole and healed and in his right mind. He wore a long white robe that fell to his feet. Around his neck, he wore a gold amulet of the fallen cross. This surprised Anam.

"My brother in God," started Galincia. "Do not speak, for I have little time and much to say. Though I am not with you now, I shall return once more and set things right in Aris-Akana. You see the cross. The symbol the priests of Foramen wore. I know you do not understand but, someday, you shall for you will set the cross straight. The woman, Zoana, is gone to the devil. But, she shall be victorious. She must do this alone. I know that you want me to come back. My chore is over on earth, but I shall return once. You shall understand later. Hear me. I have been before God's throne. His throne is of choice marble and crystal and gold. The walls are of gold the luster of which would pierce a man's eye, they are so pure. The walks and the standing-places are of gold and diamond, and more. But there is so much more. For all this is like nothing compared to the wisdom of God, and he is surrounded by thousands and millions and they all praise him. And you would have me go back? If I could, I would not want to. But you return, for your time is not yet."

Anam looked around. He was sitting on the bed next to the cold, dead body of Galincia. In spite of the heat of the day, Anam shivered as he tried to grasp the impact of what had been shared with him. Was it a dream? Of course not. He stood up and opened the bedroom door.

Mordi stood, leaning against the wall near the door, and looked anxiously upon Anam who was still speechless. There was a long, quiet moment as everyone waited to hear the news.

"I...I spoke to him," said Anam. "He doesn't want to come back." Tears began forming as he knew he could not share more.

He looked around the hall and lobby. Though his eyes met with a few patient faces, most of them were set in anger. They had expected a miracle and, now, they were listening to lame excuses. The people began getting up and leaving. The temple servants pushed passed Anam to remove and prepare the body for burial. The tears he shed were mistaken for tears of failure. He wished he could tell them everything, but he realized it would make little difference and also, he hoped, they would find out for themselves soon enough.

Anam could stand the pain no more, so he left the house and went into the adjoining garden so he could cry in peace. He sat, eyes closed, shaking uncontrollably, still unable to grasp the knowledge he had. He felt a hand on his thigh and opened his eyes to see Togorasom kneeling in front of him. He helped the boy to his feet.

Togorasom's eyes were also full of tears. "They shall," he said, "be repentant or grievous in the morning. My prayers are with Zoana."

Anam grasped the young prophet to his chest, and they moistened each other's flesh with their tears as Anam realized, again, the spiritual power of this little boy.

It was still fairly early in the morning when Zoana approached the palace. The front archway was partially broken away. She could see inside the courtyard that a great deal of destruction had indeed taken place, as she had been told. There was much activity. Workmen were attempting to lift huge slabs of concrete and marble with ropes and levers, as well as with their bare hands. As she stood by watching, they hoisted a flat slab that was several feet across, a few inches into the air. One man climbed underneath and quickly came back out, nodding his head. The huge cords were wrapped around the slab and then attached to a pulley that was suspended from the wall. In a few minutes, the piece of concrete had been hoisted six feet into the air. Several of the men carried the dead, crushed body of a soldier out of the rubble and laid him safely to one side before lowering the slab again.

Zoana felt someone's presence next to her and turned. It was Pholipi. He was still clad in the simple robe. Around his neck was an amulet with no insignia on it. It was merely a large gold circle about two inches across. He also wore a cloth headband around his forehead and was sweating profusely. She pointed to the amulet.

"A mere sign that I am their prince. It is no big deal, but I felt they should see it. This is hard, disgusting work. Yesterday, we removed all the injured and tended them. A few probably will not make it. I had decided, today, we would tend to the bodies. Unfortunately, one poor soul was trapped under the rubble and died when we tried to rescue him this morning." He looked like he was ready to cry. "This is not an easy task. I had to tell his new wife that he was dead. All this could have been spared if not for Goranus' ignorance. I don't understand what control that fat old fool had over me and everyone else." He put one hand on Zoana's bare shoulder. She didn't prevent him. "Even when confronted by that good man, Anam, he would not repent. Why are people so stubborn?"

"I don't know," she said, softly. "They prefer to live in darkness."

Pholipi removed his hand and looked down at his feet in shame. "I'm sorry I touched you. I had no right." He looked into her eyes. "But when I am near you I feel, I don't know, somehow special."

"You are special." She put the cup of her hand on his forearm. "You are the King of Aris-Akana."

"I don't feel special for that reason when I am near you. I feel chosen. You are so warm and so beautiful. Would you like to see the rest of the palace? Most of it is quite intact."

"I came here to see you and the palace."

They climbed over the rubble beneath the archway where they had been standing and entered what had been the courtyard. The wall surrounding the area was almost completely wiped out, and one could see the inside of the hallways and adjoining rooms. These areas had already been cleaned out by the palace servants. While Zoana and Pholipi had been speaking, the working crew had located yet another body, which was carefully deposited with a growing number of corpses. Lined up in two rows along a clear area were about fifty dead men. As Zoana scanned the bad situation, another dead body was discovered beneath the rubble. Pholipi took her hand.

"Come with me."

They entered a long hallway and passed through several closed doors until they reached a throne room at the far end.

"What should I do with the palace?" asked Pholipi as he spun partly around to bring attention to the gala they were surrounded with. "I don't need a palace. I don't need a hundred servants. I am not too excited about all this pomp. Perhaps, a nice house with a few trusted helpers. A good cook. A gardener." He sat down on the throne steps at her feet. "I don't need all this nonsense. Do you know that, since the plague, there are so many sick. As many as a hundred a day are dying. What a waste." He looked around thoughtfully. "We could turn this into a hospital. There are so many sleeping rooms. These could be wards and we shall get the best help available to find a cure and wait by the sick."

"Pholipi," she said softly.

"There is a doctor," he said. "What is his name?" he asked and closed his eyes in thought. "I don't remember his name. Good man. He says he may have a cure. Another thing," he said, getting up and walking away a few paces, "is feeding these people. There seem to be so many hungry. I believe they have simply given up."

"Pholipi," she said again.

He turned around and looked at her. "You think I'm mad?"

"No, I don't think you're mad," she answered, smiling. "I think you're wonderful. How could I have misjudged you? You have such a kind heart."

"Of course, I care for these people. Times are so bad. They need a patient and thoughtful leader."

"Pholipi! Your majesty!" yelled a worker as he ran in. He fell to his knees. "A thousand pardons, but I have good news. The elders of the city are gathered at the front of the palace. They are here to crown you as King."

"Rise up, man," said Pholipi, taking him by the arm. "Rise up. I am only a man who is a leader of men."

The worker looked at Zoana. "I am sorry for this intrusion, my princess. But this is of such import."

"Of course it is," she said. "Pholipi, you go to the people. I shall wait here, and you can tell me of it. Be slow. Remember, patience and understanding."

"I shall return quickly for you," he said. He backed out of the room, watching her.

Zoana got up and walked around the room a bit. Then, she walked up the steps and sat on the throne. It was wonderful.

Closing her eyes, she pictured the room full of people who had come before her for counsel or judgment, and she was quite willing to share her wisdom. She smiled at the game and heard someone enter. She was ashamed of herself being caught at this foolishness and opened her eyes.

"Mother!" she exclaimed and started to get up.

"You stay where you are." Zoana settled back into the chair. "Your royal majesty," said Asafa as she curtsied and winked at Zoana. She could play at the game, as well. "I need your advice on a certain subject."

"Say on, maid," said Zoana as she playfully raised one hand.

"I have a beautiful and very kind daughter. She has done very well for herself, in spite of an arduous life and having to live with uncertainty. She has been away from home for a long time and now she has come back, but I fear, she shall leave again." Zoana tried to interrupt. "Wait, your majesty. There is more. Her mother is old and lonely. The poor woman has no real means of support. If her daughter left now, she would be grief-stricken." Zoana again tried to stop her. "Be patient, queen. I am nearly done. But there is more. A wealthy and handsome prince has fallen in love with the young woman." Zoana sank back into the throne. "The man has a good heart and he means well. However, his evil and immoral father has recently passed away and left the kingdom a shambles. There are little children with no fathers. Sick who are in need of nursing. Hungry who need to be fed. The young woman is a holy and righteous woman of God, however, perhaps she has no time for such things. Maybe, she could get her great leader to say a prayer before they leave and the new King will be able to do it all by himself."

"Stop it!" yelled Zoana. "Please, stop it."

"Why? Does the truth hurt that much?" asked Asafa, sternly. "I understand that in another city, it was decided it would be a good thing to leave a young Rasomite woman to help lead the city. And why? Because it was convenient since she had fallen in love with a young leader herself. Are you less? Of course not. Besides, I want you to stay. You have crossed mountains and deserts looking for a home. Zoana, today you are home. Please, don't leave me." Asafa broke down into tears and started shaking. "I...I just couldn't stand it if I were to lose you again."

Zoana leapt down from the throne and held Asafa. They were

both crying. "Don't cry, mother. Please, don't cry. I'll never leave you." Asafa looked into Zoana's eyes and, though her tears still flowed, she began to get hold of herself. "Really, mother. I shall never leave you. I will stay in Aris-Akana or I shall take you to another place if that is not possible."

"I...I cannot travel far in the desert."

"I know. We'll work it out. Do not fret." A movement caught her eye, and she looked up. Pholipi was standing near the entrance.

"I'm sorry," he said. "It was not meant, I mean, I did not want to intrude."

"It's fine, Pholipi. Allow me to present my mother. The mother I thought I had lost. I have her back. I have vowed I shall never leave her."

Pholipi fell to one knee and took Asafa's hand. "I am honored," he said and kissed the back of her hand.

"Oh my," said Asafa. "Do get up, your majesty. This is embarrassing. I'm just an old beggar woman."

"You are a gem," he stated. He stood up and looked at Zoana. "I can barely stand it. Whenever I think of you, I can think of nothing else. I have a question. You have just made it easier for me to ask. I have just come from the city elders. They want to crown me as King. I told them that everything must change if I consent. I have told them another thing. I cannot be King without a queen. I will not accept the title unless..." He looked down.

"Unless what, Pholipi?" Zoana asked.

"Unless," he said looking up, "you marry me and be my Queen."

Zoana was speechless. The three of them cast nervous glances back and forth. Finally, she said, "This is a hard decision. I need time. I cannot answer it so quickly."

"Will you consider it?" he asked.

"Yes, I will consider it."

"Then, I shall consider accepting the crown. I must know your feelings very soon, for there is so very much to do." He backed out of the room. "I must inform the people. Thank you, your majesty." He smiled. "Do you like the sound of that?"

"Yes," she replied. "I like the sound of that."

Zoana tossed and turned in the spacious bed. Never had she

been surrounded by so much glamour. However, they had discussed all of this. It was all going to go, whether or not she decided to stay with the prince. He was moving along as though everything was decided, but he was being very careful not to push her into a decision. It seemed so obvious. This was an opportunity to practice everything she believed in. There was no one in the city that did not have great needs. They would build orphanages, hospitals, special homes for the old and handicapped. They would rebuild the economy from the foundation. They were brimming with ideas. She loved him. She knew he was an idealist. That a lot of his spur-of-the-moment ideas would fall short. However, whenever she was near him, she felt drawn to him like a magnet. He loved her. He told her how beautiful she was. He had even bent over and kissed her feet. He was so good-looking and so charming. His long, blond hair and deep, blue eyes excited her. She longed for him to touch her, but he was so careful about that. She had great respect for him.

Suddenly, she heard a rattle at the door and it opened. Anam stepped in and quietly closed it. He was angry. "You lied," he snapped. "Why have you done this?"

"I didn't really lie." Zoana sat up in bed to defend herself. "I did come here, but I also found my mother."

"These people have led you away from the only good people in the city. You have become garbage, just like them."

"How dare you!" she yelled. "Get out of here! How dare you slink in here and accuse him, and you don't even know him. I happen to love him."

"Shut up! I came to take you with me."

"Well, I'm not going. I have decided to stay here. I am going to stay with my mother, and I may even marry the prince."

"You'll do what I say!"

"Get out of my room!" she screamed.

The door again rattled and Anam moved aside. Asafa came in and looked at Zoana. "I heard you crying, dear. I thought you were having a nightmare. Oh!" she exclaimed when she noticed Anam. "What are you doing here?"

"I came for her," he said sharply. "Now get out of my way."

"I think she won't go unless she wants to." She tried to pull the man, several times her size, out of the room.

"Let go of my arm," he said, shaking her loose. She fell to the floor. She stood up and grabbed a leather boot lying on the floor and started beating him.

"Mother, no," yelled Zoana, getting out of the bed.

It was too late. Anam pulled his dagger and, shaking with rage, shrieked, "I said to leave me alone." Asafa backed off in fear as the dagger came down upon her. He plunged it into her chest. She fell to the floor, shaking and trying to catch her breath. He carefully swung his foot and struck her in the head. She fell backward, unconscious. "I'll be back for you!" he hollered as he ran from the room.

Zoana fell to the floor over her mother. Asafa was dead. For a second, she hesitated as to what she should do. Then, she hurried out of the doorway. Anam had just turned the corner at the end of the hallway and was now out of her sight.

"Stop him!" she screamed. "Stop him. He killed my mother. Stop him!" She fell to her knees.

Suddenly, several armed soldiers came from another hallway in pursuit of the intruder. Zoana sat in a daze and suddenly realized what could happen. She ran after them. When she reached the front entrance, she could see in the yard what had happened. The men surrounded a slumped-over figure. She slowly walked outside, stunned. In the darkness of the night, she fell to her knees over Anam.

"I can't believe all this has happened." She was beyond tears and in shock. Asafa was dead. Anam was dead. She looked around at the soldiers. No one spoke. Someone sat beside her and put his arm around her.

"Oh, Zoana. Oh, my darling," said Pholipi. She held him and put her head on his shoulder. "I do not know what to say to ease your pain."

"He killed my mother," she mumbled, "but I never wanted him slain."

"This man of God is a murderer? I know it will be hard, but you must forget him."

"He killed my mother." She held Pholipi so tight she hurt him, but he did not let go. "Oh, Pholipi, help me."

"I shall never leave you."

"Togorasom, are you awake?"

The young boy picked up his head. "Very," he said. He yawned. "I couldn't sleep well. There's too much going on."

"I agree with that," said Anam. "I am very concerned over Zoana. She has not merely gone out to seek her mother."

"I know," said Togorasom. He sat up and looked out the window. "It's late," he announced. He looked back at Anam. "She has to do this herself. You know that."

"I know," he said, nervously looking around. "Perhaps, my faith is weak. I'm not confident."

"I can think of only one thing to do," he said. "Why don't you go back to sleep?" Togorasom yawned again and stretched.

"I suppose," Anam shrugged, "we can't do much from here." He left the room.

"I guess I won't get any sleep again, tonight," Togorasom said to himself as he began to pray.

"Zoana," said Pholipi as he paced back and forth before the throne. "You must forget that man. You must forget everything he stood for. He did, I know, many good deeds. But when one can sink so low to do what he did," he stopped and looked at her, "how can he be forgiven?"

Zoana sat slumped back against the throne, only paying half-attention to the prince. She was still in shock. The events that had just taken place were beyond her comprehension. She'd had her life planned before Anam had snuck in. Why didn't he come in broad daylight, like he usually did? Why had he changed so suddenly? Pholipi was standing beside her, leaning against the throne.

"I shouldn't pressure you. I'm sorry," he said, taking her hand. She gave him a blank look.

Suddenly, she had a flash in her mind of a young boy in prayer. She looked at Pholipi as he grimaced, and then a patient smile crossed his face.

"Pholipi?"

"Yes, darling?" he asked carefully.

"Can you read my mind?"

"Huh?" he backed up and scrutinized her. "What do you mean? Of course not! How silly a question. I think you need some sleep. You've been through a great deal."

"You're so handsome."

"I said you need some sleep," he said quietly.

"I want to touch you." She smiled as her change in attitude threw him off.

"Stop it! You're making me nervous. Why are you doing this?"

"I want to run my fingers through your hair. I want to run my hands all over your beautiful body. I asked you before, this morning, how long have you lived in Aris-Akana?"

"I answered you. All my life."

"You look so much like another man I used to know. He was very good-looking also." She stood up and acted as though to hold him. He backed off. "My darling. What is the matter? I want to touch you."

"I am not afraid of you," he said slowly.

"Are you afraid of my friend that is with me?"

"What are you talking about?" He looked around.

"No. No. My friend. Right here." She placed her fist over her heart. "Even my God. Do you have a friend there? Let me see." She grabbed at his robe, but he fell away.

"Don't touch me!" he snapped. His face was red with anger.

"It almost worked, didn't it? But you failed. You didn't quite convince me. You wanted me to deny my God. Let me see your chest, Artero. Let me see the wound. You could have almost anything, couldn't you?" she said with disgust. "But you were stuck in the body of a dead man."

"You are still mine." His teeth seemed sharp as razors. His eyes were glowing like fire. "I promised you a kingdom and a kingdom will be yours. Enter my fiery domain and reign with me."

The room seemed to be getting hotter and Zoana began to perspire. "You are so stupid. Don't you give up? I am not yours!" she yelled. "I belong to my God. I won't believe your lies anymore. I'm going home to the people who really care about me. You fooled me. I admit it. You almost had me convinced. Your warlords killed my poor mother years ago. Someday, I will be with her. I'm going back to the only honest man I know."

Pholipi threw his arms up into the air. "You are mine!" he screamed.

"Nothing is yours, except it be given you of God, and I am His. You annoy me." She clasped arms around her shoulders and lowered her head. "Lord!" she called out. "Will you send this one home?" She waited for a few moments and looked up. Artero still stood near her, but the color had gone out of his face. His arms were wrapped around his waist, and he shook as though he were about to retch. Then, he stumbled to his knees and fell to his side as he twitched in convulsions. Smoke began to billow out of his flesh and from his clothing as his body was released from the possession. A terrible putrid smell of burning and rotting flesh filled the room. It was over. The decayed corpse of Artero lay motionless before Zoana. "I think it's time to go home," she said, holding her hand over her mouth, barely able to control her queasiness for the disgusting smell and appearance of the body.

There had been such a wailing and lamenting throughout the city when the word spread that Galincia was dead. Several people also felt that the Rasomites should be driven out of the city when they were told of Anam's supposed deception and inability to raise him again. However, there were many, including Mordi that trusted the Rasomites and so, there was a division. When Mordi announced that Pholipi was gone, the entire city was jubilant. The awesome satanic power he had over them was released. When Goranus had been found dead, the people were terrified of the prince. It was two years before when he had arrived in town, and it was then the reign of Goranus had gone bad. Pholipi had never told them of things like hospitals. When the elders had approached him, he had told them of executions and human sacrifices.

The people slept well, that night, though there was confusion and doubt about the future. The city slept exceptionally well that night, as God brought a deep sleep upon everyone. Even the night guards and other nighttime people slept soundly for a few hours.

It was the beginning of the day. The sun was not quite up when, suddenly, the city became alive. The people awoke as though a great alarm had been sounded. They had all dreamed a dream where Galincia had spoken to everyone at once.

"I have come to you, this way, such that you cannot flee from me." Galincia was clad in a white robe. His wounds had healed. His face shone with a great inner joy. "Today, I have found satisfaction in paradise. You are convicted by your own actions. However, today you are free. The past is dead. The evil one, for a time, has been kept away, except you decide to call on him. I adjure you by the living God to make a covenant with my Lord as soon as you awake. He will hearken unto your pleas. The past, I say, is dead. The future is alive, and it is yours. Wake up now and make this report known to all the world."

Thousands of people opened their eyes as one. Some were confused by the dream, due to their own weakness. Some, being young or still in infancy, did not understand. For a moment, the entire city lay in silence as the people wondered what of this dream. Then, eyes of bed-partners turned to each other. Many convicted by their hearts fled from each other's sights. Many others clasped each other in wonderful joy. Then, quietly at first, they began to share their dream and were amazed that the thrust of it was the same for every person who dwelt in Aris-Akana that night, both native and foreigner. A few foolish souls fled the city. A few died by their own hands. However, nearly everyone felt a surge of spiritual excitement. Even at that early hour, candles were lit, teapots were set to warm, screams of joy were noised. There were parades and tears of joy.

The evil one could not find a hiding place in Aris-Akana. The palace of Goranus was pulled to the ground by its inhabitants. The sellers of cheap sex toys and drugs and satanic objects and unfit literature burned their own shops. Foul objects and all manner of perversions were thrown into giant flames that leaped higher than most buildings.

And another people saw these flames. A number of women and children in search of a fallen dove had been led astray into the desert by Satan, but now, in the night, the light of Aris-Akana's flames could be seen and provided a torch for the Rasomites. By the time the sun was coming up over the horizon, the revival had already happened.

Chapter 9
Opathon

Zoana lay back on the sand. Even at night it was warm, so there was no need for a fire, even had there been the essentials for building one. This allowed her more time to contemplate her relationship with God and with the Rasomites. How could she have been so foolish as to lie to those who trusted her the most? She knew it was Satan who had first weakened her and then struck in the weakest spots. She prayed that he was truly defeated, but knew in her heart that she would cross tracks with the evil one again. That was her destiny. To battle Satan. But it scared her to realize she had suffered and believed such awful delusions.

The stars were so beautiful in the desert sky. Nothing interrupted their twinkling loveliness. She imagined that heaven would be like the night sky and she as one of the stars. Had she destroyed her position with God and her family because of her actions? Or had she been valiant in determining Satan's motives and, in the end, come through as a shining star in God's sky? This is why she had gone into the desert, so she could discover the truth.

After returning to Anam and explaining all that had happened in the palace to him and the others, she had partaken of the great spiritual reawakening of Aris-Akana. She remained for two days and then explained to Anam what she must do. She prayed he would trust her this time for her motives and he did. In fact, he had insisted that she go away by herself to sort this thing out and reaffirm her relationship with God.

Naturally, she traveled light. Her dagger, bow, and quiver were with her always. She carried a pouch of very strong wine. This would keep her from drinking it too quickly. She carried a small pack of dried fruits and nuts that would last her about a week. She would need water before she would need food.

"Oh God," she spoke aloud. "I pray that you would purify my

heart and make my spirit and your spirit the same. I worship you, Lord. I love you. Renew and refresh me in your steadfast love. You are my salvation and my strength. I place all my hope upon you. I cannot be strong, for I am only a woman. It is only in you that I can find strength. You have delivered me from the very jaws of evil. How can I not trust you? Your righteousness is to be my righteousness for, if I be righteous to myself, I am a fool. Let me be a fool for you, Lord. Let the sinners scoff at me and persecute me, for they shall have their day of judgment and I shall have mine. Only you know who is righteous. And you also show compassion. Hallelujah!"

Zoana cried herself to sleep.

It seemed as though only a few minutes had passed as she opened her eyes to the stabbing glare of the sun. It was day. She had slept soundly and was totally rested.

She sat up and scanned the horizon. It seemed to make very little difference which way she traveled. Everywhere was desert. The entire horizon was unbroken. Except for her footsteps in the sand and the position of the sun, it was difficult to tell from which direction she traveled. Taking a draught of wine and a deep breath, she stood up and headed away from where she had come. For a mile behind her, she could easily see her trail. It would be easy to stay on course.

However, there was life in the desert she became aware of as she traveled. At first, it was only the signs of life. Tiny paw prints of mice. Narrow channels etched by snakes. An occasional wisp of grass or struggling twig. The little animals, however, were very aware of the intruder and seemed to keep away. Finally, late in the day, she noticed a movement. She stopped. A tiny mouse, smaller than the end of her thumb, stood a few paces before her on its hind legs acting at once as defender of this domain and, cocking its tiny head from side to side, wondering what this great creature could be.

"Little mouse," she spoke gently.

The little thing panicked at the sound and darted away, however, only a few feet. He again stood up and watched her. She squatted, thinking her smaller stature would not be so ominous and the two contemplated each other for a time. Zoana grew hungry and so, taking a handful of nuts from her bag, she pulled the shells open and ate their contents. She tossed a tiny piece of nut very near the mouse, who first hopped back a few inches, but then unhesitatingly jumped back to the nut and devoured it instantly. She threw a tiny piece near her feet and the little creature dashed forward, grabbed the morsel, and darted back to his position. He devoured the second piece and proceeded to eye her. She placed a tiny piece on her knee and looked away from the mouse. Zoana was not startled when the mouse hopped up on her leg and, remaining there, ate the tiny piece of nut. Then he lay down on the flesh of her thigh, content that this was a friend.

"And what is this place called, my valiant friend? And what are you called?" She placed another piece of nut near the mouse's nose and he, picking it up with one paw, placed it in the pouch of his mouth for safekeeping. Zoana considered how the tiny creature had placed his trust in her as she looked around at the unchanging desert.

"So, which way do we go?" She frowned. "Toward the horizon, I suppose. If you have no family responsibilities," she said to her new friend, "you are quite welcome to accompany me. I seek your companionship because, I am certain, you know more of these parts than I do." The mouse never moved. She took the tiny creature on a finger and placed him on a depression on her wine flask strapped to her shoulder. "Now, behave yourself there as I do not know what to do with drunken mice." She stood up and headed away in the same direction she had been traveling.

As she walked, she began to have thoughts of those she left behind. She had hardly taken the time to speak individually to Paluqua and the others when they had arrived. She felt, perhaps, she should have delayed her departure. However, there had been two very active days. She had spent a great deal of time explaining to everyone the delusions she had suffered and how foolish it could have turned out. She knew and had expressed that Togorasom had interceded for her before it was too late. This was the second time he had interceded for one of them before they made a total fool of themselves with a member of the opposite sex with whom they had become enamored. As this boy grew, he would surely become a mighty prophet and be remembered for all ages.

As she thought, her mind wandered to the wedding of Anam and Paluqua. It had been so beautiful that day. It was unfortunate that there had been no fancy dresses or parades, as in the old days. No royalty came from afar. Nonetheless, it had been wonderful. Eric and his men had already departed for Foramen and, naturally,

Ernie had stayed behind.

Ernie had led them a few miles away to a natural garden; a field of flowers surrounded by a hedge of fir trees. There, Anam and Paluqua were wed. It was particularly jubilant because of Anam's prophesy of the fame their children would receive.

Her mind went to her childhood. She had barely known either of her parents. Her father had been killed by the Atrocene army in one of their repeated raids while she was still a baby. Her mother had been beaten and raped in front of her and her sister, finally to be taken off to Rodan and never heard of again. She had been one of six children. Every one of her brothers and sisters had eventually been taken away to satisfy the Atrocene thirst for Rasomite blood.

The painful memories were too much for her to bear. She sank to her knees and wept. She remembered the day the last of their people had come upon the slaughter of the last of their men. It all seemed so unfair. She had never known the love of a man. Suddenly, save one, there were no young men left. Only the day previous to the battle, their hopes had been so high because of the truce. However, in the end, the Atrocene kingdom had been destroyed. Why couldn't the miracles have been performed before the loss of all her once-proud and powerful people? She hated the Atrocenes, but what good did her hatred do?

She had started walking again. She wondered where was she going? Just what was she trying to prove? Now, she was lost in the middle of the desert. But she was not completely lost for, looking over her shoulder, she could still plainly see her tracks. It would be a relatively easy thing to turn about and head back. She considered the idea and almost made the decision to turn back. This was a foolish trip. Then, she remembered her lack of water. She needed water now. How stupid she suddenly felt. Why did she not bring adequate water? It had been nearly twenty-four hours since she had had a drink. The wine was no good. She suddenly was so very thirsty, she began coughing and had to sit down and take a bit of the wine. She got up and started to walk as her mind swirled. She was too weak and stumbled and fell. Attempting to push herself from the ground, she again collapsed. This time her quiver of arrows emptied itself onto the ground. Grasping one of the arrows in her hand, she thought to pick up the mess. Then, she went blank.

There was a child's laughter and the sound of people talking. She couldn't open her eyes due to the pain in her head. There was still the sound of voices, but she could not understand what was said. However, then she heard the sound of what seemed like a door closing and someone moving about. She forced open her eyes and looked up at the ceiling over her, still too weak to move. She was alive. She closed her eyes and fell to sleep.

"She's looking much better. You say you know from where she has come?"

"Aye! I know from where she comes. I wish she were awake, for I so long to speak with her."

Zoana opened her eyes to see two men standing over her. When they realized she was awake, they at first merely gaped at her and forced smiles. One was a young man, not much more than a boy. The other was an older man, perhaps fifty years of age, though it was very hard to tell due to his very full beard that was just beginning to turn white. They were father and son, as they looked very much alike.

"Quickly, Julian," said the man, "run to fetch mother." The boy was motionless. "Go!" he said firmly, and the boy set off.

"Where..." Zoana struggled to speak. "Where am I?"

"You are here in this little place in the desert. It has no name. I am called Opathon."

"Opathon is an Atrocene name."

"Yes, it is."

The boy appeared with a young woman who seemed scarcely old enough to be his mother.

"This is my wife, Malora, and my son, Julian," explained Opathon. "Malora," he said to his wife, "take very good care of this woman. Treat her as though your very life depended upon it. Julian," he said to the boy, "we have work to do."

"But, Father," he protested, "I want to hear of where she came from and why she came to us."

"She is still too weak to entertain the likes of you. She will have many things to tell us later. Come, we have ditches to dig."

"Stupid ditches for no water!" shouted Julian. "I want to stay here and help."

"You want to stay here and stare at this beautiful woman. Outdoors, now, or I'll be forced to thrash you!"

The men left, and Malora smiled down at Zoana. "We're very glad that you are here, and I'll do my best to serve you. Do you feel like eating?"

"I am hungry, but first," Zoana asked, "where are my things? I need my wine pouch."

"Everything was kept for you exactly," said Malora as she handed the flask to Zoana. "However, should you begin with strong wine?"

Zoana briefly inspected the wine flask and handed it back. "I was looking for something, but I guess, it's quite foolish."

"But what?"

"A little desert mouse. Silly, yes?"

"I don't know if it's silly or not. However, the mouse is in a little wire cage and is doing very well."

Zoana sat up in the bed and looked around. The home was formed completely of plaster, except for the wood plank floor. The walls and ceiling had originally been white but had turned a dull grey from years of lack of attention. The three windows had no glass but were completely open to the outdoors. There were shutters to be used when necessary. One of the shutters was now closed to keep out the direct sun. She assumed this was what she had heard close earlier. The doorway had no real door to it but, rather, only a heavy blanket to cover the opening and a wooden bar to secure it against the wind. The bed she lay on was one of three. The other two beds were merely blankets thrown on a matting of various furs, mostly in tatters. There was a small kitchen area with a table but no place to prepare food and very few shelves. The general appearance of the house was very unclean and run-down. Zoana took all this in at a glance and looked back at Malora.

"I need water."

Malora quickly filled a cup with water from a pot that was sitting by the door and Zoana took a drink.

"How long have I been here?"

"Not long," answered Malora. "You were found only yesterday."

"How did I come to this place?"

"Julian found you. You were only a few hundred feet from the oasis. We were surprised that you had come this far and, then apparently had turned back."

Zoana laughed. "I was not thinking wisely. I was walking with my head down and lost in thoughts."

"That is how they die in the desert. From where did you come?"

"Aris-Akana."

"You do not look like an Akanian."

"Actually, I have traveled far. I..."

Malora put her hand up to stop her. "I am sorry. I have asked too many questions. Opathon will want to talk to you before long. However, you should rest."

"I am fine now. I have learned not to travel so lightly in the desert."

"Are you hungry? There is some fruit." Malora left the house before Zoana could answer and returned with a bowl of spoiling, dried-up fruit. "I can slice an apple for you. Would you like a bath? Anything you want. We did bathe you when Julian brought you back."

"I thought so."

"That is, I mean myself and Mula bathed you. Not Julian."

"Malora, how did you come here?"

"My parents fled the oppression of the Zalandorians when I was a baby. My mother died in the desert, but my father and a few others arrived here safely."

"I do not know of the Zalandorians."

"A civilized people who, unfortunately, harbor the lawless as well. Thankfully, they have never come here. My father used to speak of them. I..." Malora stopped speaking.

"Yes?"

"I could not trouble you while you are recovering."

"Go ahead. I am feeling very well. I really want to know." Zoana took the young woman's hand and Malora sat beside her.

"All of our people were destroyed by these cut-throats. We were not warriors, merely farmers. All of my brothers and sisters are dead. I am, perhaps, the only one left. There were no other children who survived to seek refuge."

"Then you have also lived a life of persecution," said Zoana. "As with you, all of my family."

"Why is the world so cruel?" asked Malora, holding back the

tears.

"I don't know, Malora. I just don't know."

They embraced each other and both trembled from the suppressed anger.

Opathon appeared in the doorway, unknown to Malora.

"And who," asked Malora, "were your people tormented by?"

"I cannot say just yet," answered Zoana as she eyed Opathon.

Malora turned, saw Opathon and smiled at her husband.

"Malora," he said, staring at Zoana, "you'll have to leave so I can speak alone with our guest."

She quietly got up and left the house.

Opathon slowly walked across the room and kneeled in front of Zoana. He lowered his head as he thought of how to begin. Zoana closed her eyes and tried very hard not to be bitter. The man stood up and looked at Zoana. His eyes were moist with tears. Zoana opened her eyes, and they stared at each other for a long moment. Finally, he spoke.

"I hardly know where to begin. My thoughts are so run together. All I want now is for you to understand how I feel and to forgive me."

"And how do you feel?" she asked. "My heart is very angry toward the Atrocenes, but I am willing to listen."

"In the end, I became so angry." He struggled to find the words. "It was all so senseless. They, that is, we were afraid."

"Afraid? I do not understand."

"Because we knew you were right and we were wrong, but we could never say it. No man serves the devil faithfully. It is done either out of ignorance or from a misplaced fear of God. So, I ran. I simply could not stand it anymore. I knew I would have to run far or everyone would remember I was an evil man. So, I fled. Everywhere I went, they knew me or found me out, and I moved on. I suppose there is no escape from my past, save death."

"And then," she said sternly, "you shall go to Hell!"

Opathon clutched a wooden support and began crying. She got up and stood near him.

"Opathon, it doesn't have to be that way. I want to forgive you, and I know my God loves you and wants to forgive you."

He stopped crying and looked at her. "How can you say that since you know my past? I am dark and evil."

"Believe me," she said with a note of anger, "it is not easy, but it is the truth."

"I do not even know if there is a God."

"You have never asked him into your heart?"

"I don't know how," he said. "But, if you are patient, will you teach me? I so want that peace."

"You can find true peace this way. You say, 'Dear God, fill my heart with your peace'."

He smiled. "You make it seem so easy."

"You must do a difficult thing first. You must say, 'Dear God, forgive me' and you must be sincere. Opathon," she said softly, "make haste, because I sense the Lord's presence here now." She said this because she knew he would begin to ponder and become indecisive.

"Dear Lord, please forgive me," he said with little conviction.

"Father, I don't know the terror and anguish that lives in this man's mind. You know, Lord. I sense that he has tried to repair some of the damage he has wrought, but he has been doing it in his own strength. He cannot forgive himself, for he does not know how to be righteous unto himself. He cannot save himself. Lord, he is still alive and can cause much good but only if he does not hold back from you. He has a wife and a son, and he must lead them. Help him, Father. He cannot run forever."

"Dear Lord, please forgive me," he said as he collapsed onto the floor in tears. "I just can't go any further." He lay there for a long time, sobbing, and finally sat up. "I do feel it. I do sense God. I believe!" He grinned. "When I came in here, I came to send you away because I did not want anyone to know my secret. But, I don't know what to do next. I still don't know how I should live."

She crouched on the floor beside him. "What do you feel God has for you?"

"Love. Forgiveness. Many things."

"How God loves you, you should also love others. It really isn't that difficult."

"I believe you."

Zoana smiled, and they both stood up. "Then surely the God of the Rasomites is also the God over the Atrocenes and there is no sin that he cannot cover. Hallelujah! Now, let us go outdoors."

The shade offered in the house presented a false sense of the weather. Outside, the heat was stifling. The glare of the sun against the white sand was so intense that Zoana could see nothing at first and was even tempted to retreat back to the house. She wondered how she had walked so far across the desert in this heat with no water and little food, except God had strengthened her. Soon, however, she was able to discern the layout of the tiny village. There were four little houses made of plaster and covered with only thin paper roofs. Two of the houses appeared to be unused. The other two, including the house of Opathon, were sorely in need of repair. The sides of the buildings were crumbling. The window frames had been removed, since the glass was all broken. Beyond the huts, there was a grove of orange and fig trees and a variety of berry bushes. However, the plants barely clung to life, and they had no fruit. It was obvious the oasis was nearly dried up, and it had been a long time since the last rain.

"Malora!" Opathon called out.

Several people emerged from the other house.

"These are all of us," he said and identified each as they came out. "Of course, you already know Malora. This is Mula," as another woman much older than Malora appeared. "And her sons, Yuramedan, Alanto, and Meradese." All the boys were much younger than Julian.

Zoana was surprised as she had expected a real village and not merely two families. She glanced at Opathon.

"When I arrived here, there were at least six families left. Even then, they were suffering and dying. They have no food. They have no water. The sun is merciless. We continue to hope something will change." He asked Malora, "where is Julian?"

She pointed across the oasis to the solitary figure sitting on the ground. "He said he's going to sit in the sun until he dies. I simply don't feel I can deal with him anymore. I don't know what to do."

"Let me talk to him," Zoana said as she started towards him. He looked up at her as she approached him. "I wanted to thank you for saving my life."

"I had to," he explained. "I could not simply leave you out there. However, I'm sorry I had to bring you to this awful place."

She pointed at the ground next to him, wondering if she could sit next to him. He nodded his head.

"Tell me about yourself," she asked.

"Why?" He shrugged his shoulders. "Who cares? I'll be dead and forgotten soon. Nobody cares."

"You mean you think Malora would want you to die?"

"Of course not!" he said stubbornly.

"Then what do you mean?"

"I don't know. I just don't see the sense of struggling from one day to the next. You know what I mean. It's like we're just waiting to die."

"Was it always like this?"

"It's been bad forever. There were only a few good days."

"Like what days? What were your favorite days?"

He pointed across the desert in the direction Zoana had come from. "They used to come through here. The caravans from Aris-Akana. They were going to the mountains where my mother was born to trade with the Zalandorians. I hated it when they left, but at least they brought news and change and toys for us children. But, then they just stopped coming a couple of years ago. Maybe, it's because we were always so short on water and supplies."

"Julian, take heart." She put her hand on his shoulder. "The city of Aris-Akana has had a great change. The evil king is dead. The people are happy and looking forward to the future. I think they will be coming this way again, soon."

"Really?" he exclaimed, and his dull eyes came alive. "But," he said as he dropped his head again, "we have nothing to offer them. No supplies, no water, no entertainment. Nothing but a bunch of skinny kids."

She took his hand. "Come with me," she said. "I need to teach some faith in God."

"I don't know much about God," he said as he followed her. "Maybe, it's useless to try."

"Or, perhaps, it will be easier." As they approached the group which had been watching them, she told Opathon to get everyone inside one of the houses and shutter all the windows. "I'm going to help you, with the Lord, to get started."

He didn't really understand, but he herded everyone into his house and began shuttering up the windows. The women and children arranged themselves in a semi-circle on the floor around Zoana, who had taken a seat on the bed she had been using. When Opathon had closed up the house as well as he could, he leaned against the pole behind the others, awaiting the words that would come from Zoana's mouth. The house was still well-lit because of the thin roof and numerous cracks.

As soon as Zoana had sat down, she had bowed her head and

began praying quietly to herself. When she realized the room was silent and in anticipation, she picked her head up and smiled at those before her.

"Does anyone know who or what God is?" she asked primarily to the three young boys.

Alanto nodded his head and said slowly, "I think I know. He's like a monster that flies around in the dark and punishes people for not acting like he wants them to."

"We'll talk about that, but does anyone else have an idea?"

Julian spoke up. "He made everything. He's good, and the monsters were invented by men to scare us into doing what they want us to."

"Very good, Julian," said Zoana. "There are no invisible monsters like we would know them, but there are spiritual monsters. They usually work by taking over a person's heart and mind and causing them to do evil."

"Then," asked Malora, "how can not everyone be evil, since monsters, or whatever, want things done their way. We know many evil men are in the world. As well as women."

"Well, now," said Zoana, "if I am afraid that my heart and my mind were going to be filled with evil, what should I do before that happens?"

"You should fill your heart and mind with good things," said Yuramedan, "but where can we find these good things, for it seems the whole world is evil?"

"God is good," said Julian.

"Yes, but how can you take a lump of God and put him inside your body?" asked Alanto.

"God's not real, I mean, He is real," said Julian, "but not like you can see Him or talk to Him. You can fill your heart with qualities that are good."

"Like what?" asked Zoana.

"Hey," said Julian, keeping back a smile, "I thought you were the teacher?"

"But you're doing so very good," she said. "What sort of qualities?"

He closed his eyes and thought for a minute, then, still eyes unopened, said, "do good things for each other, tell other people about God and, oh, I suppose, obey your parents." Malora took his hand.

"What should parents do?"

"They must teach these things and other good things to their children," said Opathon. "It is the responsibility of the parent to raise up children who can behave in a manner that causes their parents to be proud of them."

"And also that God will be proud," said Yuramedan.

Zoana clapped her hands. "You're all doing so well," she said. "Meradese, would you like to feel the presence of God?"

Meradese had been listening intently, however, he had been silent.

"Yea," he said as he became wide-eyed and smiling.

"Then, you must pray diligently," she said. "If I promised you a mountain of gold and diamonds, would you be willing to work hard for it?"

"Of course," he said.

"The kingdom of God is much more," she said. "Are you willing to work for God's kingdom?"

He looked stunned, but he nodded his head.

"I believe," she said, "that God is dealing with your heart right now. Do you believe?"

"I believe," he said quietly.

"Mula, has God ever made his presence known to you?"

"Huh," she said suddenly. "I'm sorry. I wasn't paying attention. What were you saying?"

"How is it," Zoana said sternly and stood up over Mula, "that God is here and impressing himself upon the hearts of your own children, but you are unaware? Do you believe in God?"

"I believe in God. I believe he is the salvation," Mula answered with a serious tone to her voice. However, she had no true conviction.

Zoana got to her knees in front of Mula. "I want you to accept God," she said. "I want all of you to believe."

"I said, I do believe!" she retorted. "Please, don't pressure me."

"Then, let's all of us come together and take hands if we all are convinced of God's salvation." She stood up and they all rose with her, taking hands and forming a circle. "Dear Lord, thank you almighty God for your many gifts. Your peace, your salvation, your generosity. I ask you now to fill the hearts of everyone in this family. Give understanding." Then, she felt a tug on her heart. "I hear you, Lord," she said quietly. She dropped her hands and paused for a moment before speaking. "Very soon the caravans from Aris-Akana will be returning." Everyone looked excited. "They will be good people and much different from before. When they arrive, they will be hungry and thirsty..."

"But we have nothing to offer them," interjected Julian.

"Shh, let me finish. I will have to leave here, but I will leave two gifts behind. One is salvation. However, if the word of salvation is not spread, then it is of little value. You shall offer both food for the heart and for the belly so that the missionaries may continue their travel. You shall also have much work. Opathon, it is time to go outdoors."

"Are we done?"

"No," Zoana corrected. "In a way, we have only begun." They all started filing out the door. "Julian," she said as she took his hand. "Wait, I need to explain something about what you said earlier. Yes, you can speak to God and He shall answer you if you are diligent in your love and, someday, you shall see him."

He started crying. "I love you," he said. "Please, don't go away. Please, stay with us."

"In the morning, I will go back to Aris-Akana. Don't confuse godly love with worldly satisfaction."

"I just don't want you to go."

"Julian, someday a beautiful and godly woman shall be your wife. I believe soon. You must stay here and glorify God. You must someday manage this oasis."

"It is if no importance," he said. "It's just a dumb little place in the desert."

"So that you shall believe, go outdoors and discover what God can do for those who believe."

He took a deep breath and walked outside. He didn't have to go far. Zoana watched with joy as he beheld what had transpired during the time they had been inside. The tiny, nearly-dead oasis had been transformed. What had been merely a few hundred feet across, now stretched out for over a mile in each direction. The greenery was overpowering. The trees and bushes hung low, bearing figs, dates, oranges, apricots, grapes, and a multitude more.

"Julian," yelled Meradese from behind the bushes, "come quickly and look. There is a fish pond here."

However, when Julian pushed through the enclosure, he discovered it was actually a small lake.

"Come on," yelped the younger boy as he dashed into the water, completely dressed and screaming for joy.

"I am nearly speechless," he said, looking over the bushes at Zoana. "It is a miracle. How could any person not believe?"

Zoana merely smiled and said, "why don't you go swimming?"

Opathon and Malora appeared walking down the path with their arms around each other and approached Zoana.

"It is so much more than I could have even imagined. We shall be good stewards of this great gift. I believe, some of the travelers will want to remain," said Opathon.

"I also know that they shall remain, and their daughters will marry your sons. Someday, this shall be a great city. I urge you to take care of it as God would desire. Tell me, how is Mula?"

"Mula is stubborn," said Malora. "She shall never listen nor shall she believe. What can be done?"

"Pray for her and keep her busy," answered Zoana. "Some cannot be convinced of God."

"Will you be with us much longer?" asked Opathon.

"No," she replied, "in the morning, I shall have to return to Aris-Akana. What I went to search for, I have found. To you, my friend, has been entrusted the hearts of all the people who dwell here. You should plant grain fields, tend the fruit, do all to preserve the water supply, and teach of God. Now that the Lord is in you, this last task shall be easier. Soon, the travelers will begin to come from Aris-Akana and, eventually, from other places. The miracle of this transformation will be less than the miracle you shall perform. You must be husbandman, trader, and minister. You will be tired when you sleep each night. Malora, I urge you to do all you can to make his day easier."

She was interrupted as the boys returned from their bathing. Meradese was ahead of Julian. "Opathon," he yelled, "there's fish in the water. How do you catch a fish?"

"Go ahead," said Zoana. "I am tired and must rest for my trip back. You know the things that you shall have to do." She turned and went back into the house.

Much later, after dark had settled upon them, Zoana woke up and found it impossible to fall back to sleep. She lay for a few minutes, awake on the bed and contemplating the events of the day. Before retiring, she and the others had enjoyed a fine meal from the abundance of the oasis. She had taught them how to pray and also many songs of praise. It was clear to her that she was in God's favor. Unable to slumber, she finally got up and went outdoors. The evening air in the desert had been warm, but here in the shelter of the trees, the air was quite cool. She could not see far in the dark, though much farther than most people. She headed down the path. It was her first opportunity to see much of this place.

Even in the dark, it was lovely. The smell of the several fruit trees drifted passed her as she walked. She came to an open field. A meadow in the desert. This would be the fodder for the horses and livestock Opathon would procure. It would be easy to succeed in his undertakings and difficult to fail. After walking for several minutes, she sat down in a grove of trees with her back against one of them.

"Thank you, Lord," she said and fell to sleep.

She awoke with a start several hours later and smiled when she saw Julian standing a few paces from her.

"I want to be like you," he said.

"You are. Don't worry. You are like me."

"I guess I am," he said as he sat down in front of her. "I wish you could stay, but I also know you miss your friends."

"That's only part of it. The world is a great place, and there is so much to do."

He pointed in the opposite direction of Aris-Akana. "That way are the mountains where my mother was born. There are the Zalandorians. They need either destruction or salvation. Will you go there?"

"First, I go to Aris-Akana. Then, I do not know. One thing at a time. And what will you do?"

"I suppose I will stay here. There is a lot of work to do. Opathon is getting older and could never do it all alone. The boys are still so young. They need me. But, perhaps, other help shall come. I would like to see more than this desert."

"I understand," she said. "I think you shall travel, but I hope you can return here."

He looked around. "It seems so strange, so different," he said, "with all of this when, before, there was nothing. Who could not believe after this?"

"Yet, there are those who shall never believe. Only yesterday, you wanted to die."

He lowered his head. "I was foolish. I'm sorry."

"Don't be sorry. It's passed. But, do you see, you did not know the truth. You had given up. When I prayed with Opathon earlier, he had given up. Yet, he only wanted to know the truth, and he received salvation. It was needed for you to see a miracle before you could really understand. In spite of this, there are those among you who are more stubborn and still do not believe. But, it may be, one day the Lord shall catch them unaware and they will know. Or, perhaps, another shall come their way and minister to them a special word and heal them and they shall be saved. Some shall find salvation in a moment of time, and they will cast all behind them and go forward. Another may struggle with a situation for years in an attempt to reconcile their beliefs with God, but they will finally search and find salvation. Many will never find the Lord. It is up to you to make certain that no one is missed but, if you pass by one to minister to another, you shall be forgiven."

"It all seems so difficult," he said as he shook his head.

She laughed. "I'm trying to make it easier for you. Always remember one thing. God loves you, and he wants you to love others as he loves you."

"But God is perfect. I know I'll make mistakes. I'm not even certain what to do next. How can I be like God?"

"Don't confuse the goal with the process."

"Huh!" He shook his head again.

"God is perfect and you are not God, but you are going to God. Therefore, you should begin to emulate those qualities of God and you shall learn. I know it will be difficult, but don't concentrate on being perfect; concentrate on striving to get there. Take one quality at a time and then another. You will not get there in this world, but He is watching."

"I still hate to see you go. I think we have a special relationship," he said.

"We have a special relationship. We're both going the same way. But, don't ever get to thinking too well of yourself. You have been given a special task as a servant. In heaven, you are a prince, but on earth, you are a servant."

"I'll try."

"You go back to the others," she said. "I need to be alone for a little while."

He got up. "I understand. Breakfast will be soon. It's beginning to get light. Opathon promised us a busy day. I suppose," he said more quietly, "after we eat, you'll be wanting to start out." She nodded and he sadly turned and walked away.

"And what do you think of all this, my little friend?" Zoana sat in Mula's house, talking to the mouse in the cage. The little mouse sat up on its hind legs, looking at her intently. "You have come so far from home. I think it best that you return with me. We both have certain obligations to keep."

Breakfast had been a drawn-out affair. There had been a multitude of questions. Even Mula had begun to show an interest in the things of God. Zoana had bathed, received provisions, and filled her flask with water. She was eager to return to Aris-Akana; however, not excited about the long trek back.

She pulled open the door in the little wire cage, and the mouse eagerly hopped out and sat on the palm of Zoana's hand. She placed the tiny creature in the pocket of her water flask and slowly walked outside. It was not hot where she stood. However, she could see the edge of the oasis. A few feet beyond the edge of the last trees was an obvious line beyond which the sand became much lighter in color due to its dryness. She also knew it would be much hotter at that point.

Julian came out of the other house with the rest of the group following him. He was dressed in shorts and sandals as though he were ready for a long walk.

"It is my intention," he spoke plainly, "to accompany you part of the way..."

"Julian, I don't think that..."

"I have already made my decision. I have no intention of staying with you. However, I am going part of the way and then, I shall return."

"I don't understand what you expect can be accomplished."

"We shall decide that along the way. I just feel that I must, and I have spoken with my parents."

"Yes, we have talked," said Opathon, coming forward. "I think it would be a good thing for him to spend a bit more time with you. I cannot hold you here. Take care, Julian. Though, I know you know the desert well."

Malora handed him a water flask and a food sack that strapped to his belt. He put them on and gave her a hug. "I shall be back soon," he said quietly, looking into her eyes. "I shall be fine." He spoke to Opathon. "Don't wait for me to get back to get things started. If we don't keep at it, this place will be a mess." To Zoana, "let's go." He walked off a few feet.

Zoana took Opathon's hand. "I feel certain that the good things we have begun here will continue. There will be bad days but not all. Work hard and pray." She shrugged her shoulders. "I really can't give you any more than I already have."

"You have given us enough," he said.

"This all came from God," she corrected.

"If it were only of God, then all would have been accomplished without you getting lost in the desert. God is mighty, but He prefers to do his good works through his servants. This gave us the faith to keep trying. If it is ever possible for you to return, you shall always be welcome beyond measure."

"Our tracks may cross again," she said. "However, the goal of the Rasomites is to find a home. I fear I may be keeping the others from this quest, so I must leave now."

After the last farewells and heartfelt hugs and tears from all, Zoana and Julian headed out of the oasis and into the desert. True enough, as soon as they had crossed the line beyond the trees, they were certain they had entered an oven. The glare of the sun from the sand hurt their eyes. However, they soon began adjusting to both the heat and glare.

They both walked along in silence for a considerable period of time. It was too hot for them to perspire. The sand burned their feet, even through Julian's sandals. As they became more used to the intense heat, however, their minds wandered as to how to begin a conversation.

"Julian," she asked, "why did you accompany me?"

"Because I asked Opathon if I should, and he said, 'yes'."

"That's not a straight answer. Why did you ask him and why did he let you go?"

"I really don't know. I simply felt compelled to go. There wasn't time to search out all of the reasons."

"Have you gotten over your amorous feelings toward me?"

He smiled and laughed. "Yes, I'm quite over that. It was sort of silly. I…"

"Julian, don't lie to me."

"No! No, I haven't. I love you and I can't help it."

"Oh, Julian. Why didn't you say so? This isn't right at all."

"Why isn't it right? Isn't it right for a young man to love a woman? Is it because I'm younger than you? Is it because you're a Rasomite? I don't understand." He started to get angry.

"It's not for those reasons. It's because I don't feel the same way toward you. I just don't feel right about it."

Julian was on the verge of tears. "I would do anything for you. You're so beautiful and so special."

"I don't want you to love me because you think I'm beautiful or special. I want someone to love me because God says it should be so."

"Is it because you're afraid you'll be tied down to that oasis? I won't go back. I'll go anywhere you want me to."

"Julian, you're not listening. It's not right. I don't love you that way and I don't feel God would sanctify it. I want you to forget it. Do you understand? I am beginning to get angry."

He shrugged his shoulders and stopped walking. Zoana passed him. "Then, nothing matters," he said. "My life is empty. I don't see why I should try anymore." She tried to ignore him and continued her pace. "Don't you even care?" he yelled as she got further away. He hurried to catch up. "So what should I do?" he mumbled when he was beside her.

They walked along in silence until he asked her again what he should do.

"Perhaps, you should be asking God what you should do?"

"But I feel like you are my spiritual guide."

"Do you ask me because I am your spiritual guide or because I am the woman who scorned your love? A charge I don't feel guilty of. If you ask me as your spiritual guide, then you ought to do as I have already told you. Julian," she said patiently. "I understand how you feel. You were bored, lonely, and on the verge of suicide. I know how low you were. Then, along comes a good-looking woman and, in less than a day's time, takes your whole world and turns it upside down. You feel like you must grab out at this opportunity or your whole life shall be lost. Can't you see? Your whole life is ahead of you. I am not nor shall I be yours. I want to be your friend. I want us to feel love and compassion for each other as God does. I don't want to be your woman. You shall have so many tremendous opportunities offered to you. I know it. What can I say more to you than, don't blow it? Please, don't throw it away."

They walked on for some time in silence.

"I'll never forget you," he finally said. "I've been thinking about it, and I know you are right. I was foolish. I only hope you can forgive me and not always remember me as a love-sick fool. I know I still have a lot of growing up to do. My chances will come, and I only hope I can gain the wisdom that you have and never make a mistake."

Tears started to form in Zoana's eyes as she explained. "How little you know about me. Have you ever wondered why I was wandering in the desert? I cannot tell you everything, but I made a very foolish mistake and fell in love. If you think a person can make mistakes...Yes, I think I should tell you everything because there are lessons in it." And she expounded upon all the things she had done in Aris-Akana.

"The reason I was wandering is because I was afraid my God had left me and I could not be forgiven. How can God leave me, for He is in my heart? Nevertheless, I was afraid and confused. You know the Lord has shown me that He has not forsaken me, so all things work out for those who obey God, even when they err and must repent. When I was at the oasis, I felt nearer to God than ever, and I had to because He also needed to be shared with you. Don't ever think that I am the closest to God, for I also make foolish mistakes. I hope you can avoid some of those I have made. Look!" she said suddenly and pointed off into the distance. She could clearly see a caravan of horses coming. However, Julian's eyes not being so developed, it was some time before he could see it. "There is so much you need to know, but you shall have to follow your heart. I know you shall do well."

"I believe we shall see each other again. I pray that I shall also do well, for I want someday for you to find me and be proud of the work you have begun in me."

"Do you know," said Zoana, looking around, "we are very near to the place I found my little friend?" She looked down at her flask and saw the little animal sticking his whiskers out from his hole. "Yes, you may come out. You are home again." They stopped walking, and the little mouse darted out of his place and soon disappeared into the sand. "A tiny, humble creature," she said, "and should we not all be so? I would think that all of us would live as that little mouse, but we were created after God's image. All of the creatures in creation are obedient and submissive to the simple laws of nature God has instituted, except man. The great violator. He has placed us in charge, and we have become wicked and lazy servants."

They sat and engaged in idle conversation while they awaited the caravan to reach them. Very soon, the horses and men were alongside. There were nine horses, three riders. The leader of the group was a pleasant-looking, heavyset man clad in a white tunic and headgear. His two companions were both substantially smaller than he, but clad similarly. The other six horses were lightly laden with trade items such as cooking pots, clothing, blankets, and jugs of wine.

The leader raised both hands in the air as a friendly greeting when they were close enough to speak without shouting. "Behold, it is as the man said. We should meet a young Rasomite woman if we were to follow her footpath. What ho, young and worthy woman of God."

Zoana laughed in a friendly way. "It can only be that Anam has sent you in pursuit of me. All is well with me. I am called Zoana."

"As I know," he replied. "I am Labathar, as my father was also called."

This name caught Julian's attention. "Did your father also trade along this route?"

"That he did a number of years ago. I sense I have stirred up your memory."

"Yes," said Julian, smiling. "Your father used to come to the oasis when I was a small boy. He brought trinkets for us children. I believe he was a kindly man."

"Aye, and a good father. However, he has innocently fallen victim to the plague and left me to clean up the bits of his once-great fortune. However, you say there is still the oasis?"

"It flourishes," said Julian. "We are sure it will provide a place of refuge for man's spirit as the new trade routes are forged across the desert."

"It shall," said Labathar. "A mighty work of God has been wrought in Aris-Akana, and it was my decision to attempt to reopen outside trade with the Zalandorians, as well as others. They also need to hear the good news."

After Julian had exchanged names with the two helpers of Labathar, he was invited to ride astride Labathar's horse. One of the other men dismounted and offered his horse to Zoana to return to Aris-Akana. After some discussion, Labathar rearranged some of his items and gave Zoana a horse. They also gave her enough food and water to help the horse on his full day journey back. The men were pleased to discover relief was so close for them.

Before everyone mounted up, Julian took Zoana in his arms. "I can now reach out to you as my sister and extend to you a godly love. However, deep in my heart, I wish we never had to part. I know it must be so." He could not talk further nor release her due to the embarrassing tears that flowed. Necessity, however, soon dictated that it was time to go back. They parted with no final words. She kissed him on the cheek and backed away toward her awaiting horse. He stood motionless with his arms hanging limply at his sides. Then, he turned and climbed onto the horse with Labathar. He dared not look back until several minutes had passed.

Zoana was gone.

Epilogue

Upon Zoana's return to Aris-Akana, she immediately sought out Crazon. The entire city was in celebration. The evil King Goranus was dead. Pholipi was gone. The presence of God's Spirit was evident everywhere.

"Zoana!" called out Crazon from the midst of a crowd as she saw her friend slowly ambling along astride the horse. With tears in her eyes, Zoana quickly dismounted and ran to Crazon, throwing her arms about her.

"Is everything fine?" Crazon implored her.

Zoana laughed. "Everything is more than wonderful." She merged back into the group with her friend.

Shortly thereafter, the Rasmomites left Aris-Akana and, going a different way from that which Zoana had traveled before, they reached the country of the Zalendorians. They spent a brief period in the capitol, Taba, as guests of Prince Rodando.

It was becoming clear that God had poured his Spirit out upon Togorasom, and he continued to have visions, dreams, and answered prayer. As he spent most of his time alone with God, people sensed when they were receiving intense prayer from him.

Togorasom approached Anam. "Father..." he began.

Anam sensed from the boy's downcast appearance and voice he had been in prayer. He nodded. Anam knew in his heart, as they all did, their time in Taba would be short.

"I must leave."

"Are you certain you want to travel alone? What has happened?"

"The city of Lasapulis is not far from here. It is a city ruled by astrologers and magicians. An imminent attack from two other armies is about to flood and destroy the city."

"I have heard. But, what will you do?"

"One man, the ruler of Lasapulis, is the key to blunting the rush into war. This king and the king of Marsa are weary of war, but they will fight because of honor. I can stop this, but to do this, I must be there. I cannot stop the third army. Because of all this, I must leave."

"In a few days we will all be prepared to depart. Must you leave now?"

"I have great fear in my heart."

"Of what do you fear?" Anam asked.

"I fear a multitude of bloodshed if I do not leave quickly."

"Then, go!" Anam instructed. "Take what you need and go. I will tell the others what has happened and in three days we will follow you. I know your prayers are more mighty than all of us together."

Togorasom forced a smile, turned and left the room. Anam could not see the boy's tears.

About the Author

 Larry was born in upstate New York and raised on a dairy farm. He always loved reading and writing and desired to be a writer even from a toddler. His play involved searching for cattle in the pastures while avoiding imaginary aliens and terrorists. The Lord found him as a teenager and he began to read the Bible and wonder why God seemed no longer to be active, only to discover through personal experiences and miracles later that He was still very much active. Larry and his wife, Yvonne, now attend church at Northwest Assembly in Bentonville, Arkansas. He has been married for 31 years. They have five grown children and seven grandchildren.

Inspiration

The inspiration for this story arose indirectly from reading so many other books about godly people, but God himself was rarely present in the story. It also arose from reading the Bible where God was normally a major player in the action. The story just came to me as I often had no idea what was going to happen next or why I was creating a situation the way it was going. Then, God would surprisingly reveal himself in the story. I pray the reader is as pleased as the writer.